THE
REFUSAL
CAMP

ALSO BY THE AUTHOR

Billy Boyle
The First Wave
Blood Alone
Evil for Evil
Rag and Bone
A Mortal Terror
Death's Door
A Blind Goddess
The Rest Is Silence
The White Ghost
Blue Madonna
The Devouring
Solemn Graves
When Hell Struck Twelve
The Red Horse
Road of Bones
From the Shadows

On Desperate Ground
Souvenir
Shard
Freegift

THE REFUSAL CAMP

STORIES

JAMES R. BENN

This is a work of fiction. Names, characters, places, and incidents
either are the product of the author's imagination or are used fictitiously,
and any resemblance to actual persons, living or dead, businesses, companies,
events, or locales is entirely coincidental.

Published by Soho Press, Inc.
227 W 17th Street
New York, NY 10011

Library of Congress Cataloging-in-Publication Data

Names: Benn, James R., author. | Title: The refusal camp : stories / James R. Benn.
Description: New York, NY : Soho Crime, [2023]
Identifiers: LCCN 2022036700

ISBN 978-1-64129-451-5
eISBN 978-1-64129-452-2

Subjects: LCGFT: Novels. | Classification: LCC PS3602.E6644 R44 2023 |
DDC 813/.6—dc23/eng/20220815
LC record available at https://lccn.loc.gov/2022036700

Printed in the United States of America

10 9 8 7 6 5 4 3 2 1

For my wife and muse, Deborah Mandel.

"For she had eyes and chose me."
— William Shakespeare, *Othello*, Act 3, Scene 3

CONTENTS

THE HORSE CHESTNUT TREE

...

I REJOICE IN the Sabbath. Not for the words of the English preacher or for the hardwood bench in the rear of their Sunday god's church. Not out of eagerness to hear the sermon about the offspring of their deity who came back from the dead, or the holy ghost with a tongue of fire. Rather, to talk with my own brethren. Slaves, like me and Maame. The English in their finery do as well, since they worship gossip as much as they do their three strange gods.

We arrive in a cart with the other servants, behind the carriage of our master. It is news of the war I seek most. The war of independence these English of the colonies are fighting with the English from across the sea. They talk of freedom, and I wonder if it will extend to Africans. Likely not.

I make my way to speak with Cato. It is the name his master gave him, of course. The English enjoy giving us names from the ancients, but Maame has given me my own name, neither African nor Roman.

"Freegift, come here," a voice demands. Frederick Perkins, a proud lad of seventeen and known to all, dismounts from his horse and hands me the reins. "Be a good fellow and take Apollo for a drink. It's a warm day, and he's been ridden hard."

"But the service will begin soon," I say, even as I take the reins. The pond is not far, but it will take all the free time I have, and I cherish the moments of freedom I am granted. Frederick and I played when we were young, but as he is two years older, that childhood time was brief. I grew into my labor and he into his proper place in the society of Connecticut landowners on the banks of the Quinebaug River. Still, I hope he may grant me this favor.

"Then you must make haste," Frederick says, giving me a hard shove. This is strange, even for the haughty lad he is. "Did you not hear me, Freegift?"

"I did," I say, and turn to lead Apollo to water, having little choice.

"Hands off my horse, damn you!" Frederick bellows, and I am perplexed by this sudden change. But not as much as when he throws me to the ground and begins to pummel me.

Now, I am the younger, but I spend my days felling trees for my master, who is a cooper. Every barrel, bucket, and cask found along this stretch of river has been made by him, many from hardwoods hauled from the forest by my hands.

I am strong. Very strong. But I dare not strike back. Slaves who do so have been known to be sold to plantations in the far South, where more brutality than a New England slave may ever see greets each new day. I listen as Frederick's companions gather around and cheer him on, laughing even as their worship bell calls to them.

"Make no trouble over this, Freegift," Frederick whispers as he roughly hauls me up, grasping my waistcoat and tearing the seams. "Or I may buy you for myself."

Another shove and they are gone, red-faced shouts replaced by humble heads bowed in piety as they take the steps into the church. Mr. Stoddard, my master, looks to me but says nothing to the boys. He is not cruel, other than believing in the ownership of human beings outright. But he will not go against his own kind. These English, or Americans, as they now fancy themselves, value position, appearance, and status above all. Mr. Stoddard and Frederick's family have the great honor of sitting in the front pews as they listen to the droning preacher speak of hell and the hereafter. In those pews, all expect heaven as their due.

I dust myself off, wondering if the rip in my waistcoat can be repaired by Maame, who is able with the needle. The waistcoat is a cast-off from Mr. Stoddard, who wishes his slaves and servants to reflect well upon his house. I see a button has been torn off as well, and hope no one takes notice, for only I will be to blame.

As my hands brush the garment, I feel my clasp knife gone from my pocket.

Can Frederick be so petty as to remember the day when he wanted that knife, newly given to me by Mr. Stoddard? I was eight years old and denied it to him. He had asked his father to make me give it up and was rewarded with a swat. Can that have rankled all these years?

I mount the steps into the church where Maame waits. She smiles, weakly, patting my arm. Her eyes glisten with tears, which she blinks away. We hide our sadness as well as our rage, since our masters wish us happy with our lot, a lie we strive to tell.

I settle into the rearmost pew and watch Frederick Perkins and his family take their seats. His parents have died, and as the oldest of six brothers and sisters, he is now head of the family. An older cousin joins them, a fellow named Samuel Sawyer, who purchased a prime tract of farmland from Frederick's father shortly before he passed. It was the talk of the town when the elder Perkins lost the money from that sale to some sort of speculation, which I do not understand. Then he died, and Frederick fell into a constant state of bitterness, which I do well understand.

But why assault me today?

I have said I am strong, true enough. But there is another matter I recall now, and it was a time Frederick's father lectured him on learning his letters. Mr. Stoddard had once caught me looking through his books. At that age, it was an atlas with pictures and maps that drew me in. He never said not to touch his books, but I expected a whipping anyway when he caught me. Instead, he marveled at my interest and taught me how to sound out letters. He claimed to do so only so I might help with his bookkeeping one day, but I think he liked the idea of someone sharing his interests, even if only a slave.

What I mean to say is that I know myself to be smart. I took to reading and taught myself about the world. I have read the English Bible entire and came away little impressed. *The Odyssey*—a story of a son's search for his father—still thrills. As do the few plays of

Shakespeare owned by my master. I study *The Merchant of Venice* over and over, always cheering on Shylock, who is used so badly.

The villainy you teach me, I will execute, and it shall go hard, Shylock says, his words raging in my silent soul.

I think upon the last time Frederick and I played as boys. His father had come to visit Mr. Stoddard and chided his son, Frederick, about finding the written word so hard to understand. Frederick stumbled over a simple passage his father made him read and ran from the room in tears.

Could that be why he rained punches on me and stole my clasp knife? Retribution for that embarrassment? At least now his warning made sense. If I should protest, he will make trouble. A slave has trouble enough without seeking more. So, I work at staying alert and try to forget my loss. The sermon is about eternity, and how we should follow god to ensure we spend it in his heaven.

As we leave, I manage a few moments with Cato. He is of the Akan people, as am I. We step aside, and I address him by his secret name. Okomfo. And he by mine. Kwasi. It is what we do, as taught by my mother and his grandmother, who tell us tales of our people, so that we may remember our ancestors, even here among the English and their wars, so far from Akan.

Frederick mounts Apollo and rides close to us, so we must step aside. Apollo is a fine beast, a chestnut mare with a bridle and straps decorated with brass ornaments, all inscribed with a fine engraved *P* for *Perkins.* I admire the horse more than the rider, who does not spare me a look, even as he nearly knocks me over. A warning.

I do not tell Maame of the loss of the knife. It is enough that she saw my humiliation. Later, after Sunday supper with the family—for we all dine together, seated in order of importance, with Mr. Stoddard at the head of the table and slaves at the foot, with servants and his daughters between us—Maame presses me about the encounter. But I do not want to talk about it and aim to distract her with the question she always refuses to answer.

"Who is my father, Maame?"

"Freegift, someday I will tell you. But this is not the day." What she always says.

"English, isn't he?" I ask. As I always do. Maame has the rich, dark skin of our people. My skin is lighter, a shade of brown like the crust of fresh-baked bread.

"What does it matter?" Maame says, standing over me as she twists the locks of my hair into the long *mpese* style of the Akan people. Another way to remember who we are.

Maybe she is right. Whoever my father is, he does not know my ancestors, and they may think little of him. So I sleep.

My rest ends when I awake before dawn and cannot fall back asleep, troubled by the encounter with Frederick. I toss on my pallet until the first light of the coming day cracks the horizon. I rise and walk quietly past Maame's bed so as not to disturb her. She too has a hard day ahead, cooking and cleaning for the household. With each season, the work wears on her more, and I worry. But worrying accomplishes little, so I dress, donning the leather waistcoat made for working with wood and sharp blades. I take a sack from the kitchen, fill it with johnnycakes, a jug of ale, and take my leave before any are awake.

From the workshop I take my axe and hatchet, then begin the trek to where I labored Saturday. It is a stand of chestnut trees, densely grained, a fine hardwood for making staves, which in turn are used to build casks, barrels, hogsheads, and all manner of things to store food and drink.

A skill I have, other than swinging an axe and reading the Bard, is to find the best trees for Mr. Stoddard's craft. The one that awaits me was felled two days ago in a thunderous crash and split smaller trees in its grand descent. I'd started to trim the branches when the light faded, and it became too dangerous to send sharpened metal biting into wood. Today, I will finish that task, section the trunk, and prepare it to be hauled out by draft horses.

It is hard work, the labor of blisters, cuts, and aching bones. But I do it well, and there is something to that. In an hour I am close to the spot. The stand sits near a river that divides Mr. Stoddard's land from the parcel belonging to Mr. Perkins. Or that of Frederick and his cousin, Samuel, I should say. For although Frederick is only seventeen, he is the oldest boy and inherited his father's lands, those remaining after Samuel's purchase.

I take the path to an outcropping of rock, which gives me a view of the fallen tree and the valley below. Horse chestnuts like well-drained, fertile soil, and the streams feeding the river beyond mark this spot as friendly terrain for them. The sun is up and reddens the sky as it warms the rock where I sit. I eat a johnnycake and slake my thirst with ale.

Footsteps echo from below. I wonder who is walking on Mr. Stoddard's land so early in the day. Not a visitor, since there are no paths other than those made by deer. No route to his house from any neighbor's land.

"Come, Samuel," a voice says. It is familiar. Jonathan, one of Frederick's younger brothers. Then Frederick himself appears, by the top of the fallen tree.

"We'll teach the African bastard a lesson," he says. At these words I gather my sack and tools, retreating from sight behind a jagged rock where I hide my gear. Samuel protests, and I bring myself closer, using the rocks to cover my approach. If they aim at mischief with me, it would be best to know what they plan and what grudge they hold that brings them here. As I move, I dislodge a small stone, and it clatters away, sounding like an avalanche.

But the three of them do not hear, and I decide I am close enough. And scared, I do admit.

"Why do you need me to defend your family's honor?" Samuel says.

"To witness," Frederick says. "He used uncouth language concerning our sister Abagail, did he not, Jonathan?"

"Aye, and that's an insult to us all, Samuel—the whole family. When he arrives, you ask Freegift what he said and you'll see," Jonathan tells him.

Strange, since I have not talked with nor mentioned that girl for years.

"Come, let's hide ourselves," Frederick says, beckoning Samuel closer to the trunk of the tree, near the branches I'd trimmed. "He works early in the day. We won't have to wait long. I heard the tree fall the day before the Sabbath and spied him from across the river. He'll be here soon. We'll give him a thrashing and then take ourselves home for a fine breakfast."

I cringe at the thought of three fellows beating me, and pull back, fearful they may find me as they watch for my approach. Fright clutches my gut, and I plan my escape, wishing I had never crawled closer. I hear talk of hiding places, and Frederick tells Samuel to burrow under the wilting leaves of the thick branches still waiting to be trimmed. An excellent spot, they all decide, upon closer inspection.

Then, amidst deciding who is to go first, Jonathan grabs Samuel from behind and slams him against the bare trunk. I hear the grunting shock as air is dispelled from Samuel's lungs, the startled disbelief that fails to form into words as Frederick throws him over the trunk, pulls his cousin's head back by his hair, and wields a knife.

He hesitates long enough for Samuel to cry out, "No!" and for me to recognize the glinting blade of my own clasp knife.

He draws it across Samuel's throat, and I cannot bear to think what will happen. In an instant, my mind tells me it is a trick they are playing on Samuel, or on me, because this cannot be real.

This cannot be happening.

There is a terrible gurgling as Frederick and Jonathan step back, stumbling away from the horrible deed and the effusion of blood. Samuel turns, clutching his neck, which streams crimson red. He falls, blood gushing through his fingers, as the two brothers gape openmouthed at their handiwork.

This cannot be real.

I feel it in the pit of my stomach, in my widened eyes, and in the sweat at the small of my back. It is real. Frederick and Jonathan are murdering their cousin. Nothing can put back the blood in Samuel's body; it is not a trick. Nothing can heal this evil breach. Frederick's ancestors must be shuddering and wailing at such foulness.

Samuel collapses in one final lurch. He does not move. The blood no longer flows. Frederick takes a step and gingerly kicks Samuel's leg.

"For God's sake, he's dead," Jonathan says, a bark of laughter escaping his maw. "Have you ever seen so much blood?"

"Every time we slaughter a cow, you idiot," Frederick says. "Now open his hand."

Jonathan does as he is told. I see Frederick place a small object in Samuel's palm and close it. They drag the body to the far end of the tree, hiding it under the branches at its very top, which is further sheltered by smaller pines it snapped as it fell. Jonathan spreads cut branches to cover blood soaking into the ground.

"Now for the sheriff," Frederick says. "Remember, Samuel went off in a rage, vowing to take revenge on poor Freegift for his indecent comments about his fair cousin."

"Wait, the blood," Jonathan says, pointing to the cuff of Frederick's shirt, speckled with pink spray.

"I'll soak it in the river," Frederick says. "The blood is not yet dry, but the cuff will be by the time we get to Sheriff Harkin. Quickly now, Brother, to the river. You'll paddle as I soak this damned blood out."

They walk away, satisfied with their work. The violence of it sickens me as my mind swirls to understand why they would do such a thing. And why it was done at the site of my labors. I fear the thought forming in my head as I approach where the body is hidden. They may be a hideous pair of brothers, but they are smart. I would not stumble upon poor Samuel for hours as I worked my way down the tree, trimming branches and sectioning it.

I prepare myself as I draw closer. I have seen game killed and skinned, sheep slaughtered, and fish gutted. But all that is in the natural order of things. This is not.

Samuel is torn at the throat. I cannot bear to look and retreat instead. Bile rises, and I choke out pieces of johnnycake as my stomach protests at what my eyes have seen. I force myself back, for I must find what he holds.

Having seen Samuel once, it is not so hard the second time. I kneel and take his hand in mine. Still warm and pliable. I open it and find what I expected.

My button. A match to the others on my Sunday waistcoat. Then I study how the body lays and move Samuel's limbs. What I search for next cannot be far.

I find it under his shoulder. My clasp knife, which Frederick never forgets, and now uses to hang me.

Damn him, he will not.

I run, the knife and button secure in my pocket, knowing I am still in danger. I run along the deer trail that leads to the river, a faster route than Frederick's. They skirt the steep slope and go the long, safe way. The deer and I know better. I am familiar with these woods and foresee where a canoe would have been brought up on the riverbank.

I run down the slope, catching thin trees to avoid a fall, flinging myself from one to another, all the time calculating where the brothers must be as they walk from the ridge. I come to the riverbank through a grove of mountain laurel, and there is the canoe, pulled up in a small inlet.

I take it.

Frederick and Jonathan are ten minutes away, no more. I paddle quietly across the calm river, knowing it to have a deep channel. Though not wide, it will take a hardy swim to cross. As I reach the far bank, I place the paddle exactly as it was, and shove the vessel back. Let them think their own carelessness took it into the current. Or let them worry. I have little choice if I am to beat them.

For they will return on horseback, of that I am certain.

I run again, this time across Frederick's land, keeping to the lines of stone walls and trees that divide his fields. I run until my lungs feel as if they will burst, then slow to a walk, gasping in air, and then run again.

For my life.

The sheriff is a quick ride from Frederick's farm. Jacob Harkin is a lawyer, elected sheriff last year. Mr. Stoddard speaks well of him, but that is all I can say about the man. Other than he has a good horse.

I see Frederick's homestead ahead, smoke rising from the chimney. His two sisters keep house, and they will be about, along with the youngest of the lot, a boy of nine who should be busy with chores. They must not see me.

I run by a cornfield, the stalks hiding me from them, but not from Frederick's approach if he be closer than I think. I crouch low as the cornfield ends, and peek around the corner. I see the house and barn. I see the boy, splitting wood on a stump by the back door.

He carries a load into the kitchen, and I race to the barn, hoping his sisters are busy with their work and not idly gazing out the window. If so, I am undone. I press myself against the door at the rear of the barn, waiting for my breathing to settle. I hear an axe making kindling as the lad returns to his chore. I unlatch the door, quietly, to not disturb the horses.

I slip in and close the latch, blinking rapidly to see better in the gloom. The axe continues to fall in a steady rhythm as I look to the horse stalls.

Empty, or nearly so. The Perkinses are renowned for their horses and are known to have ten or so fine steeds. But only two remain at the far end of the barn. Apollo and one other, saddled and ready. Another axe strike, and I wish the lad strength to continue. I approach Apollo, grabbing a handful of hay. He is eager to eat and nuzzles me for more. I lean in, grasping the bridle with its inlaid brass decorations.

I reach down and pry one off with my blade, whispering soothing words to the horse.

The axe goes silent.

I make for the back door as I hear voices. Angry voices. Frederick and Jonathan tell their brother to mind his own business and return to his chores. Frederick chides Jonathan for not securing the canoe. Jonathan bemoans his sodden clothes and asks why he had to swim for it, not for the first time by his whining tone.

"Change then, you fool!" Frederick shouts. "Harkin can't see you soaked to the bone."

With that, he opens the tall barn doors wide, letting in a flood of light.

I step back into the empty stall near Apollo and crouch in a corner, hoping the shadows will hide me from Frederick's fury. He storms in and I hear him holler after his brother, calling him a vile lily-livered toad and threatening to whip him if he fails to be ready when he returns with the sheriff. Whipping and beating seem to play a large role in Frederick's life.

I hear him lead Apollo from her stall, and the horse stomps in excitement, or maybe giving warning to its master. Frederick curses the horse too, and I hear his boot take to the stirrup as he pulls himself into the saddle, leather creaking beneath his weight. Apollo neighs and stomps again, perhaps nervous at the smell of blood and death clinging to Frederick.

"Damn," he snarls as his cocked hat falls to the ground, rolling right in front of the stall where I hide. I gasp, and it sounds to my ears like a thunderous wind. Cornered, I am defenseless if Frederick dismounts.

But he does not, in a great hurry to make up lost time. He must be frantic that I might arrive and find evidence of what he has done. Let him fret. He has more worries to come.

For I have even more than I dared hope for; his fine felt cocked hat, with a black ribbon cockade held in place by a pewter pin, inscribed with that *P* the Perkins men wear so proudly.

I leave by the rear entrance, darting for the woods, hiding myself from the house. Now I have no worries of being seen until warned by horse's hooves beating the ground. Once away, I sprint across the fields, making directly for the river at its narrowest point. I cannot take the canoe a second time. One unmooring is chance. Two is clearly by design.

I halt at the riverbank, blown like a racehorse at the end of the course. My chest heaves for air, but I cannot rest. I hear the distant drumbeat of three horsemen at a gallop, coming steadily on. I plunge into the river, holding the hat above water, since it would make no sense for it to be found soaking wet by the chestnut tree.

Once I gain the other side, I stumble up the deer trail, gasping for air, hearing the voices of Frederick and Jonathan not far behind as they take to the canoe. I scramble on but slip as a stone comes loose and rattles down, clacking against rock and wood. I fall after it, sliding back on my belly, losing my grip on the hat, which tumbles away from me much as it did from Frederick.

I must retrieve it. I scurry down, wincing as more stones dislodge themselves, cursing my own weakness after these exertions. Samuel's face and ripped throat appear before me, a warning against what could happen to me, or perhaps, a plea for justice from his spirit. Both give me strength.

I have the hat firm in my hand as the scrunch of gravel announces the canoe coming ashore. "This way, I think," Frederick says, his tone changed now as he plays a different role for Sheriff Harkin.

They are off on the roundabout path again. This time, I have no burst of downhill energy on my side. I must pull myself upward against my own laboring lungs and aching muscles. *Better than the hangman's noose*, I tell myself. *Better that Samuel has justice done as well.*

And no small part of me demands to know why this happened.

What had Samuel and I done to be singled out for death? What brought forth this plan, put into motion by Frederick on the Sabbath?

I break out of the deer trail and propel myself forward into the sunlight on the hillside, vaulting over the fallen chestnut and parting the branches where Samuel lay. He'd gained the pallor of death and gone gray-skinned, sunken-eyed, cold-handed. I force open his stiffening fingers and place the brass piece within.

The hat. Where to put it?

On the side of the tree opposite Samuel's body. Where it might have fallen and not been seen by a killer eager to escape. There, lodged between two branches, hidden just enough to suggest it had been lost.

Voices. I hear Sheriff Harkin urging them on. I turn to clamber up the rocks to my hiding place, but the ground is too open, and they may come upon me in a moment. I back up, careful not to snap a dry twig, and hide behind a thick tree trunk. I lie down, watching for their entrance into this deathly scene.

They come out of the woods, Frederick first, and he seems to look right at me. His eyes pass over me, searching the length of the tree, looking for evidence of my presence. He must wonder, since by this time I should already be swinging my axe. Jonathan wears his new garments. Sheriff Harkin carries a leather sack across his shoulder.

"Well, Frederick," the sheriff says, his voice hinting at exasperation. "Where are they, either of them?"

"Freegift was working here, I am sure," Frederick says, his voice betraying a worry that the sheriff might take as concern for his cousin.

"And Samuel was intent upon finding him," Jonathan adds. He walks closer to the trunk, and I see him lay his eyes upon his brother's hat stuck down in the branches. He nearly jumps and turns to Frederick, barely able to keep from blurting out what he has seen. The boy is a poor liar indeed.

"What do you see?" Harkin asks, but before he can move closer, Frederick seizes the moment.

"My God!" he cries, pointing to where Samuel lies. "Samuel!"

They gather around where the body is hidden and pull him out. Frederick remembers to act surprised, but Jonathan is too perplexed by the hat to do anything other than glance back again and again, as if some explanation might appear the next time he looks.

"See to his hand," Frederick says, pointing. Harkin studies both the brothers, and I can see a suspicion starting to form as they act even more strangely. I think that murder must be much easier to think upon than to carry out.

"I will," Harkin says, bending down. He comes up with a small object, which he quickly pockets.

"What is it?" Jonathan asks.

"Evidence of the guilty party, I daresay. Now, let us search the area," Harkin tells them.

"Is that not enough?" Jonathan asks, his voice rising. Frederick begins to look relieved and rebukes his brother, instructing him to look more closely where the body was hidden away. Jonathan does so, and as he is within the branches, Harkin draws out iron shackles from his leather bag.

"Hold these, Frederick. We may need them at hand should Free-gift show himself."

"It will be my pleasure," Frederick says, followed by a cry as Harkin fixes the shackles hard upon Frederick's wrists, knocking him to the ground. In a second, he brandishes a flintlock pistol and orders Jonathan to stand with his hands raised.

"Brother," Jonathan says, his lower lip trembling and tears about to burst forth. "What have you done?"

"Me, you stupid swine? Mind what you say!"

There follows a torrent of brotherly abuse until Harkin silences them with a wave of his cocked pistol.

"Jonathan, go fetch whatever you saw that startled you so," Harkin orders. "Be quick about it." Jonathan sends a sneer his brother's way and steps over the tree trunk, hoisting up Frederick's cocked hat. Frederick blinks in surprise, as if he's just seen a conjuring act.

"This is yours, is it not?" Harkin demands, pointing to the pewter piece. "This is your initial engraved so."

"I have no idea how it came to be here," Frederick stammers.

"Nor this?" Harkin says, displaying the brass ornament with the same letter.

"But Freegift did this," Frederick says. "He had to."

"Your hat. Your harness ornament. Both close to the murdered body," Harkin says.

"But he is our dear cousin," Jonathan says, tears staining his sweaty cheek.

"Yes, dear cousin indeed. But not dear enough, for it looks like you murdered him to gain your family land back, and tried to lay the blame on a slave," Harkin says. "It is no secret that you are your father's son when it comes to bad investments and speculation, Frederick. And you are well aware Samuel is unmarried and has no issue of his own. Therefore, his land reverts to the blood of the original purchaser."

"No," says Frederick.

I am befuddled.

"Oh, yes," Harkin says. "I handle Samuel's legal affairs and know he has no will. Therefore, the land reverts to the original purchaser, meaning your father, who sold it to Samuel. Since your father is deceased, you inherit as his eldest son. My only question is who actually wielded the blade?"

"Not me," Jonathan cries as Harkin produces another set of shackles and tells Jonathan to wrap his arms around a tree. He secures the iron restraints and tells him he shall return with men to remove the body. At some point.

Frederick curses, Jonathan weeps, and I back away quietly, circling around to pick up my tools and take a long pull of ale. Poor Samuel, killed for his land. Poor Freegift, nearly hung for it. I take another drink, my hand trembling at the horror of what I have seen and what could have come to pass.

Soon I begin the slow walk home. I plan my story, that a muscle ache bothered me and I could not work the axe today. Instead, I searched for hickory trees near the river, where they'd be easy to float downstream close by the cooperage.

Yes, it is a good story. Although Maame knows when I tell a lie. She may see through it but will keep it to herself until we are alone. If she presses me for the truth of it, well, I shall have a fine secret to keep from her.

Then perhaps one day she will trade her truth in exchange for the tale of the horse chestnut tree.

THE TWO NEDS

■ ■ ■

"BURNETT."

The name drifted across the snow. Wind took the sound and scattered it, stabbing men's cheeks, stinging their eyes. It was also their
salvation, casting away the crunch of boots on snow, hurried whispers,
the subtle sounds of fabric and gear as each man swiveled his body,
moving head and eyes front and back, side to side. Even so, Jake
Burnett heard his name.

"Yeah." He twisted his head and felt the frozen snow tapping at
the back of his helmet. The wind danced loose granules over the
foot-deep snowpack, sending clouds of white over the surface. Good
for crawling on your belly, hell on the eyes. He shivered, from deep
inside, the spasms radiating out, rippling through his lungs and
shaking his limbs. He tightened his grip on his M1 Garand, afraid
it might leap from his quivering hands. He let the shiver run through
him, a puppet pulled on strings of frost.

Hand signals shot out. Index finger stabbing at him, pointing at
Clay Brock, five yards to his left. Keep low. Scout forward. Jake took
it in, nodded, and turned away. Cradling his rifle, he pulled himself
forward by his elbows, feeling the cold on his thighs the most. His
feet weren't bad, encased in four-buckle overshoes, combat boots, and
several pairs of wool socks. He had lost count of the layers under his
field jacket, sweaters and shirts compressed into one sweat-encrusted
stinking second skin. But even with long johns and the heavy wool
pants, crawling in the snow left his thighs numb with the cold. No,
numb would have been good. They were bruised with cold, prickly
and raw, razor blades slicing them each time he moved over the frozen
ground.

Jake watched Clay crawl to the base of a pine, raising himself on one knee. The edge of Clay's helmet and one eye peered out from behind the tree, under the first branches, heavy with snow, bent into a drift. He was still, except for his eyes. Jake couldn't see him, but he knew. He knew Clay. Knew his smell, what his cough in the night sounded like, how he moved through cover, and what he'd say next. Behind Clay was a jumble of thick brush, brown branches with lines of white snow on them weaving patterns in every direction. Patterns that a helmet edge wouldn't betray. Stick your head out with a nice clear background of white and Western Union would be knocking at the door.

Clay slowly pulled his head behind the tree trunk. No sharp moves, nothing to draw the eye. He slumped down and looked at Jake. Jake rolled and got up on his knees. Snow clung to his jacket and worked its way down the olive drab scarf knotted around his neck. He hugged his legs, willing warmth into his thighs. Clay waited patiently; he was never in a hurry. But that was Clay's nature. Slow and calm, deliberate and predictable.

"Red says scout down to the tree line," Jake whispered.

"Fuck," Clay said. Jake knew that would be his first response. If he had told Clay that they were to head back to Company HQ for hot chow, it would have been the same. Anything the army wanted Clay to do was greeted with contempt.

"Observe across that field, report back," said Jake. "Look like a hundred yards?"

"Yep. Fuck," said Clay. He leaned his head forward and tapped the front sight of his M1 on his helmet, a habit he'd started a week ago. Jake didn't ask about it. He had his own superstitions, secrets, and rituals. "Let's go."

"Fuck yeah," said Jake, trying to imitate Clay's flat Tennessee drawl. He tried to smile but couldn't tell if it showed under the frost-encrusted stubble on his face and the scarf drawn up over his chin. Clay caught himself as he began to roll over to start the hundred-yard crawl. He looked at Jake, raised an eyebrow.

"When'd you start being funny, Jake?"

A broad grin lit Clay's narrow, dirty face. The kind of face that when you gave it a good scrubbing would show a sweet country boy, more Tom Sawyer than Huck Finn. But this wasn't dirt from playing down by the stream. It wasn't the dirt of mischief and mumbley-peg. It was foxhole dirt, muddy earth overlaid with black cordite smudges, white crow's feet showing at the edges of Clay's eye where it squeezed shut when he aimed, easing his finger against the trigger, lining everything up, spinning a straight course from his eyeball through the rear sight, along the barrel, over the front sights, across the gulf separating him from the target, the enemy, the quick from the dead. Final pressure on the trigger and the slam of the shot, M1 jarring his shoulder, smoking cartridge ejecting into the air, the direct line between brain, eye, weapon, and enemy disconnecting as a gray uniform slumps to the ground, the tension releasing as if a cord was cut, like a kite on a windy day when the string snaps and falls from the sky.

Jake smiled, and it felt like his cheeks would crack from the effort. Clay could smile with ease, as if a grin were the natural set of his jaw. Jake had seen him walking a muddy road, weighed down with combat gear and pulling his boots out of the ooze with every step, all the while a half smile playing around the corners of his mouth, as if it was all so funny. *Look at us. Ain't we something?*

Jake was better known for silence. Shorter than Clay, his dark, wavy hair surrounded deep brown eyes set under eyebrows that looked permanently knitted. Jake's home was coal country, where the towns lay in cramped valleys, steep hills cutting sunsets short and letting in the morning light a full hour after dawn. Side streets ended in one or two blocks, dead ends hitting granite looming like a giant wall over skinny brick houses, the kind of landscape that got you worried just waking up in the morning.

But that was nothing compared to this country. There was so much to worry about here you couldn't afford to, not enough time or energy for that. You just tapped your helmet, made your little joke, did whatever you could do to convince yourself you'd get through this day, and that your squadmates wouldn't start a fistfight in the middle of it all.

Clay went left, Jake right, as low to the ground as they could get, heads down like swimmers doing the crawl. Elbows out, pull. Push with the knees. Butt down. They kept apart, but within sight of each other as the land sloped down, the pine woods thinning out into a field. They could see it clearly now, a wide strip of cleared land, a farmer's field. It curved to the right, rising as it did so they couldn't see beyond the small hill. Winds drifted the snow, in some places leaving only a thin covering. Stubble stuck up through the white cover. Sugar beets maybe. But the field didn't matter, unless it was mined, of course. What the lieutenant really wanted to know was about the tree line on the other side of the field. Was that the German MLR?

Main Line of Resistance. Go find it. That was their job. A simple one. Just sneak around a few outposts and keep going until lots of people started shooting at you. Not a few rifle shots, there had to be heavy stuff too. Machine guns? Mortar fire? Good, you found it. If you didn't get hit right away, or pinned down, you had a chance to hustle back, keeping an eye out for patrols, outposts, minefields, and your own trigger-happy buddies in their foxholes.

Clay cursed again, knowing that after all that, he'd probably spend the night keeping the BAR man and his ammo carrier from beating each other senseless. Loot had them at each other's throats.

Clay signaled to Jake. They were behind a big pine, branches screening them. They'd stopped short of the scrawny trunks, the smallest growth at the edge of the field, going to cover behind thick green branches coated with white, hung down to the ground, frozen. Clay pointed to a jumble of boulders five feet tall. Perfect. Hard angles between jutting rocks. Jake nodded, and they both crawled around the pine trees, giving the branches a wide berth. A slight touch and the snow would slide off, sending the green fir flying up like a penalty flag to betray them. It happened all the time when the sun warmed the ice. You heard the snow hit the ground with a soft crunch, then the whoosh of the branch springing up out of it. Only there was no sun now, nothing but grayness and wind and a white swirl along the hard ground.

They moved in front of the trees, keeping them at their backs. Jake looked across the field, as much as he could without lifting his head. Tops of trees lined the horizon, under the rim of his helmet. A mix of pines and bare branches, standing out against the sky like lattice-work. Lots of oak, old growth, thick-trunked trees in forests where you could walk with your arms outstretched.

Clay was at the rocks. Jake scuttled sideways, rolled over, and lay on the rock, helmet tilted back, mouth hung open gasping frigid air. He didn't move, except to push his scarf up over his mouth so he could create a little pocket of false hope as he exhaled the air warmed by his lungs.

"Fuck," Clay finally said.

Jake knew what he meant. He could feel the sweat dripping down his back, matting his damp hair, gathering on his stomach. The exertion had warmed him, but in a minute the sweat would soak into his clothes, chilling his skin as he lay exposed to the wind and cold.

Clay looked at Jake, who raised a finger as he brushed snow from his face with the other hand. *Gimme a sec.* Clay nodded, a slight dip of the head as he closed his eyes, then opened them as he looked away. *Okay, no problem, take your time, buddy.* They all shared a secret language. Looks, gestures, nods, a raised eyebrow, everything had a meaning that was bound up in who they were, unintelligible to anyone outside their experience of each other. Days and nights together, on marches or waiting by the side of the road, in some nameless village, sleeping in a hastily dug hole, huddled for warmth, or in a bombed-out house, maybe a barn with clean hay if they were really lucky, had given them time to decipher each other, taking in moods, reading between the lines, learning from silences, until it was second nature to know the other man from the set of his shoulders, the look in his eyes, a catch in the voice.

The shorthand of men at war.

All this took time and ability, the willingness to observe and listen. Infantrymen who came ashore in the spring and summer of 1944 without the skill of observation and listening, whether to their buddies or the sounds from the fields and woods of northern France, didn't need to worry about time. By the winter of 1945, in Belgium or Germany, maybe Luxembourg—nobody was really sure where the hell they were—they were already dead.

Two large rocks, about five feet tall, leaned against each other with a small cleft at the top. Clay flattened his face on the rock and peered sideways through the space. He looked down the edge of the tree line and watched. Not a sound, no movement to catch the eye. He crouched and slowly moved his face to the bottom of the cleft, looking straight out across the field. He felt the wind blowing on his face, heard it swishing the pines and drifting up snow in front of the rocks. The wind lessened and he heard another sound. Scratching? The wind rose and he heard it again, his ear tuned to it.

Scritch. Scrittttttch.

Jake took off his helmet, not risking the telltale *clunk* of metal helmet against rock. He moved slowly, as Clay leaned to the left. Their heads joined, one right eye and one left eye each with a clear view.

Scritch.

A leaf, brown and curled, from one of the giant oaks across the field. Its sharp lobes turned downward so it looked like a prehistoric insect, teetering on its pointed tips, stem straight out like a tail. The wind pushed it along the top of the crusted snow, the sound unnaturally loud in the silence.

Then it was gone. Jake blinked. Clay raised his head an inch, tilting it back to get a better angle on the field. Jake looked at him, saw his eyes widen. Then he saw it too. A line of footprints, almost obscured by the drifting snow. They raised their heads as high as they safely could, and from this added vantage saw clusters of brown leaves caught in a clear trail of footprints that led along their edge of the woods, right in front of them, heading across the field to a spot where the woods jutted out onto a small rise. They eased their heads back behind the cover of the rock. Jake shivered.

"Fuck," whispered Clay as he raised his binoculars. He wished he had his helmet on, so he could hold his M1 butt to the ground and tap it on his helmet two or three times. Three times would be good. Fuck, fuck, fuck. Clay could hear his daddy say it clear as day. *Fuck this tractor, ain't worth shit. Fuck this engine, and fuck Henry Ford, too. Fuck that banker man.*

Clay's stomach was in a knot, like it always was when his daddy swore like that. But he'd come to understand his daddy never used it in a nasty way. When he said it, it was to mean, *I ain't got nothing left but this awful, terrible swear word, and by God you ain't taking that from me.* That's how Clay used it, never to mean something dirty, but to show his daddy, wherever he was, that he too still had something left when he stood at the end of the road.

In the tree line, past where the sugar beet field turned to brush and pine seedlings, Clay spied logs, stacked up about three feet, with cut pine branches strewn around to soften the straight lines, German helmets, bobbing up and down, rifle snouts sticking out, and two heavy machine guns. The Germans had good fields of fire in either direction. He scanned left. No log emplacements. The rise was either a strong point on the MLR, or an outpost in front of it. He knew what that meant. Fuck. He slid down, head low.

"MG-42s, two of them, with plenty of Krauts, in the woods, on the right, up on that rise."

"See anything else?" Jake asked.

"Nope."

"Shit. I'll tell Red."

Jake went flat, crawling back on his own track, figuring the odds. He knew he could count on Clay, but he was unsure of the Neds.

Something had come between them, and he hoped it wouldn't get in the way of keeping them all alive. Red was a good officer, and Jake liked that his foxhole was right up with theirs, not as far back as he could get and still say he was at the front. Like some. Jake put his arm over Red's shoulder and pointed across the field.

"Two MG-42s, camouflaged behind logs, buncha Krauts around 'em." Jake kept his fingers pointed until Red got out his binoculars.

"Yeah," Red said. "Anything else?"

"Can't see on the right, and Clay couldn't find anything on the left. Could be dug in."

"Let's find out," Red said. He looked at Jake, and the others gathered around. He wasn't asking, but Red liked everybody on board.

"Okay," said Jake. The Neds nodded.

"Big Ned, Little Ned," Red said. "Get the BAR set up over there, under that fallen pine."

Ned Warren and Ned Kelleher were a team, and it was obvious who was who. Big Ned handled the Browning Automatic Rifle, a sixteen-pound monster that looked like a toy in his big, beefy hands. Big Ned was the strongest guy in the platoon, a Michigan lumberjack who almost split the shoulder seams of his field jacket. A jagged scar ran from his left ear across his cheek, the result of either a faulty chainsaw or a knife fight with an Indian from Mackinac Island, depending on how much Big Ned had had to drink. Little Ned was his ammo carrier. Besides his own gear, he had to carry a heavy ammo pouch for the BAR. Little Ned was a small guy, but there was wiry muscle on every bone, and Little Ned could walk lighter than any man in the squad. His union card said he was a structural steelworker, used to climbing on I and H columns floating far above city streets, bolting steel beams with a spud wrench. Little Ned was great with tools and could fix a jam in the BAR faster than Big Ned could get his gloves off. The Neds stood side by side, not looking at or speaking to each other.

"That fallen pine is a little exposed," said Little Ned, not arguing, merely stating a fact.

"Yeah, but you can crawl down to it, dig out a little snow, and fire from underneath it. It's good cover, don't worry," said Red.

"I ain't worried about getting there, Red," he answered, looking out at the field and not bothering to say the obvious. They could crawl to the pine easy enough. It had toppled over and lay at an angle, facing the machine-gun nest. Broken branches held the tree up off the ground, leaving space to fire through.

"I got two smoke grenades," Red said, willing himself to speak slowly and calmly, as if explaining to a kid that a shot at the doctor's wasn't going to hurt. "When I throw them in front of you, haul ass out. Jake, you and Clay on our left flank. Open up on my signal, and we'll find out what they got. Smoke is the signal for the Neds to clear out, plenty of covering fire. Understood?"

They understood. Big Ned and Little Ned avoided each other's eyes and moved into position. Jake signaled to Clay to crawl back and explained the plan.

"Sounds easy," said Clay, trying to catch his breath. Plans always sounded good. They were soothing, gave you the illusion of something to count on. "What about the Neds?"

"Not sure," Jake said. "They aren't talking, but they're listening okay."

"Fuck," Clay said, summing it up. It was bad news when the Neds were at each other's throats. The patrol had to work smoothly, everyone firing on all cylinders, not nursing grudges.

Clay settled in, resting his M1 in the snow, twisting the sling around his forearm to steady his aim. At this distance, aimed fire didn't mean much, but it was how Clay did things. Jake gave the high sign to Red. All set. They watched Big Ned and Little Ned snake their way down the slope to the fallen pine.

Big Ned dragged the BAR by the barrel, too big to cradle in his arms like a rifle. He moved over the snow like a plow, flattening it as he went. Little Ned scuttled like a crab. He didn't have the best technique, too much elbow and butt above his head. But he'd stop often and freeze, so if his movement caught a Kraut's eye, maybe he'd blink and look again before he shot, and think, *Damn, I'm too jumpy, it's nothing.*

Big Ned and Little Ned didn't like each other. Big Ned was an outdoorsman, a backwoods boy. Little Ned had a few years on him, and at twenty-five thought he knew everything. He'd worked in Philadelphia, Richmond, and Baltimore, seen more people from up on those beams than they had in all of Michigan. Some guys, with different backgrounds like that, would pepper each other with questions about home, eager to learn about a part of the country they'd never seen, wouldn't have known about, except for the war. They'd write their mom and dad about this swell fellow from Idaho, or a great pal from Georgia, and stories about distant states would be scattered around the nation like fireflies on a summer night.

Not the Neds.

They tolerated each other. They depended on each other, knew the other guy pretty damn well, and could count on him in combat. But they grated on each other, having nothing in common but a desire to live. They understood that if they lived through this, they'd shake hands at the end, turn away, no regrets.

They'd argued yesterday about loot, and it had turned into a fight. They'd found a dead Kraut with a collection of rings in his pocket. Gold rings, diamond rings, all sorts of rings. They looked valuable. The Kraut had them on a string, wrapped in a piece of soft leather so they wouldn't jangle. GI gold bands, French engagement rings, rich lady rings, a man's wedding ring with a showy diamond. Expensive, small stuff. Good loot.

The Kraut was still warm, and that should have been a warning. Mortar rounds started to drop around them, curses in German rang out from the next ridgeline. Bullets smashed into the trees as Little Ned tossed a smoke grenade for cover. They ran.

Once they were safe, Little Ned went berserk. He'd had the rings, he said, was certain he'd put them in his pocket, but now they were gone. He tried to go back, but Big Ned stopped him, catching the sound of Germans coming through the woods. Their small fortune was lost, and without much of a friendship to fall back on, things got worse. They accused each other of being at fault and got into a fight that left them bruised around the cheek and jaw. They drank, collapsed, then got up and went on this patrol, sullen, angry.

The Neds knew this patrol wasn't about being pals. This was serious, a job to be done like so many others, one that could get them or the whole squad killed. They finally looked each other in the eye, and with a brief nod, acknowledged they understood. Big Ned moved off, going wide so his trailing BAR didn't snag on a half-buried branch. He was almost to the tree now, and Little Ned scurried forward, flailing his arms too much as he always did.

Jake could feel his heart thump louder in his chest. Sweat broke out on his forehead, feeling like it might freeze before it dripped off. He shivered, trying to still himself. Any second now.

Little Ned stuck his elbow in the snow and pushed off with his left leg, aching to get behind that big pine, aching even more to be running up that slope with clouds of smoke between them and the Kraut gunners. His foot hit something.

Clump.

Jake saw it, a tremor at first, then the achingly slow slide as heavy snow slid down a thick pine branch. He saw Little Ned turn as the snow hit him and buried his legs.

Whoosh.

The green fir flew into the air, freed of its snowy burden. The tip of the branch had been buried, but Little Ned had pushed off on it, kicking off a clear signal, green against white and GI brown.

Jake knew light traveled faster than sound, but he didn't think he'd ever see it. Everything became crystal clear, intense, as if it were suddenly blue skies and sun, all color and clarity. He saw the twinkling bright sharp whiteness from machine guns, and sparkling lights all along the woods, hundreds of them. They were everywhere, silent, incandescent. Then the sounds exploded.

Clay heard the snowfall from the branches. He didn't wait for Red to fire. He squeezed off his first shot, then the second, breathing in and out, not wanting to be some trigger-happy fool firing into the air. Take aim, fire at the enemy. He knew it was useless.

"Jesus Christ," Red said. He grabbed a smoke grenade and threw it. "Jesus Christ."

Big Ned turned in time to see Little Ned try to pull himself out from under the snow. The MG-42 chopped up the top of the dead pine, and he had to duck. He fired and tried not to think.

The German machine-gunner aimed his bursts at Little Ned and so did every other Kraut dug in under camouflaged trenches and foxholes along the MLR. Little Ned and the tree were the only things moving, and they drew fire. He was hit, and hit again, killed twenty times over as swarms of bullets chopped the branches and brush all around him. He never had a chance to say a thing, to curse the branch, think about home, wonder about the rings, or see the bright bursts of gunfire that Jake saw as a strange thing of distant, terrible beauty.

Red pulled the pin on the second smoke grenade and flung it out in front of Big Ned as a round caught his left arm, passing through it, spraying blood on the snow. Red saw the blood, didn't feel a thing, couldn't get his arm to work.

"Pull back!" Red yelled to Big Ned. Bullets thrummed around them, steel wasps buzzing their ears. Snow flew up in clumps and pine bark rained on their heads.

Big Ned saw the first smoke grenade hit the ground in front of him and rammed a fresh clip into the BAR. He fired, amazed at being alive, wondering how many of those fuckers they had over there. The second smoke grenade hit, bouncing and rolling as smoke spewed out. He let the BAR hang from his neck and ran over to Little Ned, grabbed him by the collar, and pulled him up the slope into the tree line.

They gathered deep in the darkening woods. Jake was bandaging Red's arm. Big Ned had dragged Little Ned through the woods and was looking for branches to make a litter.

"I ain't leaving him here," said Big Ned, to himself as much as the others.

"He's dead," said Red, as if that settled everything.

"I know he's dead, but I ain't leaving him here."

They found pine branches to make a sled. Clay had a length of rope and cut it into pieces to tie the branches together. Little Ned was shot up bad. Only his clothing and web belt cinched tight kept him in one piece. When they were done, Big Ned looped the rope around his shoulders, refusing help.

They set off, trudging through the woods, hoping to get back to their lines before dark. Jake heard Big Ned talking to himself, whispering, the words rising and falling on currents of quiet anger. Straining to hear, he realized Big Ned was talking to Little Ned.

Shit . . . what am I supposed to do . . . you stupid fuck . . . Put up with you for five long months and what do I get? You go and get yourself killed. What a fucking stupid thing to do. I always told you, you crawl like a fucking recruit. Now I'm going to have some asshole replacement carry ammo for me and he'll point me out to some Kraut sniper . . . I'm fucking dead . . . Thanks for nothing, shithead. I never could stand being around you, and now that you ain't here, I'm screwed. God damn it.

The cursing continued into the night, long after they made it through their lines. Clay and Jake took Red to battalion aid; Big Ned took Little Ned back to Company HQ so Graves Registration could get him in the morning. He covered him with a tarp, pulled up an ammo crate, sat down, and lit a Lucky. He thought hard while he smoked, about fortunes lost and gained, about life and death, right and wrong. About guilt, and all the things he wanted. Now, all he felt was regret, all he wanted lay dead before him.

Clay and Jake came upon him as snow began to fall. It covered Little Ned like a blanket and sat on Big Ned's shoulders like a shawl.

They stood, silently paying their respects, curious about Big Ned's mourning of a guy he'd never really liked and had come to blows with the day before.

They watched as Big Ned unbuttoned his jacket, dug around in the layers of wool until he found it. The string of rings, tied to a bootlace around his neck, close to his heart. His fortune. He untied the string and removed one ring, the diamond wedding band. He secured the rest, pulled back the tarp, lifted Little Ned's neck gently, and placed the bootlace around it, stuffing the leather sack deep under his clothes, against his cold skin. He took Little Ned's cold, gray hand in his and worked the ring onto his finger.

"They might rob him," Big Ned whispered, aware of Jake and Clay. "But they won't take a ring off a guy's finger." They'd all heard of rear area slobs stealing from the dead and wounded.

He put the tarp back, pulled out another Lucky, and lit up. The snow became thick, and Clay draped a blanket around Big Ned. Jake laid a hand on his shoulder, and then they left him alone.

As the quiet whiteness graced the Neds, the cursing began again, in the cadence of a prayer, the repetition like a hymn.

You fucking bastard . . .

GLASS

■ ■ ■

THE PROTON MOVED at an insane speed. If it had been capable of fear, it would have been terrified. Contained within an oval tube, traveling just short of the speed of light, it whipped around the 54.1-mile circuit ceaselessly as other protons shot past it from the opposite direction. Collisions sparked all around it, sending smashed protons against the smooth metallic surface, which contained its universe.

If the proton could have felt pride, it would have beamed at its speed, staying ahead of the bundle of particles it had started its journey with. It would have marveled at its agility, avoiding the oncoming protons that would have meant cataclysmic destruction.

But it never could have considered the sterile neutrino attracted to the gravitational force the fast proton generated. Sterile neutrinos have no regard for matter, but this one found the pull of gravity irresistible, following in the proton's wake like a mad suitor, enveloping it as they approached the speed of light at 0.999999991c.

For a microportion of a nanosecond, the neutrino and the proton bonded—the neutrino caring only for gravity, bound to no other laws of nature. The proton spun even faster; the kinetic energy of its component quarks spurred on by the absorption of the sterile neutrino. Neither could know it, but at that less-than-a-moment, they—or it—were unique in the universe.

The collision ended that. Another proton smashed into the union of neutrino and fast proton, releasing immense energies that could not be contained within the oval universe. The reaction obliterated the proton and neutrino duo, generating a Higgs boson field that simultaneously threw off a Higgs singlet. Formerly only theorized, the singlet was now real, responding to nothing but gravity, unaware of any other natural forces.

Or dimensions.

The singlet burst out of the contained oval and took with it enormous mass and energy, enough to prevent any object near it from achieving escape velocity and the pull of the quantum mechanical black hole the singlet had created.

The black hole was small. A micro black hole, if you will. Powerful, as all black holes are, but short-lived. The elementary particles of electrons and gluons evaporated, leaving nothing behind.

The Higgs singlet swirled into *elsewhen*, propelled through space and time, vanishing into the depths of the unknown universe.

"TUPPER, YOU'RE FIRED," John Lee Hardy said, not missing a beat when Guy Tupper stepped into the store. "If you can't sell goddamn electric fans in a Waxahachie heat wave, then you can't sell shit." Hardy mopped his ample and sweaty brow with a worn handkerchief, even as a dozen fans kept up a whirlwind inside Hardy's Fans, known far and wide in central Texas as the purveyor of SPRING COOLNESS INDOORS AND FREEDOM FROM HEAT AND SWEAT.

Window fans, ceiling fans, oscillating fans, pedestal fans, and floor fans all labored to bring that freedom to John Lee, but it wasn't working. With suffocating humidity and the temperature topping one hundred, there was damn little spring coolness indoors or anywhere else.

"John Lee, I tried," Guy Tupper said, stretching his hands out in supplication. "I hit all the shops down to Mustang and Silver City. I even called in at a few farms on the way back. Almost sold a rotating fan to the lady of the house, but she couldn't buy it without her husband's say-so."

"On the route all day, and you *almost* sold one unit," John Lee said. "Sweet Jesus, Tupper, you're wasting your time and mine. Unload the van, then you're done. I'll give you a ten-spot to speed you on your way, since I'm in a generous mood."

Guy Tupper knew there was nothing he could say to get John Lee to change his mind. Tupper wasn't sure he wanted him to anyway. His salary was next to nothing and the commissions few and damn far between. He stepped out into the blazing heat and unloaded the van, carrying the fans into the storeroom, disgusted with himself for not telling John Lee what he could do with his sawbuck. He needed it too much.

"Thanks," Tupper said when John Lee handed him the Hamilton.

He hated himself for that. Why the hell hadn't he told John Lee off?

'Cause that wasn't how Guy Tupper was wired, he admitted to himself as he shuffled along the sidewalk to his pickup. The door creaked as he opened it, and a flood of blistering hot air hit him square in the face. He cranked open the window and waited to get in, the steering wheel too hot to touch anyway.

Guy didn't like fights. He didn't like arguments. And he didn't like telling people what he thought. Probably why he wasn't a good salesman. He kept things to himself, unlike John Lee, who could convince a rancher to shell out good money for a ceiling fan by telling him it made the air healthy and fresh when all it did was move the dust motes around.

Guy hated John Lee for his bullshit, and he hated himself for being unable to pull off the same crap. He slid into the truck and started it. It took a couple twists of the key as the motor tried to turn over. He pumped the gas, the rusted and rotting floorboard almost giving way beneath his heel.

What a hunk of junk. Just like his life.

Guy pulled out into the street, squinting into the sun's glare as he headed for his rooming house. He passed the Ritz Theater, its marquee advertising ICE-COLD AIR-CONDITIONING right above *Dr. Zhivago*. Most windows in the brick buildings along his route were wide open, catching what little breeze there was. But a few sported window air conditioners. They were expensive, but they weren't just for movie theaters anymore. In a few years, John Lee might be out of business if they caught on.

It was time to pack up. To get as far out of Waxahachie as he could, as fast as he could. Go stay with his cousin Jerry up in Fort Worth until he figured things out. Jerry had a little repair shop where he fixed radios, televisions, any kind of electrical appliance. Guy hadn't seen him in a few years, but Jerry did nothing but work six days a week and drink on the seventh. Tomorrow wasn't Sunday, so he'd be sober and in the shop.

Jerry had been good to him when Guy and his mother had moved to Texas from Denver when he was a kid. Almost like an older brother. One summer when Guy was in high school, he had stayed at Jerry's and worked at his friend's gas station pumping gas. They hadn't seen each other since his mother died, but Guy was sure Jerry would help. Maybe get a job again.

Back at his rooming house, Guy went through his possessions. Not much to show for more than a quarter century on this earth. He packed everything in a duffel, counted his cash—a grand total of thirty-three dollars and some loose silver—and vowed to make a new start.

Whatever it took.

SUPERCONDUCTING SUPER COLLIDER
UNITED STATES DEPARTMENT OF ENERGY
NO TRESPASSING
AUTHORIZED PERSONNEL ONLY

Brandon Cory passed the sign as he took the access road into Desertron. That name wasn't on the billboard, but it was what everyone called the new particle accelerator complex. First, it was out in the desert, at least as far as Brandon was concerned. Just south of

Waxahachie, Texas, it was hot, flat, and surrounded by scorched grass, nothing like the rolling green hills of Vermont where he'd gone to college. Second, it sounded cool. Futuristic.

At least it had when he'd first arrived, fresh out of graduate school with a physics degree and notions of taking part in breakthrough research in quantum physics. Desertron was the largest particle accelerator in the world. At fifty-four miles in circumference, it made CERN's Large Hadron Collider in Switzerland appear puny at a mere seventeen miles.

Brandon's job had been entry-level, but that hadn't worried him. He'd make a name for himself, pay off his college debt, then go for his doctorate.

Yeah, he thought, as he slowed and lowered his window. *Right*.

The hot air, dense with mugginess, hit his face like a blast of reality. He showed his ID to the guard, who studied it from behind his reflective sunglasses, taking his time before handing it back to Brandon. The gate opened, and he drove the last mile to his parking spot out under the fiery Texas sun. The air conditioner labored to overcome the heated air, but it hardly made a difference. By the time he got to the entrance and another identity check, he'd be drenched in sweat.

Security was tight, and, last week, warnings had been issued again—verbally, not on paper or email—to never discuss work with outsiders.

Not that Brandon would have much to talk about. His job was to monitor systems. They'd built up the job, but, basically, he babysat computer screens, watching numbers and graphs as particles sped around the supercollider, completing their circuit in two hundred microseconds. His workstation was far underground, close to one of the quadrupole electromagnets, which kept the particle beams focused to increase the effectiveness of the collisions. If the numbers stayed within parameters, there was nothing for him to do. For hours and hours. Brandon thought he'd be part of a grand quantum physics experiment, a partner in one of the greatest discoveries of the age. But he was a cog, an observer of numbers, a flunky who knew nothing beyond his assigned post. The worst part was, he'd gotten used to it.

Multicolored wires ran riot up the ceiling and down to his workstation, linking the electromagnet and supercollider data, displaying it on an array of large screens. It had all been so cool when he first arrived. Now, it was mind-numbingly boring. Numbers and lines scrolled across his field of vision, a never-ending thread of information that went in circles, just like the particles behind him. The beam pipe was as tall as he was, shining steel and bright blue paint. It was like being in the cleanest, fanciest basement in the world.

Which basically summed it up.

Brandon ran the usual diagnostics. His supervisor came by, making a circuit of her dozen subordinates, asking the same questions she always did at the start of a shift.

Readings on the superfluid helium-4 levels? Check.

Power consumption and luminosity levels? Check.

Super Proton Synchrotron teraelectronvolt acceleration? A little on the high side, but within proscribed limits. Check.

Brandon went over the rest of the numbers with her, noting that a few readings were higher than yesterday, but nothing was about to red-zone. She tapped a few things into her tablet and took off in her electric cart with a curt comment about monitoring the teraelectronvolt levels.

Brandon said he'd keep an eye on them, but she was already yards away, the soft purr of her cart casting a faint echo in the cavernous chamber. She wouldn't be back for two hours.

Brandon sighed, giving his monitors a quick glance. The teraelectronvolt levels were a touch high, and a few numbers spiked before they settled down again. He thought about calling his supervisor back but decided to wait. If it happened again, he'd report it.

In the meantime, Brandon had other plans. He'd received a birthday present yesterday from his older sister Haley. It was the latest iPad, an expensive gift to be sure, but she was a lawyer and could afford it. Something she didn't mind reminding him of as often as she could. Haley had downloaded all the books by her favorite author, Stephen King, which probably cost more than the iPad. She loved King's stories and was constantly urging Brandon to try them.

He hadn't had a chance to set the iPad up yet, but he had charged it overnight. There wasn't any Wi-Fi underground, not even a wired internet connection. No links to the outside world, no way for data to escape or for outsiders to hack in. An internal, hardened network. No games, no amusements, just endless data and drudgery.

Brandon took the iPad from his backpack and plugged the charger in. Even if he couldn't get online, he could at least read some scary stories. A perfect way to spend a few hours in a chamber deep underground surrounded by particles accelerated to nearly the speed of light.

One of his computer screens began to show red flashing numbers. Power consumption was surging. The SPS teraelectronvolt acceleration levels were crazy fast. Then all the monitors began to flash red as a siren kicked off, the emergency warning wailing like a wounded coyote.

The air began to shimmer. The beam pipe looked as if it might ripple and flex like a rubber hose. Brandon felt a quiver flash through his body. Then a moment of fear as the noise and colors around him swirled and danced, breaking into pieces and scattering into the universe.

Finally, Brandon had become part of a very grand, but purely accidental, experiment in quantum physics. Too bad no one would ever know.

Least of all, Brandon Cory.

GUY TUPPER HAD tiptoed out during the night and put his stuff into his truck. In the morning, he left home at his usual time, as though he was going to work. He owed a week's rent but saw no reason to settle his debt, since the landlord was a jerk and the place was a dump. From now on, Guy Tupper was going to look out for number one, and no one else. He tried to peel out as he pulled away from the curb, but the pickup wasn't capable of much more than a sputter and a puff of blue smoke. Guy satisfied himself by rolling down his window and giving the finger to the house, to the street, and to anyone stupid enough to spend another day in Waxahachie.

Guy took Route 287 out of town toward Fort Worth. The heat of the day was already starting to shimmer on the road ahead, but he didn't mind. This was a new beginning, a chance to make something of himself. What, he had no idea, but it had to be better than working for John Lee. Hell, even sweeping up in Jerry's repair shop would be an improvement.

Guy twirled the knob on his radio, trying to find a Top 40 station among the constant stream of gospel music the hicks around here went for. He finally gave up. Then he saw it, just as "Wings of a Dove" vanished in a blazing burst of static.

A flash in the brown scrub up the road on the right. No, not a flash, that would be bright and vivid. This had been a sudden darkness, a deep chasm of black that opened, pulsed, then disappeared. Guy blinked a few times, uncertain of what he'd seen. Had it been something huge and far away, or small and close?

He pulled off the road, rolling to a stop about where he'd seen whatever the hell it was. There was not one house or a farm for miles. The only other traffic was a big rig barreling down the road. It blew past Guy, swirling dust and blasting its horn.

Quiet settled in as Guy watched the truck recede in his rearview mirror. He squinted hard, scanning the dry landscape and brittle scrub for any sign of what he'd witnessed.

His radio came back to life, and a cold shiver grabbed hold of his spine. But it was only Ferlin Husky crooning about that damned dove and a sign from above.

"Dammit," Guy said, getting out of the truck, his heart thumping from the surprise. He felt strange, uncertain of what to do. He thought about driving off and not stopping until he hit Fort Worth. But then he'd never know. Was he seeing things, or had something really happened?

"What the hell," Guy muttered and headed into the low brush, watching out for snakes and having no clue of what else he might find.

He smelled it first, about twenty paces in. The odor of burnt vegetation. A few more steps and he saw it. A circle of charred ground about ten yards in diameter, wisps of smoke rising from the remains of grasses and shrubs. The odor rose in his nostrils, an odd mix of soot and electricity, the lingering sharp smell of lightning.

Guy didn't like it. He shivered, even in the hot, dry heat. Sweat sprouted in the small of his back as fear gnawed at him. What if it happened again? He'd be burned and God knows what else. He turned away, the thought of some soothing gospel music suddenly appealing.

Then he saw it.

What the hell was it? Black glass? It sat at the far edge of the charred ring, a coating of dust and soot doing little to disguise the shiny brilliance of the reflective surface under the sun's glare.

Guy stepped into the circle, his boots scrunching on brittle tufts of blackened grass. He stopped, wondering if it would be hot to the touch. He knelt, inspecting the strange object more closely. A thin white wire ran out the side of it. Right at the edge of the blackened area, the wire had been sliced clean through, leaving about five inches dangling.

He stepped out of the ring, looking for the other end of the white cord in the scattered clumps of dry grass, but there was nothing. Guy walked back into the circle, rubbing his chin, trying to puzzle out what had happened. The cut was clean, a precise edge. How had that happened? Where was the rest of the cord?

Maybe it had fallen that way. An accident.

He got down on his knees and looked at the cord close-up. Nope, not accidental. Whatever he'd seen had made this burned-out spot and cut off the cord right at the edge. How, Guy had no idea.

But he knew he wanted this, whatever it was. He reached out a hand and tentatively rubbed his forefinger against the surface. It was cool. Glass. He tapped his fingernail against it. Definitely glass, but softer than window glass. He blew the dust away and was rewarded with his own glossy black reflection.

Satisfied it wasn't hot, he picked it up. It was a rectangle, less than a foot long, and very thin. He turned it over. The other side felt like molded plastic. Hard and smooth to the touch. Light but solid, with some heft to it. The plastic side was scuffed, with a smudge of something dark running across it. Guy turned his attention to the wire and saw it was plugged into a small slot at the side. Whatever this thing was, that had to be the power cord. The short end of it, anyway.

He looked to the bright sky and wondered if it had fallen from an airplane. But that didn't explain the burned circle. Maybe the air force was testing a new weapon. Not very powerful, from what he could see. Even so, they might be back. Guy edged away, checking the ground around him for any other strange objects. Then he got nervous thinking about death rays and more weird stuff the military might be working on. Clutching the shiny black object, he ran for his truck and took off.

He gunned the engine and left the Waxahachie city limits behind him. The black glass made him nervous, so he stuffed it in the bag next to him, wiping his hands on his jeans, leaving dark smudges from whatever had coated the contraption. Jerry knew all about electronics. He'd help him figure out what the hell it was. And if it was dangerous.

A few hours later, Guy parked in front of Jerry's repair shop. The place looked exactly the same. And not in a good way. There were some new additions in the window, but only if you counted the dead flies.

As Guy opened the door, the overhead bell rang one single *ding*, as if it was too much effort to sound the cheery chime he remembered. Jerry was behind the counter, a toaster in pieces before him.

"Howdy. Be with you in a sec," Jerry said in a distracted monotone, as he stared through his thick glasses and worked a thin screwdriver. He was heavier than Guy remembered, by at least twenty pounds, and the mustache was new as well. Guy wandered the cramped aisles, wondering if he looked as worn down as Jerry. There were large radio sets, console TVs, toaster ovens, and vacuum cleaners, all coated with a layer of dust. At least the dust never had a chance to settle at John Lee's shop.

"Whaddya need?" Jerry said, setting down the screwdriver and looking straight at Guy without a glimmer of recognition.

"Damn, Cousin, that's a helluva hello," Guy said, going for his biggest smile.

"Guy!" Jerry finally said, squinting through his glasses and extending his hand. "Sorry, my eyes are gettin' worse. Starin' at these tiny parts all day is hell on 'em. What brings you to Fort Worth?"

"Looking for a new line of work," Guy said as they shook hands. "The circulating fan business is a dinosaur."

"What you got in mind?" Jerry said, picking up the thermostat switch and holding it a few inches from his face. "Oil? Stockyards, maybe?" His voice trailed off, his attention already wandering.

"Thought I'd check in with you first," Guy said, leaning on the counter, trying to look relaxed. "See if you're tuned in to anything. Maybe you need some help around here?" Guy coughed out a half laugh, ready to say he was kidding, of course.

"Only help I need is to bring in payin' customers," Jerry said, setting the thermostat down and giving Guy a serious look, as if he'd just taken notice of him. "Half the stuff for sale in here has been left behind. People bring in their appliances, I fix 'em, and they forget about 'em. Gettin' to be cheaper just to buy a new toaster or radio, even though the new stuff is all crap."

"Yeah. Progress, right?" Guy said, not liking what he was hearing from Jerry. He'd hoped his cousin would've had something to show for all the years working in this shop. Instead, he sounded a lot like Guy. One thing Guy didn't need right now was more of himself.

"So, where you livin'?" Jerry said, picking up the thermostat again. "We should go out for a few brews one day."

"Just got into town, man," Guy said. "Thought I might bunk with you while I look for work. Like old times, you know?"

"No can do, Guy, sorry. You know that room you stayed in? It's filled with junk I can't sell," Jerry said, shaking his head slowly. Guy couldn't tell if the gesture was aimed at him or the thermostat that seemed to be demanding most of Jerry's attention. "You ain't a kid no more, Cousin. You'll do fine."

I'm not doing fine, Guy wanted to tell him, but he had a better idea.

"I've got something to show you," Guy said, slapping his palm on the counter, trying to get Jerry to focus on something besides the toaster. "I'll be right back."

"Suit yourself," Jerry said, tapping the solenoid switch attached to the thermostat with a continuity tester. No circuit. The damn thing was dead. Like his business.

Guy came back carrying his duffel. Jerry sighed.

"Listen, Guy, I just can't do it. The apartment is a dump, I got no room, and the shop ain't doing so great. You'll be better off somewhere else, believe me," Jerry said. It was all true, but mainly Jerry didn't want to be saddled with his cousin, who wasn't all that much fun when he was a teenager. A decade probably hadn't made him any more interesting.

"I just want to show you something, get your opinion," Guy said. "Okay?"

"Opinions are easy," Jerry said, pushing the toaster parts to one side and, with a magnanimous wave of his hand, inviting Guy to use the space.

Guy opened the bag and dug out the glass. He had no idea what it was for, or what to call it. Black glass had come to mind at first, then simply glass. It felt right.

"I found this in the desert," Guy said, at a loss to describe what had happened. He set it down in front of Jerry, glass side up, black plastic down. Jerry touched the object, his forehead furrowing as he ran his finger across it.

"What the hell is this supposed to be?" Jerry said, noticing a thin layer of soot on his fingers. He wiped his hand on a rag and picked up the glass.

"I was hoping you'd have an idea," Guy said. "Looks like the power cord was cut clean through. If that's what it is."

"Might be able to splice that, if I knew what voltage it took. First off, what does it do?"

"No idea. I just know I've never seen anything like it," Guy said. "That's why I headed here in the first place." As if a bed and a meal weren't part of the plan.

"Hmmm," was all Jerry said, as he worked the rag and wiped off more of the soot on the back. The carbonized remnants left behind by Brandon Cory, who had yet to be born. Most of the dark matter came off, but some of the plastic was pitted and scraped.

"Look, there's some writin' at the bottom," Jerry said, rubbing energetically.

"What's it say?" Guy asked, leaning closer.

"Can't make it out. Looks like a capital *P* there, and maybe *22* after it. But the rest is unreadable," Jerry said, buffing the plastic with a clean cloth. "But lookit this."

"What the hell? An apple?" Guy said, squinting at the design as it became visible. Smack in the middle of the hard plastic—or was it metal?—there was an apple, or at least the outline of one. "With a bite taken out."

"Like the one Eve chomped on in the Garden of Eden," Jerry said. "What is this, some kinda satanic thing?" He laughed, and Guy joined in, but it was a sound meant only to fill the strange silence surrounding the glass, and it vanished in a second.

Jerry ran the rag over the glass, shaking it out and giving the reflective surface another rub. Along the thin side of it, small rectangular silver buttons appeared when the sooty grit was cleaned off. Jerry blew on the edge, dislodging the last of the particles. He buffed the silver parts.

"Holy shit," Guy said. Jerry dropped the object on the counter, where it clattered. Guy's hands shot out and steadied the thing. He held it at the edges as if it had to be contained, so strange and bizarre was the sight in front of them.

Incredibly vivid colors had sprung from the glass. A deep, bright blue background with rows of tiny pictures, each labeled with words like *News*, *Weather*, *Camera*, *Books*, *Contacts*, *Docs*, *Clock*, *Help*, and others that made no sense at all.

"Goddamn," Jerry said. "Is that a miniature television? Did you steal this, Guy?"

"No, I found it, really. Out in the desert."

"Tell me the truth, Guy. What happened? You saw this in someone's car and swiped it."

"Jesus, Jerry, no. I was driving along, and something caught my eye. I pulled over and this thing was on the ground. There was a circle where the ground was charred, and this was inside, right at the edge. That's where the power cord was as well."

"Listen, Guy, look at this," Jerry said, pointing at the glass. "These colors aren't like anything on any TV, and I should know. I've repaired a bunch of color televisions, expensive ones, and they don't have color like this. Look at the clarity, for God's sake. And, obviously, there's no space for vacuum tubes."

"So?"

"So don't tell me this dropped out of the sky. This is some advanced shit. No one's going to leave it lyin' around in the desert," Jerry said. "This could be a government project. Old LBJ is gonna pitch a fit about you runnin' off with a top-secret TV, or whatever this is."

"Hey, I'm telling you the truth, Jerry. Sorry if I spooked you. I haven't stolen anything, but I'll go, don't worry," Guy said. He could tell Jerry was in even less of a mood now to help him out. He'd hoped to pique his interest as an electronics fan, but that had backfired. So badly that now Guy himself was getting nervous. What if this *was* some James Bond gadget?

"Okay, okay, I believe you," Jerry said, taking a deep breath. "This thing is freakin' me out, that's all."

"I call it Glass," Guy said, making the name into a proper noun in his mind. He stood still, his hands flat on the counter, waiting for Jerry to go one way or the other. Guy could see his cousin was real scared. But he wasn't. This was *his* find, and if Jerry didn't want to help, that was okay. He'd find someone else.

For the first time in his life, Guy felt a sense of purpose. Glass had been there for him to find, no one else. It was his mission to unlock whatever secrets it held. He picked up the mysterious object.

"It's been good to see you, Jerry," he said. "I'll let you get back to work."

"Hey, let me have another look before you go, okay? I am a little curious, I have to admit."

"Sure, I'm in no hurry," Guy said, setting Glass down facing Jerry. "What'd you do to turn it on?"

"Must have hit one of these," Jerry said, pointing to the silver tabs. One was longer than the other. "I think the short one." He pressed the long tab, and a picture appeared.

"Settings," Jerry whispered. A line sat beneath it, a small bell-shaped object on its left. Then it vanished.

"Set what?" Guy asked, and they both shrugged at the same time.

"I wonder if there's a remote control?" Jerry said, rubbing his chin. "Otherwise, how would you switch these channels?"

"Never saw a TV remote control," Guy said. "Hell, I'm not sure those are channels. A whole channel for weather? That's crazy."

"Could be somethin' else—you're right. But TV remotes are gettin' better, so maybe there's some advanced design that would operate Glass. I just repaired a Zenith remote last week. Pretty fancy stuff."

Guy noted Jerry had called it Glass. He was hooked.

"Shouldn't there be knobs? There's no way to watch anything," Guy said, leaning on his elbows and staring at the bright colors and images. "There's no static, no movement, no nothing. And books? Why would a TV have a whole channel about books? I don't get it."

"This isn't a normal TV," Jerry said, tapping his finger on the reflective surface.

Something happened.

The picture changed.

Rows of images popped up, all in different colors.

"What'd you do?" Guy asked, taking Glass and trying to comprehend what he was seeing.

"I hit the thing that said Books, I think."

"*Carrie, The Dark Tower,*" Guy read. "*The Shining.* Hey, these are book covers." He read off the others. *The Tommyknockers, The Dead Zone,* and a dozen or so more.

"They're all by the same guy. Stephen King. Never heard of him," Jerry said. "And I read a lot." Guy remembered the stacks of science fiction paperbacks in Jerry's apartment upstairs.

"Maybe Glass belongs to this Stephen King," Guy suggested. "So he can show pictures of his books. Like a slideshow."

"Hmmm," Jerry said, not paying much attention to Guy's theory. "These all appeared when I pressed on Books. I wonder what happens if I touch one of these." He placed his finger on the first one. *Carrie.* Nothing.

"You hit it harder before," Guy said. "Give it a good tap."

That did it. First the surface went black, with a small line of indecipherable symbols at the top. Guy and Jerry exchanged horrified looks, each wondering if the thing was broken. Then the image turned into a crisp white background.

With words.

CARRIE

STEPHEN KING

DOUBLEDAY

NEW YORK   LONDON   TORONTO   SYDNEY   AUCKLAND

"I don't get it," Jerry said. "What exactly is this thing?"

"Glass," Guy said. "It's special. I'm not sure in what way, but it is. And I found it."

"Doesn't make you special, Cousin. Let's try something else," Jerry said, picking up the apparatus. He tapped it again. Nothing. Then harder.

"Hey, be careful," Guy said, grabbing Glass. But Jerry held on and pulled it from his grasp, Guy's fingers sliding across the shiny surface.

The page turned. The picture of the page, that is. It moved exactly like real paper, curling at the corner as the next page became visible.

"Whoa," Jerry said, easing up on the tug-of-war. He held the edges and Guy ran his finger back across. The title page reappeared. *Flip*, just like a book. Then again, and the next page, and the next. Flip, flip, flip. It was a book. An entire book, or at least pictures of the pages. Incredibly crisp, clear, readable pictures.

"Glass is full of books," Guy whispered. "It's a book machine."

Jerry set it on the counter with great reverence. Books meant something to him. They were good company, better than most people in his life. And here was the strangest collection of books he'd ever seen. He flipped the pages slowly this time, scanning the words as they magically appeared.

Jerry stopped. He lifted his face to stare at Guy, eyes wide.

"Lock the door," he said.

"Huh?"

"Lock the damn door, Guy, and turn that CLOSED sign around!"

Guy responded to the urgency in Jerry's voice, locking up and wondering what his cousin had seen. Glass was full of surprises, but this last one had left Jerry in shock.

"What is it?" Guy demanded, watching Jerry tap and flip with an easy familiarity.

"Look. *Carrie*, verso of the title page," Jerry said. Guy gave a blank look. "The back of the title page, Cousin. What's it say?"

"Copyright 1974," Guy said. "That can't be right."

"That's the first one. There are plenty of others. The copyright dates keep going. Here, look at the last book. Copyright 2022."

"That's crazy," Guy said, backing away from the counter. He wanted Glass to be unique, a puzzle only he could solve, but this was taking off in an entirely strange direction. Another cold shiver ran up his spine. This time it left a trail of fear.

"It's not crazy," Jerry said. "It's either a damn clever hoax, or . . ." His voice trailed off. He couldn't say it.

"Or it's from the future," Guy finished, in a whisper.

IT WENT WITHOUT saying that Guy would stay with Jerry. They trooped up the steep, narrow stairs at the rear of the shop, floorboards creaking and groaning beneath the weight of their treads.

Guy hadn't recalled Jerry's apartment as being particularly neat and clean. But if it ever had been, things had gone downhill. The kitchen counter was filled with dirty dishes, with more soaking in a sink full of scummy water. Two worn couches faced each other like old, sagging men waiting to be put out of their misery. Books were stuffed onto makeshift shelves of cinder blocks and pine boards. A table and a workbench were strewn with electrical parts, their purpose unidentifiable in the jumble of wires, switches, and tubes.

"You can have the couch," Jerry said, without indicating which one. "Like I said, the spare room is filled with stuff."

"Fine," Guy said, tossing his duffel on the sofa with the fewest lumps. Jerry handed Glass to him and swept aside the components he'd been working on, making a place of honor on his workbench. Guy set Glass down gently. They stood in silence for a moment, taking in what they'd learned.

"It's not a hoax, is it?" Guy said. He realized he'd hoped it was. A mechanism from the future was too much to take in. At first, he'd thought it was something that would make him special. Give him a purpose. Now, he had no idea how it would change things.

"No," Jerry said, with a hard certainty. "There's no electronics I know of that look like this. No television set has this clarity. If it was a single book, I'd say someone printed it up as a joke. But we've got over forty books in this thing. Do you realize what this means, Guy?"

"Time travel?" Guy answered.

"That's how it got here, Cousin. I don't know how, and I don't really care. What I care about is what we can do with it," Jerry said, his eyes glinting with excitement.

"Read it?" Guy said, but even as he did, he began to understand what Jerry was excited about.

"Sell the damn books, Cousin! We've got years on this guy. He hasn't even written them yet. We have the finished product, and we know which publisher to go to. It's easy money, man."

"A lot of easy money," Guy said. He gave a fleeting thought to whoever the hell Stephen King was, but it didn't last long. He could write other books. Guy was the one who needed a break in life, and by the looks of Jerry's place, so did he. Glass had fallen into their hands. They'd be fools not to use it. "I mean, they pay writers a ton of money, don't they?"

"Oh shit," Jerry said.

"What?" Guy asked, the look on Jerry's face interrupting his dreams of wealth.

"That," Jerry said, pointing to the top of the pictures. Along the small line of squiggles, which looked like alien symbols to Jerry's sci-fi-filled mind, was a thin rectangle. It had just turned red. "It's shaped like a battery, see? It must be low on juice."

"You couldn't fit a battery in there," Guy said. "No room, no opening. You have to get it plugged in."

"First we turn it off," Jerry said, pressing the silver band on the edge. Glass went dark.

"No! What if we can't get it back on?"

"Think, Guy. If it loses all power, who knows what will happen? We might never get it workin' again."

"Okay, okay," Guy said, feeling dizzy at the prospect of his dreams fading to black. "Can you splice an electrical cord and plug it in?"

"I *could*," Jerry said, his tone telling Guy it had been a stupid question. "If I wanted to fry these advanced electronics. We have no idea what voltage it takes, or can take, without damage. Household current would likely burn it out. We've got to start really low and work from there."

"How do we do that?" Guy asked.

"Let me think about it," Jerry said, his tone confident. Guy didn't like that much. Glass was his, and Jerry ought to be consulting him about what to do. But he needed Jerry, for his knowledge if not his couch.

For now.

Jerry told Guy to clear off the table for his own workspace, then turned back to his workbench and stared at Glass.

"What am I going to do?" Guy asked, not happy at Jerry giving orders, even if it was his place.

"There's a Royal typewriter in the back room," Jerry said. "All cleaned and repaired, but the customer never came to get it. Set it up, and you can bang on the keys once I get Glass powered up."

"I don't know how to type," Guy said, quickly regretting his admission. So far, his only contribution had been finding Glass and bringing it to Jerry. He needed something to do before his cousin declared himself the boss. "But I'll practice while you're working."

Guy boxed up the array of appliances Jerry had been working on and lugged in the heavy Royal typewriter. He'd typed up forms and a few letters at John Lee's store, but that had been it. He wondered how long it would take to type out a whole book. A damn long time, Guy figured, as he listened to Jerry drum his fingers on the workbench.

The drumming stopped. Jerry snapped his fingers and jumped up, making a beeline for his bookshelves and the piles of magazines at the bottom.

"What?" Guy asked, but all Jerry did was hold up a hand to silence him. He pawed through the pages of *Mechanix Illustrated*, *Popular Mechanics*, and *Popular Science*, tossing them onto the floor until he came up with what he was looking for.

"I got it!" Jerry shouted. "I knew I'd read about this somewhere! There's a tool kit in the closet. Grab me some galvanized nails."

"Nails? What? Are you crazy?" Guy said, not believing what he was hearing.

"Like a fox, Cousin, like a fox," Jerry said, grinning and scooping up pennies from a bowl of loose change on the bookshelf. At the workbench, he unspooled a length of insulated wire and set out metal alligator clips. He began stripping one end of the wire.

"Tell me what you're doing first," Guy said.

"All right. Don't blow a fuse," Jerry said, taking a second to let out a snort of laughter at his own joke. "I'm makin' a very low-voltage trickle charger. Low enough it can't possibly hurt any electronics."

"With nails and pennies? I don't believe it," Guy said.

"There's one other ingredient," Jerry said, handing Guy the magazine, open to the article he'd been hunting for.

"Potatoes? Now I know you're crazy. How can a potato be a battery?"

"It's not," Jerry said. "But it's got electrolytes. The moisture inside the potato, that is. Electrolytes can conduct electricity. All we have to do is add a pair of electrodes made of the right materials. Copper from the penny and zinc from the galvanized nail. One produces free ions and the other attracts them. Presto, you have an electrical current. Very low."

"From a potato," Guy said, trying to follow what Jerry was telling him.

"It's all there, read it yourself. We'll get about one volt of power from a single potato. Can't hurt a fly," Jerry said, as he nodded approvingly at his work. With the plastic sheath stripped away, the copper wires shone brightly.

"Will it be enough?"

"That's the beauty of this," Jerry said. "We can add other potatoes to the circuit, one at a time. We watch that battery outline, and as soon as it changes, we know we have enough juice to charge it. One potato, one volt. It's safe, believe me."

"I've never heard of this. Why don't people use potatoes for electricity if it's so safe?"

"It would take too many, Guy. Think about it. This article is about an experiment for schoolkids to get a small flashlight bulb to work. But it's perfect for Glass. Remember, this comes from the future. Their engineering and electronics are probably super advanced. I'm betting it won't take that much voltage. Even if we have to link a hundred potatoes together, we can do it."

"Okay," Guy said, scanning the article. It had pictures of a nail and a penny driven into a potato, just as Jerry had said. "I guess a potato or two can't hurt electronics from the future, right?"

"Good man!" Jerry said, with just enough superiority to get under Guy's skin. "But now we need to remove the wire so I can splice it. Okay?"

"Okay," Guy answered, mollified that Jerry had asked his permission. The wire fit into Glass along the edge, a small nub of molded plastic snug up to the side. It looked like it would unplug easily, but they had no way of knowing. Jerry nodded, took the nub between thumb and forefinger, and pulled.

It came away easily. A small metal prong, rectangular in shape, came into view. Jerry held it under a light and pointed out the indentations, telling Guy that was how the internal connection was made.

Now he had to strip the cut end and reveal the wires, so he could splice in the new power source.

"Ready?" Jerry asked, grasping the few inches of wire. Guy told him to go ahead. Jerry used his blade to cut away the covering. Inside were three wires, each sheathed in plastic. He stripped each of those back, leaving two inches of exposed wire. He spliced strands of the unspooled wire around each one, sealing them with electrical tape.

"Do you think all three will take the same amount of electricity?" Guy asked. He didn't know much about electronics, but the three wires all had a different color: white, red, and green. It had to mean something.

"Can't be a hundred percent certain," Jerry said. "I'm not from the year 2022, am I? But the voltage will be so low it shouldn't matter."

Next came the potatoes. Jerry had about half of a five-pound bag in the cupboard. The spuds were starting to sprout eyes, but he said that wouldn't be a problem. He pressed a penny into the end of one and a nail into the other. Then he attached alligator clips to the penny and the nail. Once that was done, he connected the other end of the clips to a voltmeter.

"See, not even a full volt," Jerry said. "We'll start with one potato, even though nothing will happen, probably, at eight-tenths voltage." This time he didn't ask Guy if it was okay. He connected the alligator clip to the spliced cord. Then he inserted the prong into Glass.

Nothing.

"Maybe it has to be turned on to charge," Guy said.

"I don't think so. Anyway, we don't want to run the risk of it running all the way down. Let's add another potato to the circuit."

Another was added. The wire from the penny on the first spud was connected to the nail on the second. The circuit was completed when Jerry attached the alligator clip to the spliced wires.

Nothing. Nothing happened with three potatoes, or with four. They were generating nearly three and a half volts, enough to create a slight tingle in Guy's fingertips when he touched the clips.

The fifth potato was a big one. They went through the same wiring procedure. Jerry plugged in the circuit. Still nothing.

"I think we should turn it on," Guy said. "Just to check."

"Okay," Jerry said, nodding in the direction of the button. He wasn't sure about this, and better for Guy to do it if something went wrong.

Guy pressed the silver button. It took a moment, but the display popped into life in all its brilliant colors. Including the red outline of the battery symbol.

"Damn," Jerry said.

"You sure you spliced the wires right?" Guy said, frustrated that his idea hadn't worked out.

"How the hell can I be sure? We're doing stuff no one has ever done before. This is science, man. Experimentation."

"We need to be certain, not experiment, dammit!" Guy said. Now he was worried Glass might get fried, and he'd be left with nothing.

"Fine," Jerry said, locking eyes with Guy. "But where else you gonna go? Who can you trust? Who do you know with any smarts when it comes to electronics? Tell me that, Guy!"

If Glass hadn't been between them, they would have started throwing punches. It had happened before, but they'd always been drunk, and always had been quick to forgive and forget. But they were older now, and the burden of failed lives gave their anger a tinge of nastiness that might not fade as quickly as their hangovers had.

Guy looked away, unwilling to take the next step, unwilling to get himself thrown out, with or without Glass.

"Christ," Jerry whispered. Guy saw him staring at Glass. The battery outline was flashing red. "What does that mean?"

"Flashing red is never good," Guy said, leaning in and watching the rhythmic pulse. "Wait. That wasn't there before. The little lightning bolt."

"Shit, you're right. A lightning bolt! Electricity! It's charging!"

"You're a genius, Jerry," Guy said, slapping his cousin on the shoulder.

"Hey, you turned it on in the first place," Jerry said. "That took smarts."

They congratulated each other as they watched over Glass.

They drank beer. They ate baloney sandwiches.

They cheered when the flashing stopped. The battery turned a calm shade of yellow, the lightning bolt still assuring them of a steady, if slow, stream of power.

They slept on and off, checking on Glass every hour or so.

Sometime before dawn they replaced the potatoes.

As sunlight hit the living room window, the battery turned green. Green was good, they decided. Very good.

Then they began to experiment. They turned Glass off and detached the power cord. They powered it up, the battery symbol glowing green. Jerry tapped the Books image, and Guy tapped *Carrie*.

The pages were all there.

Jerry made coffee, and then they made the rules.

Glass never leaves the room.

One of us is with Glass all the time.

Never speak of Glass in front of anyone, ever.

No one is allowed upstairs unless we both agree ahead of time. No surprise visitors.

By the looks of the place and Jerry's casual approach to hygiene and grooming, Guy didn't think that one would be hard to manage.

Next, they had to buy more potatoes. Then typing paper, carbon paper, and typewriter ribbon. After Guy did some practice typing, Jerry added correction fluid to the list.

"We need to talk about money," Jerry said, as he prepared to go out.

"I don't have much," Guy said, pulling out his wallet and giving Jerry a ten-spot.

"Thanks, but that's not what I meant," Jerry said. "I mean the split from the book money. I was thinkin' fifty-fifty."

"We don't have a dime yet, Jerry. Half of nothing is nothing."

"Listen, Cousin. I'm happy to put you up and keep Glass juiced up. You'll have everythin' you need right here. But I'm not doin' it for free. If it wasn't for me, you'd be out on the street still wonderin' what that thing was."

"Okay, okay," Guy said. Jerry was right. He needed a roof over his head, and he had to admit, Jerry had done pretty well with Glass. "Fifty-fifty."

"Shake," Jerry said, extending his hand. They shook.

"How exactly do we go about it?" Guy asked. "Ask them to write us each a check?"

"No idea," Jerry admitted. "I'm going to stop at the library and see if they have a book about publishers. I'll try and find out how this stuff works. Then I'll be back with food and paper."

Guy took a shower. Maybe he should have bargained, gone for a two-thirds share. But Jerry had his good points. He was family, a known quantity. Smart with electrical stuff. Maybe there'd be so much money a few percentage points wouldn't matter. It'd be a lot of work doing all that typing, but it sure beat driving around under the hot Texas sun selling John Lee's circulating fans.

Then it hit him. Glass was worth a lot even without the books. Hell, IBM would pay a fortune for electronics more than half a century ahead of its time. But how to even approach them? How could he describe Glass without showing it? Guy knew he wasn't a wheeler-dealer businessman like John Lee, but he knew enough not to walk into corporate headquarters with an invaluable piece of electronics. He might never walk out.

Not Guy Tupper, unemployed nobody. But Guy Tupper, bestselling author, he might have a chance. Get a nice suit, nice car, then they'd take him seriously.

Guy liked that idea. Let Jerry have his fifty percent. One day he might just take Glass and disappear. Fully charged, of course.

In a few hours, Jerry came back with potatoes, paper, and pizza.

"I got the address for Doubleday," Jerry said. "They had a book in the reference section with all sorts of stuff about publishing. If Doubleday doesn't pan out, there are plenty of others."

"Okay," Guy said, opening the pizza box on the coffee table in front of the couch.

"Plain cheese. I didn't remember what you liked," Jerry said. "Plus, I'm pretty tapped out myself. The shop isn't exactly a money machine. And people with expensive stuff don't want to come to this dump of a neighborhood. Too many lowlifes around."

"No problem," Guy said. "Pretty soon we'll be dining on rib eyes. What else did you find out?"

"Publishers pay an advance when you sign the contract. How much depends on the book and if you're a big name. So the first one might not make us rich, but after that, we'll be in the driver's seat."

"Hey, right now a thousand bucks would be a fortune. Any idea how we can work a split?"

"Yeah, one," Jerry said. "You're the author, I'm your agent. I contact the publisher and your name goes on the book."

"How does that help?"

"Agents get fifteen percent," Jerry said. "So we each get money nice and legal. You can make up the difference to me later. We'll probably have to factor in taxes, but it'll work out."

"Wait, fifteen percent of everything? For doing what?"

"Making a phone call or two, I guess," Jerry said. "I don't really know. It sounds like the publisher sends me the money. I pass on eighty-five percent to you."

"You sure about this?"

"It's the way things work, Guy. Besides, this gives us some protection. I'll say you're shy, or a hermit, maybe. You don't want to talk to the press or do interviews."

"Why would I talk to anyone?" Guy asked.

"Because you're going to be famous, Cousin! Did you read the reviews on the covers? People love these books. We're gonna get rich!"

"Okay, I get it," Guy said. He really hadn't thought this through, not like Jerry had. There would be a lot of questions, from the publisher and others. He could get tripped up real easy. "You're the agent. I'm the hermit writer. Let's get to work."

THEY WENT AT it. Guy worked the typewriter keys and managed to become proficient, after a fashion. He remembered a few things from high school typing class. He'd taken the course to get close to a girl he liked, but she'd never given him the time of day. When he got tired of typing, he would imagine what she'd think when she saw his name in print. His photograph on the book jacket. It helped.

Jerry was a whirlwind. He kept the shop open to bring in what money he could. He went to the public library to read magazines about writing and to consult *Writer's Market* in the reference area, and, soon, he began to sound like he knew what he was talking about. He had letterhead and business cards made at a print shop down the street in exchange for free repair work. He put together a contract they both signed, making everything legal and protecting them both. So Jerry said.

Jerry kept Glass juiced up, constantly checking the charge from the potato circuit with his voltmeter, keeping it as close to five volts as he could.

Jerry had all the angles covered. Guy began to worry about that. He kept typing, but he couldn't shake the feeling that Jerry had him dancing to a Texas two-step tune. For all his years in the Lone Star state, he'd never cottoned to country music.

Was Jerry going to pull a fast one, or was Guy feeling the pressure of all this work, not to mention the isolation and deception? Maybe Jerry had the same idea about selling Glass to the highest bidder.

Hell, maybe Jerry would get rid of him. Guy was a recluse now. Who would ever know?

No, no, he told himself. It's this damn story. Spending time with *Carrie* wasn't the most uplifting way to spend his day. Carrie White was an unsuspecting victim, humiliated by people she'd convinced herself to trust. Pretty close to home, that one. He put those thoughts away and kept banging on the keys; the stacks of paper—one original and one carbon copy—grew steadily as the days passed.

Then came the day. Jerry wrote a letter to James Holly, editor at Doubleday. Guy typed it up. Jerry was the one to go to the post office, leaving Guy in the apartment feeling more like a secretary than a partner. He began to read the next book, *The Dark Tower*. He'd found reading the story first made the typing easier.

This story was about vampires. Guy liked that, until an unbidden thought crept into his brain. Jerry was like a vampire, sucking the work out of him, leaving him exhausted and alone. He trusted Jerry most days, but some days, like this one, the thoughts preyed on him. Was he being a chump? Was Jerry smarter, more cunning, than he was? Could he have been plotting a double-cross all this time?

Yes, Guy decided. If only for the simple reason that he'd thought about it himself. Jerry had to have had the same thoughts; it was only natural. But was Jerry actually planning something? Guy couldn't say. What he did know was that he was useful to Jerry, if only as a typist. He'd have to start watching, analyzing everything Jerry said and did. When he closed in on the last pages of the last book, then he'd have to act.

That was a long time from now, Guy told himself as he rolled a sheet of paper into the platen and began typing. The story began with two guys on the run. It made Guy uneasy, and he realized this whole thing—Glass, Jerry, the constant typing—was keeping him on edge. Nervous. The characters on the pages were becoming too damn real to him. Victims at the mercy of deadly forces they failed to understand. The constant exposure kept Guy worried he was making the same mistake.

But they were just stories. Weren't they?

He wished he was back doing a lousy job as a circulating fan salesman. He was busted most of the time, but he hadn't been shaky and scared the way he was these days. He used to see people, have a nice chat now and then, and breathe in fresh air. All he had now were these four walls and the company of a blood relative who might be up to spilling his.

But as he did so many times in his life, he pushed the unpleasant thoughts back into the dark corners of his mind and got to work. *Clickety-clack, clickety-clack, clickety-clack,* then the ring of the carriage return. It was as soothing as the story was frightening.

The weeks dragged by. Guy typed and, every day, asked Jerry if he should call the editor. Jerry said no, that's not how it worked. As if he'd done it all before.

Then came the letter. The Doubleday editor wanted to talk. Jerry made the call, and, by Jerry's grin, Guy could tell it was good news. Jerry spent a lot of time agreeing, nodding, saying *sure, sure.* He went on about the new book Guy was writing, and how it was almost done.

"Twenty-five hundred bucks!" Jerry shouted as he slammed down the phone. "We're in! And he wants to see the next book soon as it's done. He's in love with this stuff, Guy!"

"Shouldn't you have asked for more?" Guy said. It was more money than he'd ever seen all at once, but for a whole book? Just typing it was hard work. He couldn't imagine doing the actual writing for so little.

"That's the advance, Cousin," Jerry said with a heavy sigh. "There's more comin' once it starts to sell. But we get that money now. Once we sign the contract, they cut a check. Cash in hand, Guy!"

"Right, you told me that before," Guy said. "Sorry. I've been cooped up here for so long, I can't remember anything but the story. That's great news, Jerry."

"It's all coming together, Cousin. And to think we owe it all to the humble potato."

Guy thought they owed it to him. If he hadn't found Glass out in the desert, none of this would have come to pass. But all he did was bang the keys harder, tamping down his anger at a starchy tuber getting more credit than he did.

Jerry took a photograph of Guy. The publisher demanded it, so he took one of Guy at the typewriter, hunched over and in shadow. You could hardly see his face. Jerry said it was perfect. Guy wouldn't be recognized out on the street, and it fit the bill as the portrait of a genius recluse at work.

Guy thought it might make his body harder to identify.

The money came. They each took fifteen percent for themselves and used the rest to make the apartment more livable. New furniture and a new color television set. All they had to do now was wait a few months for the book to come out, and the money would start rolling in. Meanwhile, Jerry kept the shop going while Guy worked to finish the next book.

Jerry was big on laying low and keeping everything looking normal. He lived in fear of Glass being discovered and began to talk about what government agents would do to get their hands on the technology. Where Guy had envisioned a suitcase full of cash from a grateful corporation, Jerry was fixated on the military and the CIA.

"They've covered up the UFOs," Jerry said. "They'd take Glass in a heartbeat and leave us in shallow graves out in the desert. We gotta keep this quiet, Cousin."

That got Guy typing faster. Whether it was due to fear of government agents or Jerry's craziness, he couldn't tell.

Then the big news came, just before the publication date.

Another publisher made an offer for paperback rights to *Carrie*.

Four hundred thousand dollars.

It had to be split with the publisher, but even so, two hundred thousand was unimaginable.

"It'll be a while," Jerry said, after getting off the phone with the publisher. "But once we sign everything, the check will be on its way."

"To you," Guy said, suspicion edging into his voice.

"Of course, to me. I keep my percentage and pass on the rest to you. Then you give me the rest of my share. Minus taxes you gotta pay, of course. I've got it all figured out."

I bet you do, thought Guy. Funny, but he ought to be on top of the world. Instead, he obsessed about his older cousin cheating him. Or worse. Bashing his head in and burying him in that shallow grave out in the desert. The CIA weren't the only ones with shovels. Or poisoning him, that'd be less messy. Who would ever look for Guy Tupper? Who even knew what he looked like? John Lee, maybe, but his reading material mainly featured naked women.

He banged away, getting to the end of *The Dark Tower*. Maybe he'd just take the money and run. Grab Glass and go.

Or leave the damn thing here.

Or smash it to pieces, Guy thought, and laughed. The notion gave him pleasure. He'd have his share of the two hundred thousand. And the advance on this next book along with the royalties they'd get in a few months. Then he'd free himself from all this before Jerry could pull a crazy stunt of his own.

He typed so hard the periods pierced the paper.

Publication day for *Carrie* finally came. They'd printed thirty thousand copies. It sold well. Not terrific, but a solid start. Their editor loved *The Dark Tower* and gave them a big advance right away.

Money was no longer a problem.

The new problem was privacy. Doubleday hadn't liked Guy not being available for interviews or appearances, but Jerry had sold them on the hermit writer routine. However, the publicist had mentioned Fort Worth as Guy's hometown. Now the local paper wanted to do an article on the reclusive writer and his creepy story. A reporter called Jerry at the shop and asked if he could drop by.

Hell no, Jerry had said. *The author may not be disturbed.*

A few more calls came in, but Jerry handled them. Guy had to give him credit for that; he did a good job keeping people away. Which, of course, meant Guy was isolated. A prisoner at the type-writer. *For his own good*, he'd been reminded.

He began typing out *The Shining*. It was frightening, but not as frightening as staying in this apartment. Guy secretly planned how he would leave, right after the next payment came in. He didn't know where he'd go. But he was certain about one thing.

He'd leave Glass behind in pieces. Let Jerry repair that.

GUY WORKED INCESSANTLY on *The Shining*, the story of a writer working in an isolated mountain home during the winter. It was not good for his mental state, but he was desperate to see how it ended, to find some hint of salvation or hope within the pages. The empty hotel was driving the guy crazy, which Guy totally understood, being cooped up inside, much of the time by himself. Whether it was a hotel in a mountain snowstorm or Jerry's apartment baking under the Texas sun didn't matter much. He finished a page and stood up to stretch. He walked to the window and looked down at his new truck. It wasn't too flashy, nothing that would attract attention. But it was his first brand-new vehicle, and he always sighed with content-ment when he looked down and saw it parked in front of the repair shop.

But not today. Across the street was a beat-up Ford Fairlane. A tall, lanky young guy with a head of thick black hair was leaning against it, checking a piece of paper in his hand. He wore glasses, a scruffy T-shirt, and old jeans. The stranger scanned the street and his gaze settled on Jerry's shop. He looked at the paper again, then stuffed it into his pocket. He glanced around one more time. Not much to see except for a few boarded-up shops and a liquor store. Traffic was sparse, so he didn't bother to look as he pushed himself off the Fair-lane and crossed the street.

Guy didn't know who he was, but he was pretty sure the man was intent on something other than toaster repairs. He looked like he was gearing himself up for something. A robbery? Guy thought about hiding Glass, but there wasn't time. He grabbed a kitchen knife and eased down the steep staircase. He didn't want Jerry to hear him, to find him sneaking around with a knife, in case this was an innocent visit.

"Is Guy Tupper here?" Guy was startled at the mention of his own name.

"Sorry, he can't be disturbed," Jerry responded. "You from the newspaper? I told them, no interviews."

"No, I'm not. They gave me his address though. My name is Steve King, and I'd like to talk with him."

Guy gasped. It was so loud, he was sure he'd been heard. But the sound was covered up by Jerry's confused response.

"Ah, what for? Why do you wanna talk with Guy? What's this about?"

"Just want to chat, that's all. I'm a writer too. Thought maybe I could have a few minutes of his time," King said.

"King?" Jerry said, making it sound like he'd never heard the name. "Stephen King?"

"Yeah, that's it," King said. "So, is Guy Tupper here?"

"No, no he ain't. He comes and goes. Rents a room upstairs. His office, ya know."

"Any idea when he'll be back?"

"Nope. No idea. He don't much like to talk to people. A real private guy. No interviews, nothin' like that. It's why he works here, to get away," Jerry said, his words coming out in a breathless rush. He was nervous. Guy was petrified. It was like a ghost had come to visit. This guy hadn't been real before—he'd been some old guy from the future. But here Stephen King was, wanting to talk to him.

This couldn't be happening. Guy gripped the knife and wondered who knew King was here.

No, he couldn't do it.

He was pretty sure he couldn't.

Jerry and King went back and forth for a while. It was all the same. King just wanted to talk, Jerry was apologetic, saying he'd pass the message on, but not to count on anything. King said he'd come back later. Jerry said, "Suit yourself."

As soon as he heard the door slam shut, Guy ran upstairs.

"Guy! You hear that?" Jerry shouted as he made his way up the steps.

"Yeah, I heard it all," Guy said. "I'm getting outa here. I've had it, Jerry. I've had it with you and this goddamn Glass."

Guy ran to the tool chest on Jerry's workbench. He wasn't thinking about the money; he wasn't thinking about having a purpose. He was only thinking about ending this crazy scheme, the endless typing, and men from the future showing up at his door. It wasn't supposed to be like this, not at all.

He grabbed a hammer. Knife in one hand and ball-peen hammer in the other, he advanced on Glass, which was surrounded by wires and a circle of potatoes like some unholy pentagram.

"No!" Jerry yelled, waving his arms as he stood in front of the table. "Are you crazy?"

"We have enough, Jerry," Guy said through gritted teeth. "I want this thing gone."

"It's not enough," Jerry said. "Now put the knife down."

"No," Guy said, hardly realizing he still held the blade. "Get out of my way."

Guy raised the hammer, pushing at Jerry with the hand that held the knife. Jerry grabbed the knife hand, pulling Guy away from the table. Guy tried to swing the hammer, but he was off-balance. Jerry tugged at his arm, begging him to drop the knife, but Guy wasn't hearing him. All he could think about was smashing the thing and getting away from Fort Worth, somewhere far away where the future didn't come calling.

Jerry kept pulling at Guy, moving him away from the table and the precious Glass.

"Come on, Guy, let's talk this through," Jerry said, huffing and puffing with the effort it took. "Let's go downstairs, okay?" He maneuvered Guy to the landing, holding on to his arm with both hands, pulling and pulling.

"No!" Guy shouted, and turned the hammer on Jerry, swinging wildly, missing his head but sending them both careening against the wall at the top of the stairs.

"Guy," Jerry said, his voice a whimper as his fear grew. "Let go of the knife."

Guy tried once again to break free and swung the hammer at Jerry, but the blow didn't land. It did shift their center of gravity and sent the men tumbling in a deadly embrace, Jerry's foot slipping off the top step.

On the third step, Jerry fell hard on Guy, who still held the knife in his grasp. It entered Jerry's chest between two ribs and sliced into his heart, flooding his body with blood and dropping his blood pressure precipitously. On the ninth step, oblivious to the fact that his cousin was dying, Guy's head hit the woodwork as Jerry's weight pressed down on him. Dead weight. It snapped his C2 vertebra.

By the time they hit the bottom of the landing, both were dead.

STEPHEN KING SAT in his car. It had been a helluva long drive from Maine, and he didn't intend to give up so easily. *Carrie* was *his* story, and he needed to find out how this Guy Tupper came to write it.

Not that King had written it, not yet, anyway. But he'd been thinking about it for a while. The women's liberation movement had made its mark at the University of Maine, and he'd thought about writing a story with a young woman who was feeling her strength for the first time, with the twist of her coming to grips with telekinetic powers. *Carrie*.

How had Guy Tupper come to write the full version of what he'd only thought about? King couldn't remember telling anyone about his ideas. Yet there they were, in print for all the world to see.

Carrie, by Guy Tupper.

It didn't make any sense. He had to know.

He got out of the car and walked back to the repair shop. This time, he wasn't taking no for an answer.

"Hello?" King said as the bell over the door gave out its anemic chime.

Nobody answered. He looked around. No one behind the counter.

"Hello?" Nothing. He walked to the end of the counter, then saw the bodies in a heap at the bottom of the stairs. He froze at the sight of blood pooling beneath them. They had the look of absolute death about them. Still, he felt he ought to check.

The guy from the counter was on top. King lifted him and saw the knife between his ribs. He also saw the unnatural angle of the other fellow's neck. He felt both for pulses.

Zilch.

How had this happened so quickly? He'd just been in here five minutes ago.

What would the cops say? he wondered. How would he explain himself?

Guy Tupper. Was that the fella with the broken neck? He hadn't gotten a good look at him, not that the photo on the book jacket had been much of a likeness.

Maybe he should check upstairs. Maybe Guy Tupper or someone else was up there. Then it would be time to leave and keep going. This was nothing but trouble.

King gingerly stepped over the tangled corpses, taking the stairs and calling out for Guy Tupper.

There was no answer. It had to be Tupper down there. He reached the top of the steps and looked into the apartment.

What the hell was that?

Potatoes wired together? Hooked into a dark rectangle?

The potato setup looked familiar. Some kind of science experiment, a kid's school project. But what was this black object?

King's eye was drawn to the typewriter and the pages stacked next to it. *The Shining*, by Guy Tupper. He shuffled through the sheets, skimming what had been written. But then he felt the call of the dark device and lifted it up for a better look, careful of the wires attached to it.

He studied it for a few minutes, nearly forgetting about the two dead men. He touched a shiny button on one side, and the unit sprang to life. Words on a page, or at least what looked like a page.

The same words as on the typewritten sheets.

His fingers traced the words on the surface, trying to understand what he was seeing. Symbols appeared suddenly at the bottom, and he set the mysterious thing down, unsure of what that meant. As he did, a new image appeared. Small pictures of books. Very colorful and clear.

Carrie.

The Dark Tower.

The Shining.

By Stephen King.

More pictures of book covers. All by Stephen King.

He sat down, the breath knocked out of him.

These were *his* books. That's how Guy Tupper had written *Carrie*. But . . . ?

There were too many questions and no time to answer them, not with two bodies cooling at the bottom of the stairs. King studied the wiring, memorizing the arrangement of pennies and nails. He unhooked the alligator clips and grabbed those, along with the strange contraption. Plus the typed pages. Guy Tupper would have no need of them. Nor any right to them, not that this would ever be decided in court.

King took the stairs, stepped over the corpses, went out the door, climbed into his Ford Fairlane with the rusty fenders and knocking engine, and got out of Fort Worth as fast as he could.

Several days later, King crossed over the Maine state line. Once he got to his hometown, he stopped at Hannaford's Groceries.

And purchased three ten-pound bags of potatoes.

RED CHRISTMAS

...

BLUE ROCK, OHIO
December 24, 1953

ETHAN SHARD SHUFFLED through the fresh white snow.
Barely an inch, and the temperature already above freezing as the
late-afternoon sun broke through the fleeing clouds. People were
bundled up, thick scarves around their necks, gloves and mittens
warming their hands.

They had no idea.

The shimmer of snow gave Blue Rock a look of newfound purity,
like a penitent woman wearing her white veil over a low-cut dress. The
whole town was nothing more than a few stores, a diner, and a cluster
of houses surrounded by farmland on the banks of the Muskingum
River. Brightly colored lights decorated streetlamps, inviting shoppers
to stop at the Ben Franklin Five and Dime for last-minute gifts.

Shard stomped his boots free of snow on the sidewalk in front of
the diner. Time for a homecoming, such as it was.

"Coffee," he said, taking a stool at the counter, near the cash register
and the rack of candy bars. He was the only customer. A solitary
pine—needles already littering the floor—stood in the corner, draped
in tinsel and gaudy ornaments.

"On the house, pal," the counterman said, pouring Shard a mug.
"I'm closing early, so the grill's shut down. On account of it's Christmas
Eve."

"No problem. Hey, is Sully around?"

"Naw. I bought the place from him a coupla years ago. He's up in
Ashtabula now. You from around here?"

"I was," Shard said. "He told me to see him when I got out of the army, said he'd give me a job. I used to work weekends here when I was in high school."

"Sorry, buddy, I run the place myself, not that I have a lot to show for it. Blue Rock ain't exactly a boomtown, but you must already know that. You were in the war? Korea?" As if Shard might not have heard of it.

"Yeah," Shard said. "Just got out." It wasn't a job he'd come looking for; he had plenty of back pay.

"Must feel good to be home. You got family here?"

Shard shook his head, sipping at the coffee. Hearing the question out loud, he wondered why he'd come at all. After the army released him from the hospital, he'd made for Ohio without much thought, looking for familiarity, the illusion of a home to return to.

"Not anymore." They were all in the ground.

"You got no place to go?" The counterman looked like he was ready to offer sympathy, or worse yet, charity.

"I can go anywhere I want," Shard said, knowing charity offered on Christmas Eve might sour by morning. His eyes wandered, taking in the pies in a glass case, the soda fountain, candies by the register, the refrigerator stocked with everything from hot dogs to cheese and eggs. Maybe to this guy it didn't mean much, but to Shard it was heaven.

"Suit yourself," the counterman said, topping off Shard's coffee before turning to clean the grill. Shard added sugar, watching the crystals fall like thick snow, his mind's eye filling with the swirling Siberian storms that had coated their compound last winter. He had his hands around the warm cup, and he shivered as the memories returned, unbidden and relentless, as vivid as that day one year ago.

POW CAMP II, NORTH KOREA
December 24, 1952

ETHAN SHARD WOKE from his dream, gasping for breath. Schuman had visited him again. Schuman had been dead for two years.

To the day.

Shard nudged Skitter awake, motioning toward the rice paper door of their hut. They rose, hunching against the sloping roof, their heads bowed. Shard stepped over the prone bodies of his hut mates as they groaned and cursed quietly beneath plumes of frosted breath.

Skitter danced across the twelve-foot room, his feet finding the small bare spaces between bodies, avoiding the straw mats that marked the boundary of each man's tiny territory. He was small, quick, and wiry enough to move easily through the dark and cramped chamber. He slid the rickety wooden frame open, drawing it shut behind them before the men inside could summon up a complaint about the sharp blast of cold, bleak, biting wind.

Skitter followed Shard without hesitation, a habit born out of greed and avarice, cemented in terror, horror, and survival. They walked the snow-packed path along the wire, toward the high ground, the crumbling cliff face, and the garbage dump.

The men stared at what was left of the refuse pile. After being picked clean by guards and prisoners, then scavenged by civilians who trudged up the hill from the village below, there wasn't much.

"Hardly the Ginza, Skitter," Shard said.

"This whole damn country ain't worth shit," Skitter said, squatting on his haunches and intently watching one of the villagers scrounging for firewood. A young woman, obvious even at this distance. Skitter's eyes lapped her up, not out of lust, but in hopes of keeping the memory of lust alive. Shard sat next to him, lifting his head to the sky, willing the clouds to part and grace his face with winter sunshine. "Now Japan, that was something else. We were kings there, remember?"

"Yeah," said Shard. "I remember." It was what he said every time, reliving their heyday as black market operators, stealing the army blind, getting rich off Uncle Sam. Memories and talk were all the living had left. They spoke their lines like actors, giving it all they had, wondering if the play would ever end.

"What's wrong?" Skitter asked, sensing Shard's unease.

"I dreamed about Schuman last night," Shard said, watching the woman plod back to her hooch. "Remember him?"

"Sure. Died that first winter, didn't he?" Skitter said.

"Yep. Christmas Eve. Exactly two years ago."

"Weird," Skitter said, standing and beating his arms against his torso. "What'd he have to say?"

"I couldn't understand him—his voice was muffled. Can't figure out why he'd be in my dreams," Shard said, rising and dusting off the snow that stuck to his blue quilted POW jacket. He couldn't bring himself to mention the blood, the bright crimson gash on Schuman's cheek from where the Red Chinese guard had struck him before he was hauled away. "Can't stop thinking about him now."

"Dreams are bullshit," Skitter said, staying close to Shard. It was automatic, like taking a piss in the morning. Get up, see what Shard is doing. Keep in his shadow. It had worked so far. "So why we out here, anyway?"

"There's a new guy, transferred in from another camp. He knew Coop."

"Coop?" Skitter said. "Jeez, I haven't thought about him for a long time. Poor guy."

"Yeah, he deserved better," Shard said, walking along the cliff edge.

"Don't we all," Skitter said, working to keep up with Shard's long strides. Back in Japan, Skitter had wanted to be the boss, the brains of their black market operation. But here, deep in North Korea, Skitter had always known his chances would be better in Shard's shadow. "How'd this guy find you?"

"Asked around when he was brought in," Shard said, picking up the pace as he turned up his collar against the cold. "He knew Coop was missing in action and hoped he was here."

Coop was a sergeant who'd stayed with his men, discarding his chevrons to disguise his rank and help maintain discipline against the divide-and-conquer tactics of their captors.

"That's a long shot," Skitter said. "Hey, what's the hurry?"

"We got a job to do," Shard said. "Hauling supplies into the officer's camp. Let's go." He headed to a line of trucks by the camp gate. The officers' compound was surrounded by barbed wire six feet high. To protect the common soldiers of the working class from the corrupt ruling-class officers, according to the political lectures the Reds insisted they attend. A lot of guys liked that. If you had to be a POW, at least you only had to worry about the Commies bossing you around, not your own brass as well. Communication between enlisted men and officers was punishable by execution.

Shard gave a nod to Horseface as he slipped him four cigarettes, the going rate for a spot on the supply gang. Horseface, a senior guard, was named for his equine looks: big ears, a long nose, and eyes set far apart.

"So we see Coop's buddy after this?" Skitter said as he shouldered a sack of soybeans.

"No," Shard said. "He's here. A lieutenant with the 5th Marines."

"Jesus Christ," Skitter said, walking through the gate under the scrutiny of guards, their bayonets fixed.

POW officers were housed in a series of dilapidated farmhouses, not much more than mud huts with straw roofs, surrounded by wire. Skitter and Shard carried in burlap bags of soybeans, kidney beans, turnips, and sorghum, a sack of onions, and one case of canned meat.

An officer in marine fatigues checked off the items on a list as guards watched for any forbidden communication. When the last of the supplies were in, Horseface ordered the other guards out. He took one of the tins of meat, put it in his pocket, and left.

"We have three minutes," the officer said. "I'm Lieutenant John Cooper. You're the guys who knew Freddie?"

"Yeah," Shard said. "Me and Skitter were in his company."

"You mean Coop?" Skitter said. "Never got his first name. You related?"

"Yeah," the officer said. "He's my cousin. I heard he was taken prisoner, but he's listed as MIA. You were in another camp with him?"

"I was half-dead with dysentery," Shard said. "I never saw him. Skitter did."

"How was he?" Lieutenant Cooper asked.

"Not too bad, considering," Skitter said. "He and Sergeant Kelso had gotten in among the enlisted prisoners and were trying to organize things. Someone must have spilled the beans. First they came for Kelso and took him away. Then they shot Coop."

"You sure?" Cooper asked. "I heard he was alive at someplace called the Mining Camp."

"He was there all right," Skitter said. "But that's where they killed him. Sorry."

"Shit," Cooper muttered, the light of hope gone from his face. "Do you think this Kelso guy talked?"

"No," Shard said. Skitter shook his head in agreement. They'd never seen Kelso again. "Not Kelso."

"Any idea who did?"

"Coulda been anyone," Skitter said. "Guys in his barracks must have known. Hard to say." He looked around nervously, waiting for Horseface to come in and beat them for fraternizing.

"You both knew, right?" Cooper said.

"Hey, watch who you're accusing," Skitter said. "Coop was our pal. And Shard was delirious when it happened."

"Sorry. You're certain?" Cooper asked, a hint of desperation in his hooded eyes.

"Saw the body myself," Skitter said, walking to the half-open door and peeking outside. "We should go."

"Sorry, Lieutenant," Shard said, his eyes lingering on the supplies stacked on the shelves.

Soup. A memory of soup came back to him. He'd been sick in that camp when he heard of Coop being shot for the crime of hiding his stripes. Skitter had brought him soup, with onions.

Horseface hurried them out of the enclosure. There was another job.

"I always wondered who betrayed Coop," Shard said, as they climbed into the empty truck.

"It's hard to get upset about someone who's been gone almost three years. Coop missed a lot of suffering," Skitter said.

"True," Shard said. "But he also missed everything good that could happen, after the war. Home and family."

Skitter didn't answer. Things so distant and unattainable were unworthy of comment. If it couldn't keep him alive today, it had no value. He knew what happened to guys who forgot that. They drifted into apathy. *Give-up-itis* the POWs called it.

Their vehicle stopped in front of the camp warehouse where the Chinese stored their supplies. Horseface pointed to another truck, larger and stacked with food, then to the open warehouse.

"No stealing," Horseface warned with a wagging finger. Shard spread his hands and grimaced, as if offended by the warning. Horse-face laughed, a good sign.

Shard and Skitter finished with the heavy crates and began moving sacks of rice and flour, stacking them on pallets. When they couldn't be seen by the guards, Shard searched for something to steal.

"No," Skitter said. "You heard Horseface."

"Horseface was only acting tough. He might pat us down, but he's not going to make a big deal out of it. He selected us, so it would make him look bad if we got caught." Shard took his time, checking the stores of food. Under the rice sacks he found heavy burlap bags filled with cabbages. He worked a finger into the thin material and pulled, exposing the vegetables. Shard took off his blue cap, ripped leaves off, and stuffed them inside the hat.

"We need greens," Shard explained. "Cabbage has vitamins." Skitter reached up and tucked an errant cabbage leaf under Shard's cap, shaking his head at the chance his friend was taking.

They finished unloading and found Horseface and the other guards laughing and smoking, paying them no attention. Horseface told a joke, or so it seemed by the tone of his voice. As Horseface grinned and drew on his cigarette, a look of stunned horror spread across his face. Comrade Yuan rounded the corner, followed by two other senior comrades. Political officers.

Horseface dropped his butt at the same time he raised his voice at the other guards, berating them for smoking on duty. They stood to attention as Yuan drew closer. Horseface advanced on Shard, yelling incoherently. He swung his rifle butt, determined to show Comrade Yuan he was on top of the lazy recruits and even lazier prisoners. The rifle caught Shard on the shoulder, sending him tumbling to the ground. Shard's cap flew off, revealing the hidden stash of bright green cabbage.

Shard instinctively curled up as boots and rifle butts crashed into his torso. He heard Skitter begging Horseface to stop, but all else was lost in a torrent of high-pitched yells, Horseface screaming his lungs out, hoping his fury would distract Comrade Yuan from his lack of diligence. A prisoner could be shot for stealing food. A guard could end up in the front ranks of a human wave attack for letting him get away with it.

Yuan's voice broke through the melee, and the blows stopped immediately. "Stand, Prisoner Shard!"

"Yes, Comrade Yuan," Shard said, wincing as he spoke.

"You are stealing the people's food."

"Capitalism is theft, isn't that what you taught us?" Shard asked, remembering a phrase from the indoctrination classes. "I was brought up a capitalist. It's a hard habit to shake."

"At least you were paying attention," Yuan said, stepping closer and studying Shard's face. Then he backed up, perhaps uncomfortable at having to stare up at the tall American. "But tell me, why steal a few cabbage leaves? Is that worth a life?"

"I apologize, Comrade Yuan," Shard said, hating himself for the bow he gave. "I failed to control myself." Shard figured it was worth a try. Maybe Yuan would be in a merciful mood.

"I do not sense sincerity," Yuan said with an irritated sigh. He spoke to the guards, and they grabbed Shard by the arms. "Now you will be shot."

Shard twisted his arms as the guards held him tight. He felt fear in the pit of his stomach, and relief at the back of his mind. He didn't know which was more frightening.

"Comrade Yuan, please wait," Skitter said, as Yuan unbuckled his holster.

"What?" Yuan snapped. Skitter was one of the leading progressives, a valued prisoner who eagerly participated in political classes and showed interest in the Marxist line. If anyone else had interrupted an execution, it would have meant two corpses.

"You asked for prisoners to come forward and confess," Skitter said, his eyes darting from Yuan to Shard, then back to Yuan's hand on his pistol. "About the germ warfare. I'm ready. I helped load the planes in Japan."

"Good," Yuan said, extending his arm, aiming the pistol at Shard's forehead.

"But Shard is my friend. He's misguided, that's all. Please, spare him, Comrade Yuan."

"You will make the recording? A full confession?" Yuan kept the pistol trained on Shard.

"Yes."

"Good. Tomorrow, then," Yuan said, holstering his pistol. "Or you will both be shot."

Yuan turned on his heel, barking orders to the guards. They began to beat Shard, on Yuan's instruction or on general principles, it was hard to tell. Shard felt himself go unconscious as he hit the ground. A minute or an hour later, Skitter was helping him get up.

"What'd you do?" Shard said, wincing as Skitter helped him walk.

"I made a deal," Skitter said. "I'm going to confess, about germ warfare. Yuan's been after someone to do it."

"But there's no germ warfare, it's all Red propaganda."

"That's exactly why I can do it," Skitter said. "Everyone knows it's bullshit. So why not?"

"Because it's aiding the enemy," Shard said, doing his best not to hobble as they made their way back to their hut. "What the hell do you know about germ warfare anyway?"

"Well, we were right next to an airbase," Skitter said. "Close enough."

"I shouldn't complain," Shard said. "Thanks for saving my life."

"Works both ways. I owe you," Skitter said, helping Shard to sit on the log bench outside their hut.

Minutes later, four guards marched double-time out of the administration building, rifles at the ready. Shard watched their approach carefully, calculating at a certain point that they were not coming for him, but heading for the officers' enclosure.

In ten minutes they returned with Lieutenant John Cooper, prodding him with bayonets toward the admin building. He looked at Shard as they passed, accusation burning in his eyes.

"Christ," Shard swore. "He has to think I betrayed him so Yuan would let me go."

"It had to be Horseface," Skitter said, as they watched the guards shove Cooper. "Cooper'll figure it out. Maybe he doesn't even know what happened."

"News travels fast," Shard said, standing and groaning. The story of Shard, his cabbage leaves, and his near execution probably went through the camp in minutes.

"Horseface might've reported that Cooper tried to bribe him, to get back in Yuan's good graces," Skitter said. "It would have been a good move."

Yuan descended the steps of the admin building. They were close enough to see Cooper struggle in the grip of the guards.

Saw the guards lean away as Yuan drew his pistol and fired.

Cooper's head snapped back and his body slumped, then crumpled as the guards let go. A blossom of bright red blood fed the snow, the crimson color fading to pink as it soaked into the soft whiteness.

"Shit," Skitter said. "One more for the list."

The list of the dead. At first, they'd memorized the names of the dead, chanting them under their breath as they marched. After fifty, it was impossible to remember all of them, so Shard and Collier started a secret list, using whatever scraps of paper they could scrounge. The Chinese didn't want to admit how many POWs had died in their care, so it was a forbidden activity. Only Shard and Collier knew where the list was hidden. It was their mission to bring the list out when they were freed, to bear witness to what the North Koreans and Chinese had done.

"You sure the list's safe?" Skitter said, pulling at Shard's sleeve. There had been two lists. The duplicate was discovered by the Chinese three months ago. The reprisals had been ferocious.

"We're fine," Shard said, shaking off Skitter's grip. "I'm going to take a walk. See you in a few."

"Sure. I'll see if I can find out anything about Horseface. Be good to know if more trouble's brewing." Shard didn't answer. He was too stunned by the execution. An hour ago, it could have been his blood and brains in the snow.

He limped toward the garbage pit, thinking about what he knew and what he guessed. He caught a glance of Skitter moving fast, making a circuit around the administration building, head down and hands bunched in his pockets, a shadow darting from one dark corner to another.

Shard feared Cooper would join Schuman in his dreams tonight. He sought a distraction, anything to stop the mad swirl in his brain. He walked to the kitchen. No guards at the door. Maybe all the commotion had disrupted things. Worth a look. It was locked between mealtimes, the penalty for breaking and entering, death.

But the door was open, inviting. No guards in sight. He took a step inside, ready to retreat, bribe, grovel, whatever he had to do, the lure of food too great to resist. He stood in the hallway leading into the main kitchen, the cooks intent on their tasks. He laid his hand on the pantry latch and pressed, quietly and slowly, holding it tight as he pushed the door open.

He froze.

Horseface was on the floor, straddled by a chunky Korean girl, her back to Shard. She was naked from the waist down, Horseface's pants down around his ankles. She moved languidly, her long black hair caressing Horseface in undulating silence. Shard edged back, one hand reaching for a can of tinned pork as the other pulled the door shut without a sound. He waited for a moment, listening for any sign he'd been heard. Then he left, the can in his pocket, and the image of the girl's buttocks burned into his mind.

Later, Shard and Skitter sat hunched in their hut. Skitter had come back saying he'd seen Horseface getting a tongue-lashing from Yuan. He claimed that gave credence to his notion of Horseface fingering Cooper for attempting to bribe a guard. But Shard had seen Horseface, and it wasn't Yuan who'd been lashing him.

Shard spoke after the silence had become too heavy. "Someone's gotta pay."

"Sure," Skitter said. "But it ain't gonna happen. It's not like the last war where we won and put people on trial."

Shard didn't reply. He inhaled deeply, drawing the cold air into his lungs. The faint aroma of fried fish rose in his nostrils.

Then, he understood what Schuman had been trying to tell him.

The truth came at him hard, and he retreated into another deep silence, until Skitter roused him to search for firewood. The guards let them wander as far as they wanted; after all, there was nowhere to run.

"How'd we ever make it that first winter?" Shard said as they picked up branches and twigs. "No boots, rags for shoes, never enough to eat."

"You taking a trip down memory lane today, Shard?" Skitter said, hefting his load of branches. "More ghosts?"

"Ghosts are just bad memories," Shard said. "The bad things burned into our minds."

"I try not to think about it," Skitter said, uneasy with talk of things past.

"Does that work?"

"No. Not really."

"You got boots that winter, didn't you?" Shard said, his eyes watching Skitter, taking his measure.

"Yeah. Traded a pocketknife to a guard."

"You were lucky he didn't turn you in."

"It was Cho, remember him? Crookedest Commie you'd ever want to meet."

"Yeah, Cho. He'd trade anything, not that we had much," Shard said. "How'd you get that knife anyway?"

"Traded up for it. Started out with hard candies in the first Red Cross parcel we got. Christmas, remember? Then got some cigarettes, and the guy who had smuggled the pocketknife in was dying for a smoke, so he traded. I showed it to Cho, and he wanted it right away. I knew he wouldn't snitch, since that way he'd get a pat on the head but no jackknife. He came through with the boots and a couple pairs of socks, remember? I gave you a pair."

"Best Christmas of my life," Shard said. All POWs had been stripped of their combat boots, many of them marching barefoot in snow and ice. Finally, Shard had been given a pair of worn-out North Korean sneakers. With the wool socks, he had an edge, enough to avoid frostbite.

"You took a chance to get those boots," Shard said, holding his bundle of firewood under one arm as they walked. "Cho could have turned you in; what do you think they would have done to a prisoner with a weapon?"

"Aw hell, it was only a little pocketknife," Skitter said. "The real risk was getting frostbite."

"Yeah," Shard agreed. Frostbite was a death sentence. "Who did you trade with for the knife?"

"Uh, Schuman. John Schuman," Skitter said, after a moment's thought. "Hey, the guy you dreamed about. Funny, huh? I almost forgot his name."

They walked in silence back to their hut, memories of that terrible winter swirling in Shard's mind like remnants of a nightmare, a vision that remains even as you tell yourself you're fully awake.

After dumping the firewood at their hut, Skitter made for the recreation hall and class with Comrade Yuan while Shard waited for the afternoon meal. Rice balls with millet for the reactionaries, while the progressives ate rice with vegetables off real plates in the rec hall. A lot of guys attended the sessions for the extra food, but many got kicked out. You had to show interest in the class struggle, be willing to criticize yourself, your buddies, your country, over and over again until Yuan was satisfied. But he never stayed satisfied. That was the problem with giving in; the demands never ended, there was always another bit of your soul to surrender.

"Look," Shard said, as he met up with Skitter after class. "I went into the admin building while you were critiquing the ruling class and asked about hot water for baths. They threw me out, but not before I got these off an orderly's desk." He opened his pocket, showing Skitter a pack of Chinese cigarettes. Skitter told Shard he took too many risks, and that the big news was that the Chinese were looking for volunteers to refuse repatriation when the war ended. They wanted some American soldiers to make Red China their home, to counterbalance the thousands of North Koreans and Chinese who were likely to decline repatriation. No one had raised their hand.

They walked through the crowd of progressives leaving class. They had a fullness to their faces from the extra midday rations. Shard got whatever fullness he had from thievery and trading, while half-starved POWs suffered with gaunt, sunken cheeks, night blindness, and swollen gums.

It began to snow. They made it to their hut as heavy flakes fresh from Siberia draped the compound.

"Hey, O'Hara, you're back," Shard said. O'Hara was one of the prisoners from the original group.

"Been to the Yalu River, unloading barges at night," O'Hara said.

"Feed you okay?" Shard asked.

"Yeah, we ate pretty much what the soldiers got. Rice with beans and some kinda greens. Wasn't bad." O'Hara shrugged. "Not as good as what the birdies get, though. Skitter, you're looking well."

"I don't mind listening to the Reds," Skitter snapped. "And I don't mind eating their food. Small price to pay."

"If you say so," O'Hara said. Skitter glanced at Shard, eager to leave, even with the snow.

"Hey, O'Hara," Shard said, as if he'd just thought of it, "weren't you and Schuman buddies?"

"Yeah. We were together since basic."

"Me and Skitter were talking about him and his jackknife," Shard said. Skitter shuffled his feet in the enclosed space, staring at the floor. "Skitter traded with him about then, didn't you?"

"Yeah," Skitter said.

"I told him a million times, he was taking a chance keeping that jackknife," O'Hara said.

"That's what he traded with me," Skitter said, looking to Shard.

"Naw," O'Hara said. "His granddaddy gave him that knife. He'd never have traded it. But the damn Chinks found it. Threw him in the hole for that little knife. Lasted three days before he froze."

"No, really, I traded with him," Skitter said. "I gave him stuff from my Red Cross parcel. Food. A pocketknife doesn't do you much good if you starve to death, does it?"

"You still got it?" O'Hara asked.

"I traded it on to Cho. For boots."

"They shipped Cho out last spring. Bastard always was good for a trade," O'Hara said.

"Yeah. My feet were in bad shape," Skitter said. All he could think was how much his feet had hurt on that first march after they'd been captured. He'd watched men with black, frostbitten feet wrapped in rags, limping through the snow as tears froze on their cheeks. Saw them fall and welcome death.

Shard recalled the last time Skitter told the story of the jackknife. Before, he said he'd traded cigarettes for the knife. Now it was food. Shard felt sick, the certainty of betrayal like a rock in his gut.

"Let's go see Marty and Hughes," Shard said. "They'll want to trade for these cigarettes."

"You could trade with anybody," Skitter said. "Why them?"

"Because they're new," Shard said, tossing a wave to O'Hara, who'd grown silent. "They haven't had time to shake the nicotine habit, so I'll get the most from them."

"Yeah, makes sense. And the sooner you ditch those Chinese cigarettes the better." Skitter shoved his hands in his pockets and hunched his shoulders against the cold, shuffling through the freshly fallen snow. In one of the huts, men sang half-hearted Christmas carols. "I'll Be Home for Christmas," with the mocking refrain, *only in my dreams*. "Why are we making the grand tour today, anyway?"

"It's like that story, Schuman had to be the Ghost of Christmas Past," Shard said, watching as glints of sunlight broke through the rapidly moving clouds. "You know, *A Christmas Carol?* Hell, he died on Christmas Eve, and I saw his ghost. And Cooper, he has to be the

Ghost of Christmas Present, since he died today. Right?" He watched Skitter out of the corner of his eye, catching the frightened look on his face, there and gone.

"You're crazy," Skitter said, shaking his head.

"Could be. Can't even remember the whole story. How about you?"

"I don't know," Skitter said. "Some little crippled kid died, I think. Drop the ghost stuff, okay?" Shard ignored his plea, watching a group of prisoners light a fire outside their hut. They had two rats ready to roast. Catching, gutting, and cooking a rat, without benefit of a knife, was a valued skill in Camp Eleven. Country guys were the best at it, and this hut was lucky enough to house three backwoods boys and a cook from Brooklyn.

They found Marty and Hughes sitting outside the next hut.

"Hey guys," Marty said, raising a hand in greeting. Shard and Skitter took a seat on a log. Marty was thickset, with dark wiry hair and the scarred hands of a mechanic. Hughes was younger, thinner, and wary. He nodded a greeting and went back to staring off in the distance.

"Thought you boys might want to trade," Shard said, after they'd settled into the silence for a while. "Chinese cigarettes, a dozen."

"Wouldn't mind," Marty said. Hughes nodded his assent. "What're you askin'?"

They settled on a packet of crackers and a cube of cheese from a recent Red Cross parcel. Shard passed them the cigarettes, the pack decorated with a pagoda and Chinese characters.

"Don't hang on to that pack," Shard said.

"Sure," Marty said. He gave one cigarette to Hughes, took one himself, and struck a match. He put the pack away inside his tanker's overalls as he drew on the cigarette with a denied smoker's delight.

"Not a lot of tankers in here," Shard said. "You ever notice that, Skitter?"

"Guess so," Skitter said, shrugging.

"Occupational hazard," Marty said. "If a tank is hit, the whole crew gets it. If they bail out, there's a ton of small arms fire going on. Hell to pay if you gotta run."

"How'd you get captured?" Shard said.

"We hit a mine. Blew a tread clean off. Me and Hughes got out to check the damage, and artillery starts dropping all around us. We dove into a ditch, and the next thing we know a round hits our tank dead center. The Chinese swarmed all over us."

"You were lucky," Skitter said. "Sort of." Hughes nodded. Luck was a relative thing. Here he was, smoking with his buddy on Christmas Eve, while his pals decayed on some forgotten hillside.

"We knew a couple of guys back when we were first captured," Shard said. "They were from a Pershing tank. Remember them, Skitter?"

"Yeah, I think so. Don't remember their names."

"Miller," Shard said, "and Lefkowicz. You guys know them?"

"When was this?" Marty asked.

"Back in '50, late September," Shard said.

"Never heard of 'em," Marty said, blowing smoke. "Hell, Hughes was still in high school back then." Hughes closed his eyes, a distant smile crossing his face.

"When the North Koreans interrogated them, they claimed they were from a disabled Sherman. Why'd they do that, I wonder?" Shard said, as if he didn't have a clue.

"The M26 Pershings were new to Korea back then," Marty said. "The Reds wanted the dope on 'em real bad. Armor thickness, gun velocity, all that technical stuff. When we first got Pershings, the brass told us to avoid capture at all costs. Easy to say sittin' on your ass in Tokyo."

"What happened to them guys?"

"The camp commander took them one day," Shard said. "Maybe someone talked, told him they were from a Pershing. Never saw them again."

"Guys shoulda kept their mouths shut," Marty said. "How many GIs knew about them?"

"Everyone in our section," Skitter said. Shard nodded his agreement. A dozen of them. Some had been sick, too weak to do anything, others killed shortly after by the North Koreans, making it unlikely they were informers. They were the only two left.

"Miller and Lefkowicz," Hughes repeated. "They on that list of yours?"

"Yeah."

"How many names?"

"Four hundred plus," Shard said.

"That's one dangerous list," Marty said.

Skitter and Shard left after a while, stopping to watch the rat feast in progress. Men were peeling off tiny shreds of meat and licking fat off their fingers.

"You add Cooper to the list yet?" Skitter asked, his voice nonchalant as he blew warm air on his fingers.

"Not yet," Shard said. He moved closer to the fire, watching one guy toss rat bones into the flames. The fire danced higher, charring the carcass until there was nothing left but the lingering smell of rat.

"WE NEED TO talk," Shard said to Skitter. "Where no one can listen."

"What's wrong with right here?" Skitter said. They were back on the log outside their hut. The wood was shiny and cold, worn down by months of sitting, watching, and waiting. Moonlight cast long shadows across the camp like a searchlight.

"I don't want someone hearing us. Come with me," Shard said, standing and waiting for Skitter.

"Jeez, Shard," Skitter said. "Is this another ghost story?"

"Yeah. It's about the Ghost of Christmas Future. Let's head to the rec hall."

"We're not supposed to be in there alone," Skitter said, jogging to catch up with Shard. "And stop with the ghosts."

"You're one of Yuan's prize progressives," Shard said. "He won't mind."

"Yeah, well, I didn't spend all that time listening to Yuan to blow it at the last minute," Skitter said, checking the area for guards. He hugged himself against the cold, his legs jittering in place as Shard opened the door. The sound of Christmas carols, sung low and quiet, drifted across the frozen ground.

"Sit down," was all Shard said, hard, between clenched teeth. He moved to a table near the window. He motioned for Skitter to take the chair across from him.

"Shard, I'm fed up with this," Skitter said, slumping in his seat. His eyes took in the darkened room, searching for a reason as to why they were there, as red silken banners hanging from the rafters rippled in the draft.

"I know," Shard said, the words like a sigh from deep within.

"You know what?" Skitter said, leaning forward, his voice barely a whisper.

"I know it all, Skitter. I know what you've done."

"What?" Skitter spread his arms and laughed. "What have I done?" His eyes darted back and forth, and Shard felt a childhood memory wash over him. When Pa accused him of some misdeed, he'd played it the same way. Buying time, trying to figure out what his old man knew, his mind racing to make sure he didn't reveal anything Pa hadn't found out about.

But this was North Korea, not an Ohio farm. It wasn't broken windows or skipped chores.

"Schuman, Kelso, Coop, Miller, and Lefkowicz. You betrayed them to keep yourself alive," Shard said. "And today, Cooper."

"No."

"I know," Shard said, nodding solemnly. "You kept me alive to watch out for you, to make sure you were protected."

"Shard, this is your buddy Skitter you're talking to. What's come over you, pal?"

"We aren't buddies, Skitter," Shard said, slamming his palm down on the table. "We're criminals. We stole from the army and made a lot of money selling to gangsters. You were crooked in Japan, and I was a fool to think you'd be different here. Miller and Lefkowicz, the two tankers. Far as I recall, you and me were the only ones who knew about them."

"What is this, an inquisition?"

"Kelso and Cooper, they were your big catch. You told the Reds about Kelso. Then you saw Coop was there too and turned him in."

"Shard," Skitter said. "How can you believe that?"

"You got extra rations for us," Shard said. "You needed me alive so I'd watch your back. Like today. You didn't want me killed, so you snitched on Cooper and promised a germ warfare confession. What was your reward for that?"

"I only offered the confession to save you," Skitter said, panic entering his voice. "That's all I did, I swear."

"You came back smelling of fried fish," Shard said, leaning into Skitter's face and sniffing the air. "You're an informer, a rat, and they feed you for it."

"No," Skitter said, his eyes wide with disbelief, unable to take in his best friend turning on him. "I saved your life. Dysentery would have killed you. You needed those extra rations; you needed to live!"

"Yes," Shard said. "Yes. God forgive me, I did. I can still feel that soup filling my belly. The taste of betrayal. Onion soup." They faced each other across the moonlit table, neither man moving.

"Shard, we're a team," Skitter said, his voice almost breaking.

"What about Schuman? You told Yuan about the jackknife, didn't you? For a pair of boots. What did that have to do with us being a team?"

"I gave you a pair of socks," Skitter whispered, his head bowed. He was acting like a child, his voice a whine, as if socks answered all questions.

"Coop and Kelso dead," Shard said. "Miller and Lefty tortured and killed. Schuman. Cooper shot today. What else, Skitter? What else have you done?"

"You can't tell anyone, Shard, please," Skitter said, folding his trembling hands as if in prayer.

Now it was out in the open; the blood on Skitter's hands.

"I haven't told anybody, Skitter." That seemed to calm him. Skitter looked up at Shard, eyes gleaming with tears.

"I've been so afraid," Skitter said, the words tumbling out. "Yuan hounds me every day, and I worry about the guys finding out. I'm dead either way if I screw up."

"Hounds you for what?" Shard said.

"The list, he knows there's another list," Skitter said. Shard didn't have to ask how he knew. "What are you going to do? You're not going to rat me out, are you?"

"No," Shard said, shaking his head. "But there's something you have to do."

"What?"

"You have to refuse repatriation. You're a progressive; you'll do well. It won't be a prison camp, they'll treat you like royalty. If you don't agree, I tell the whole camp what you've done." Shard laid his hands on the table. He wished Skitter had taken a different path, but he hadn't, and here they were, Shard playing the ghost of Skitter's Christmas future.

"No. No," Skitter cried. "They'll tear me to pieces."

"Exactly." The hardness was back in Shard's voice.

"I can't go to Red China. What would my folks think? They're decent people. Please tell me you don't mean it."

"I do."

"Why me? Why not you? You took the soup, didn't you? You knew!" Skitter stood, his body quivering, his mouth twisted.

"I figured things out," Shard said. "Too late. There's a line, Skitter. I don't pretend to know where it is, but you crossed it."

"I kept us both alive," Skitter said.

"And I'll remember the price other men paid for the rest of my life," Shard said. They sat in silence, alone in the cold moonlight.

Shard rose and walked to a desk, bringing back paper and pencil. "If you want to write to your folks, go ahead. I'll take it to them myself. Write their address out and I'll hand-deliver it." He set the paper and pencil in front of Skitter and placed a hand on his shoulder. Gave a reassuring squeeze.

"You won't say anything to my folks about the other stuff?" He wiped his sleeve against his nose, cleaning away tears and snot. Shard knew Skitter. He was quick to agree, but he'd try to find a way out later, to skitter out of trouble. The list would be Skitter's ace in the hole. The final betrayal that could get him out of this jam.

"I promise, not a word to anyone," Shard said, meaning it.

"Okay." Skitter wrote out his parents' names and address in Lewiston, Michigan, then stopped, his hand hovering over the page. "I don't know what to say to them."

"Tell them you're sorry," Shard whispered, his hand resting on Skitter's shoulder. "How very sorry you are."

Skitter craned his neck back and smiled at Shard. He took a deep breath, and began to write, lead scratching against coarse paper.

Shard watched from behind, the slanting rays of moonlight casting his long shadow over the table. Skitter bent to the task, a schoolchild facing a tough assignment. As he wrote, Shard murmured *good, good*, nodding in rhythm to the soothing words, patting him on the shoulder.

He lifted his hand from Skitter's shoulder and swung it across his throat. He dug his right elbow into the shoulder and pushed against the back of Skitter's head with his right palm. He grabbed his right arm with his left hand, as he'd been trained, and with one sharp push, Skitter's neck broke.

The pencil still in his hand.

Gently resting Skitter's head on the table, he patted his hair. All that remained was to be sure there was no retribution for the death of a prized progressive.

He took the sheet of paper and carefully folded and refolded it until he could tear off the address and salutation in a neat straight line. He took it and left the remainder on the table.

I am so sorry.

Hoisting Skitter's body onto the table and climbing up, he grabbed the nearest red banner. He twisted the silk fabric until it was tight, then knotted it in several places. He tied it around Skitter's neck, holding up the body as high as he could.

He let go. Skitter's feet, still in the boots he had traded for Schuman's life, rested on the tabletop. Shard moved the table away, leaving Skitter dangling two feet above the floor.

I am so sorry.

Outside, several huts had chimed in on the same carol, the words drifting over Shard like new-fallen snow.

> *God rest ye, merry gentlemen*
> *Let nothing you dismay*
> *Remember, Christ, our Savior*
> *Was born on Christmas day*
> *To save us all from Satan's power*
> *When we were gone astray*
> *O tidings of comfort and joy,*
> *Comfort and joy*
> *O tidings of comfort and joy.*

It brought Shard no comfort. Joy wasn't even in the cards.

BLUE ROCK

HIS COFFEE HAD gone cold. The counterman was busy cleaning the stainless-steel fixtures, whistling to himself, ignoring Shard. It was time to go. He had five hundred miles between him and Lewiston, in Michigan's northern woods. He saw no reason to linger in Blue Rock.

"Merry Christmas," Shard said, leaving a dime tip on the counter.

"Merry Christmas," the counterman echoed as he rubbed down the refrigerator door.

Shard glanced back, then out the window. The afternoon light was already fading, the cheery colored lights in the street struggling against the approaching grayness. No one was looking.

He did a double snatch. Two Hershey bars disappeared into his coat pocket, nestled against the worn paper with Skitter's note, written out last Christmas Eve. Outside, he gave Blue Rock one last look.

"I am so sorry," he said, watching the words turn into plumes of frosty breath and vanish into the air.

They always came back.

THE REFUSAL CAMP

■ ■ ■

THE FACTORY FLOOR was thick with noise and odor. The clatter of metal and the squeaky wheels of heavy trolleys on cold concrete. The stench of acetylene cutting steel and the sharp, oily tang of scrap metal. The smell of bodies crammed together along workbenches, women in striped dresses worn over filthy layers for warmth.

Malou worked quickly, assembling the machine parts that were brought to her table in a never-ending stream of metal and wire. She had no idea what they were for. No one did. Not the prisoners, not the guards. A Nazi secret weapon, some said. What else could it be? Why else would the Germans transport the women here every day from Ravensbrück, even issuing them extra rations?

Weapons. It was horrible enough to be a prisoner in the Ravens-brück concentration camp for women. Being forced to build weapons for the Nazi war machine was far too much to bear. But this was not the time to think about it. They'd already decided.

Malou looked across the table to Ohla. This was Ohla's plan. When she gave the signal, they'd act.

At the other workbenches, women gave slight nods of acknowledgment. The Slovaks at the next table. The Dutchwomen. The Ukrainians around Ohla Eliashevska. And beyond them, the Poles, where Lena watched the guards with quick, furtive glances. Some kept their heads down. One of the new workers, a young girl from Reims, looked like she might break down as she fumbled with the metal parts in her trembling hands. Malou was new herself, arriving in camp less than a week ago, but she wasn't anywhere near her breaking point. Not yet.

No matter. Not all would go along, but no one had betrayed their plan.

A metal door clanged open. Herr Barth swept in, his white lab coat swirling behind thick hips as he grasped a clipboard like a deadly weapon. Armed guards with truncheons at the ready followed, a familiar routine during visits by the general manager of this Siemens factory.

Malou, with her sharp eye for potential threats, spotted an unfamiliar figure trailing Barth. A stocky man in a gray SS uniform, his indifferent eyes nearly hidden behind tortoiseshell glasses. He looked like a bureaucrat. They were the worst, but perhaps not an immediate threat.

Malou looked down at her work. It did not pay to be noticed.

"Ladies," Herr Barth barked as he halted at the end of a table. One of the guards thumped his truncheon on the workbench, nearly knocking over a pile of electrical parts. Barth shook his head and motioned the man back. "Ladies, your work falters. We are behind schedule."

Ohla set down her component with a thud, stood, and, stepping back from the workbench, folded her arms across her chest. As did the half dozen Ukrainians.

Malou did the same. Other Frenchwomen at her table followed suit, and like a ripple spreading across a pond, women at other tables did as well. Valerie, the new girl from Reims, wept but kept working, her shaking hands barely able to hold the electrical cables. Malou doubted she'd last long. This place showed no mercy, tolerated no weakness, and Valerie had little strength to fall back on. She wasn't political or part of the Resistance, simply a girl who'd been taken in one of the roundups. The Germans went for city girls with small, delicate hands, and pretty hands were Valerie's misfortune.

Lena was first among the Poles to stop working. Most followed her example.

"What is this?" Barth roared. "What are you doing? Get back to work!"

"No," Ohla said, looking straight at Barth, her voice unbelievably calm. "We refuse."

"You cannot refuse!" Barth sputtered, motioning for the guards to deal with the women. "It is not allowed."

Barth's bodyguards hesitated, unsure of what to do. This had never happened. The other guards in the room, German women from the camp, moved swiftly, striking their charges whether they were working or not. Barth backed away, his eyes flitting nervously toward the exit.

"Stop." The SS officer spoke, his voice breaking through the growing cries and clatter.

"Halt," Barth repeated somewhat uselessly. The guards had already backed off, but Barth was intent on asserting his authority. "Sturmbannführer Morgen says to stop."

Malou looked to Ohla, who raised her eyebrows in surprise. Everyone stared at the SS major, shocked at this unexpected turn. Everyone except Lena, who whispered to the woman next to her.

"On what basis do you refuse?" Morgen asked, walking between the tables and addressing Ohla.

"We are prisoners of war," Ohla answered, her chin jutting forward. "As such we should not be required to work on weapons. It says so in the Geneva Convention."

"Interesting," Morgen said, nodding. "What is your rank? Your branch of service?"

"I have no rank," Ohla said, which was true. That she was a member of the Ukrainian Insurgent Army was also true, and a secret worth her life. "And I refuse to make weapons for the enemy of my nation. It is my right as a prisoner. We refuse, those of us who stopped working. We are in the refusal camp."

"You are in my factory," Barth said, shouting more loudly than he needed to. "And you will work."

"Wait," Morgen said, holding up a hand in Barth's direction, then turning to Ohla. "Tell me, what weapon are you working on?"

"I do not know its precise function," she answered. "But I am certain we are not here to make refrigerators for the Reich."

"Doubtful, I agree," Morgen said, his tone conversational. "As for your status here, were you captured in uniform? As a combatant?"

"I was not captured in the sense you mean," Ohla said. "I was picked up, that's all. I have no idea why I am here, and the camp officials do not either."

True enough, thought Malou. Ohla had been the first to befriend her when Malou arrived. She'd confided to her that Ohla Eliashevska was her real name. She'd had so many false identities in her resistance work that when she was delivered to Ravensbrück she simply gave her real name, which thoroughly confused the Germans.

"And you cannot tell me what you are constructing here, can you?" Morgen asked.

"As I said, no, not exactly."

"Well, this is an interesting legal question, but one that cannot be settled today," Morgen said. "I suggest you return to work for now. I will be back tomorrow."

"Sturmbannführer, these women should be punished," Barth said.

"You say you are running behind schedule, and you plan to punish your workers?" Morgen said. "If you wish, but it seems unproductive." With that, Morgen shrugged and turned away from Barth.

"Back to work, everyone!" Barth shouted, immediately obedient to the SS major's suggestion. Ohla and Malou looked at each other. Was there anything to be gained by continuing? From across the room, Malou saw Lena pick up her tools and return to work. Others followed, as did Ohla.

Malou did the same. It was over, and it had been very strange.

Morgen moved among the prisoners, chatting as if he were a welcomed visitor. He was greeted with frightened stammers, blank looks, and the occasional forthright response.

"And you," he asked Malou, "were you taken in uniform?"

"An evening dress," Malou said, her eyes on her work. "In Paris."

"A whore," one of the guards told Morgen, pointing her truncheon at Malou. "In league with the Resistance and selling drugs on the black market."

"Are they feeding you well here?" Morgen asked, ignoring the guard, who appeared deflated.

"The bread has very little sawdust," Malou said. "The vegetables in the soup are only half-rotten, which makes this food haute cuisine compared to the camp's. Is there any other way in which I can assist the SS?"

"I doubt it," Morgen said, moving on to speak to two more workers before leaving.

Barth waited until Morgen was gone, then retreated to a corner of the room, whispering to his bodyguards. One departed, the other joined the Ravensbrück guards as they circled the prisoners, watching for any sign of renewed disobedience, slapping their clubs against their legs, and muttering curses.

Guards and officers didn't like anything that threatened their position. The work stoppage and Major Morgen's response had done just that, making everyone nervous and on edge. In the cramped confines of this machine shop, the dread rose as each prisoner waited for retribution. It might not come now, with all the delicate parts close at hand, but it would come.

MALOU SORTED INSULATED cables for the next round of assembly, her attention suddenly drawn to slammed doors and shouted orders. The female guards took up position around the workbenches as Barth and his men stormed in.

"To the mess hall," Barth ordered. It was early for the midday meal, but no one objected. Extra rations were part of the reward for working at Siemens. A piece of black bread and actual vegetables floating in the soup. The difference between living and slowly dying.

Guards shouted for them to hurry, pushing and shoving the

women as they lined up to exit the side door. Barth stood close by as a guard counted off the prisoners.

Valerie was ahead of Malou and stopped suddenly next to Barth.

"Please, Herr Barth, I want to go to the refusal camp," Valerie cried out, grasping his arm. "I'm no good here, please, can I go?"

"Get off me," Barth yelled, stepping back as a guard clubbed Valerie.

"No, Valerie, that's not what I meant," Ohla cried out from behind Malou.

"I want to go to the refusal camp," Valerie bawled, tears streaming down her face as she reached again for Barth, the false vision of some safe place driving all reason from her mind.

Guards streamed to the disruption, truncheons crushing bone as Valerie fell. Blood splattered against Barth's white coat, and a great pool of it seeped from Valerie's head.

"There!" Barth raged at Ohla. "That is what you accomplished today. You made this poor girl mad!" He stepped back, the blood coming close to ruining his shoes, and pointed at Ohla. "Take her back to camp. Now. Let Commandant Suhren deal with her."

Ohla was bundled away, alive, at least.

"Enjoy your luncheon, ladies," Barth said as Malou filed by.

IN THE MESS hall, Malou dipped her bread into the broth, softening it. Her stomach was in knots, but she had to get the food down. It was life.

"She wouldn't have lasted long, you know," Lena said from across the narrow table. "She couldn't adapt."

"Who could adapt to this place?" Malou said, focusing on her soup. There was little time to eat.

"You. Ohla, certainly. I did," Lena said. "Most of the others selected for this job. At least it was quick. She was out of her mind, probably a blessing."

"A smashed skull is as much a blessing as a visit from an SS officer," Malou said, draining the soup from her bowl. She took a crust of bread and rubbed it over the bottom, soaking up any residue. Chewing the bread, she ran her finger inside the bowl, rescuing the few crumbs left behind.

"What do you think of the food?" Lena asked.

"What a ridiculous question," Malou answered.

"No, I am serious. What's your assessment?"

"The same thing I told that SS bastard," Malou said, realizing the Polish girl was genuine. "There's more sawdust in the bread. Last week it was almost decent. There were more vegetables as well. There's fewer now, and some are rotten. Why?"

"We used to have meat; can you believe that?" Lena said. "Not much, but it was there."

"Wonderful," Malou said. "Are you going to share recipes with Major Morgen?"

"What brought you here?" Lena asked, ignoring the sarcasm.

"A train. Now leave me alone, will you?"

"Don't ignore Morgen," Lena said. "If he returns, there may be some value in it."

"Right. I might be able to strangle him with an electrical cord before they get me."

"You won't. You're not ready to give up," Lena said, licking her spoon.

"How old are you?" Malou asked. The girl's face was smudged with grease, but beneath the dirt was a young face.

"Seventeen," Lena said. "Old enough."

"For what?" Malou asked.

"To see what's going on," Lena said. "I've been here almost two months. They put me to work here the first day I arrived."

"Get up! Now! Back to work," guards yelled, thumping their truncheons on tabletops. The prisoners queued up silently. Talking while moving between buildings was forbidden, and the line shuffled to the machine shop, the evidence of the morning's violence still vivid.

Malou vowed she would survive and take her revenge on Barth and as many others as possible. How, she had no idea. But she would not forget Valerie, or the other girls she had witnessed being brutally beaten since she'd arrived.

Lena's questions about food gnawed at Malou as she worked. And why was Morgen asking the same thing? What possible value could there be in an SS officer snooping around and asking questions about prisoners' meals? There was no love lost between Barth and Morgen, but what did that mean for the survival of even a single prisoner?

Nothing, as far as Malou could see. She put away those thoughts and focused on her work. Too many mistakes, and it was the punishment detail. The severity of the punishment depended on the severity of the mistakes. Sometimes women came back in two days. Sometimes never.

If she knew what they were building, she might be able to sabotage it, but she had no idea what all these wires did. Even so, as she connected one of the cables, she cut away the sheath surrounding the conductors and snipped one of the inner wires short. Perhaps it made no difference. Perhaps something would blow a Nazi to bits.

Malou smiled. She caught Lena watching her from across the room. That girl seemed very sure of herself. Did she know what they were building? Did she have her own ideas on sabotage? Lena had some odd ideas about the SS, but there was something about her Malou admired.

It was common knowledge that the Germans picked up young women with small hands to do this delicate work. Lena had mentioned she'd been taken in just such a sweep, not for any specific resistance activity. But how true was that?

Just as Ohla was hiding from the Gestapo in plain sight, so was

Malou. She had her own secrets. Was Lena more than a prisoner brought in for slave labor?

Lena wore a red triangle with a *P* for Pole. Malou's was plain red, marking her as a political prisoner. There were other colors as well. Blue for forced labor, black for asocial, brown for the Roma, pink for homosexuals, and purple for Jehovah's Witnesses. And the yellow double triangles for Jewish prisoners.

Malou earned her red triangle by working at a high-class brothel in Paris. A hostess who greeted clientele and entertained them while they waited their turn. Germans, mostly. It was the perfect job for an agent of the Special Operations Executive.

Before it all fell apart on the eve of Liberation.

She shook off the memories, thankful that the Gestapo thought of her as a small cog in a Resistance cell doing black market work on the side. She'd been interrogated but managed to stick to her identity as Malou Lyon. Her worst fear was that based on her past employment, she'd be sent to one of the concentration camp brothels operated for SS guards.

She'd kill herself first.

"Zofia Janicki!" shouted Barth as he entered the room, this time escorted by four guards armed with rifles at the ready. He carried one of the electrical components, trailing multicolored wires.

A girl working near Lena stepped back from her workbench, eyes darting to the exits. They were all guarded. She let out a heavy sigh and waited for the inevitable.

"Prisoner Janicki, this is sabotage," Barth shouted, holding the component. "The cable is not connected at all. Did you think we would not check your work?" He removed a metal plate and let the unattached wire dangle for all to see. He snapped his fingers, and two guards grabbed the girl roughly, dragging her to the door.

"Niech żyje Polska!" shouted Zofia, before a guard struck her from behind with the butt of his rifle.

"You have been warned," Barth said, tossing the component on Lena's workbench. "Repair that immediately."

Two shots shattered the air, echoing against the brick building.

Long live Poland.

HOURS LATER, THE women were ordered to the trucks for the journey back to the Ravensbrück camp. Zofia's body lay crumpled on the ground in plain sight. Two prisoners, men with hollow faces and glazed eyes, stood by with shovels. It was obvious Barth wanted the women to see Zofia's corpse, to make plain the penalty for sabotage. She'd be buried nearby, along with others who'd died while at the Siemens factory. Murdered, all of them, whether by overwork, beatings, starvation, or bullets.

Valerie. Zofia. Malou envisioned Barth at her mercy. There would be none.

Malou hoisted herself into the truck bed. There were no benches, the women forced to stand and grip the rails. Night was falling and it was cold. Hope was at an ebb, and she wondered if she'd be able to make it through another day. She caught Lena's eye and saw something familiar once again. It sparked a curiosity in her that had been tamped down by violence and fear. What game was Lena playing at, and why was she interested in the SS officer?

Maybe she was part of an active resistance cell within the camp.

Or perhaps she was looking for a way to collaborate and save her own skin. If so, there were all sorts of unfortunate accidents that could happen in a factory. For an SOE agent trained in the killing arts, it would be easy.

Malou watched Lena as the truck rumbled through the main gate, past the guards and the administrative building. Lena leaned in to whisper to her fellow Poles, careful not to have her conversations overheard. What secrets were they passing back and forth?

As the trucks halted in front of the barracks square, prisoners were pulling carts filled with corpses. The daily haul of the dead from the barracks, those who had succumbed to starvation or disease. Limbs as thin as sticks dangled and bounced as the carts negotiated the uneven ground. There'd be more in the morning when the prisoner detail collected the overnight dead.

Three girls, none older than sixteen, held on to one another as they hobbled between barracks. Rabbits, the Germans called them, for their hopping gait as they walked. Their legs had deliberately been infected to test bone, muscle, and nerve regeneration. Not all lived through the procedures, but all were severely crippled.

The girls looked away as their tormentor passed them. Dr. Herta Oberheuser, her white lab coat flapping lazily in the breeze. Fair-haired, in her thirties, and with a protruding upper lip that gave her a permanently sour expression, she ignored her victims.

This camp devoured women. That was its purpose.

Malou stumbled wearily to her barracks to stand in line for the evening meal. She'd seen so much death and destruction in this war, but nothing prepared her for the horrors of this camp. She collected her meal. Another slab of black bread with a piece of sausage. The bread was supposed to last until morning; solid food wouldn't be issued again until midday. But no one could wait.

Their meager meal consumed, women collapsed into their thin mattresses. The cavernous room held tiers of bunk beds three high, most holding exhausted women who'd returned from heavy labor details. Soft moans and the sound of sobbing floated through the space, where only the most determined moved with any purpose.

Lena was one of those.

She came to Malou's bunk. When Malou first arrived, she'd had to take a top bunk. But it hadn't taken long for death to clear a lower berth for her, so the two women sat side by side.

"Who are you?" Lena asked.

"A Parisian whore, no better than that, as you know," Malou answered.

"If you want to play that game, fine," Lena said. "But do away with your calmness. You watch everyone very carefully and never seem shocked. I'd say that shows training, the kind of training the British give their spies."

"Who are you that you wish to know?" Malou asked. "And forgive me if I don't respond as you think I should. I will try to better show my shock and disgust at your interest in our SS visitor."

"Ohla has been taken to a punishment camp. Königsberg," Lena said, without responding to Malou's derision.

"How did you come by this information?" Malou said. "It's quite precise."

"Mury," Lena said, lowering her voice.

"What's that?"

"Mury is a secret unit of the Polish Girl Scouts," Lena whispered. "About one hundred members. They have many jobs, including work in the administration building. And the kitchens." With that, she nodded to a young girl a few rows over. She was spooning broth into the mouth of a painfully thin woman. They were surrounded by other girls on the watch for guards.

"Ohla is alive, you're certain?" Malou asked.

"Yes. They beat her, of course, but she got into the truck on her own," Lena said. "If I know her, she'll find a way to survive."

"How well do you know her?" Malou asked.

"I trusted her enough to join in on the work stoppage, as you did," Lena said.

"With some people, it is immediately obvious that they can be trusted," Malou said. That had been true with Ohla, but she wasn't entirely won over by Lena. After all, the strike today gave the Germans a perfect reason to take Ohla away. Lena could have informed on her. The punishment camp would be where they'd torture her for information about her network. No, it wasn't time to trust this girl, as ardent as she seemed.

"I'm sorry you feel that way," Lena said. "We need your help."

"To do what?"

"Never mind," Lena said. "Trust works both ways."

"All right," Malou said, resting her head against the bed frame. "I was involved with a Resistance cell. The brothel was a cover. But the bastards took off and left me there when they heard the Germans were onto them. It was just days before the Liberation."

"They left you to be arrested?"

"Yes, while they took off with false identity papers as members of the fascist militia," Malou said. "They left a message for me to join them in Rotterdam, at a hotel run by a friend. But the Germans came before I could get out the door. Bastards. I wish I could get my hands on them."

"Bad luck," Lena said, as a group of women gathered at the next bunk and began to sing a slow, mournful song in Polish. "We'll talk more tomorrow."

Malou smiled, watching Lena join the singers. Yes, tomorrow there would be more to talk about, one way or the other.

There was no friend in Rotterdam, no safe house within a hotel. She chose a city in Holland only because it was still occupied by the Germans, and they'd want to track down any Resistance fugitives. If Lena *was* an informer, she'd sell that information to the Gestapo for whatever they paid turncoats. A piece of cheese, perhaps. Life was cheap in Ravensbrück. So was death.

Malou would know by morning. If the Germans questioned her, that would be the end of Lena. If Malou still breathed.

As she waited for sleep, Malou felt her spirits rise. For the first time since being delivered to Ravensbrück, she had acted of her own accord. She had a plan, and tomorrow she would know if Lena was trustworthy. There might be an interrogation and a beating, but physical suffering was nothing compared to the sense of absolute powerlessness that clung to every prisoner like a cloak of heavy chains. Malou was making something happen. Something was going to happen tomorrow because of what she did today. Not the guards, not Barth. Malou.

Exhaustion finally put her to sleep.

THE MORNING WAS a blur of rushed preparation, as it always was. Roused before dawn, the prisoners had work to do. Beds must be made, and the barracks left perfectly clean. Hundreds of women waited to use toilet facilities with only dirty water for cleaning. The dead were collected and left in a row outside the barracks. The work detail picking up the bodies looked like the young women from the Mury Girl Scouts. Malou watched as they loaded the corpses onto carts, quickly going through pockets and scrounging anything useful. A crust of bread or a slice of sausage could help someone live another day.

Only after the dead were removed could the women line up for breakfast, a half liter of grain-based coffee substitute. Malou held the tin cup close to her breast, letting the warmth seep into her bones as she watched Lena and her friends. They stood in the sunlight, the weak rays of the autumn sun lighting their features as they whispered and laughed.

A spark of joy, even here, Malou marveled. She hoped her suspicions about Lena were wrong. She ached to join in and be part of that group of brave young women. But that was a weakness. *Not yet, Malou*, she told herself. If she were an informer, Lena could have gotten word out about her via one of the guards.

It was time for the count. Prisoners lined up in front of the barracks. The number of dead was reported. The guards counted the living, twice. An officer noted the numbers on a clipboard and nodded, satisfied with the morning statistics of life and death.

The formation broke up, guards herding groups to their designated work details. Two trucks rolled in, the Siemens transport for Malou's detail. Two new girls were added, to make up for yesterday's losses. City girls by their looks and their thin, uncalloused fingers.

They began to board the vehicles, Malou about to haul herself onto the truck bed.

"Halt!"

Two guards elbowed their way through the line of prisoners and grabbed Malou, pulling her roughly away from the truck. Even though she'd half expected it, she gasped in surprise and shock. The women around her edged away, their gazes fearful and perhaps suspicious.

After all, this would be how the Nazis communicated with their informers. Drag them away as if for interrogation, or worse, and then transact their business in secrecy. Malou caught a glimpse of Lena watching her, her face impassive.

Pushed and prodded, Malou was taken to the Political Department. This was where she had been interrogated when she'd first been brought to Ravensbrück. She'd played the part of a fallen woman in over her head, and the SS quickly tired of her. After a few blows, they were done.

Now she was back. Her guards opened a door and led her into a room empty except for a table and two chairs. And an SS officer in one of the chairs. Light streamed in from the windows behind him, casting a glow around his head.

Malou squinted, approving of the technique. She stood before him, blinking, as he dismissed the guards with a wave of his hand.

"I am Major Krantz," he said, not looking up from his file. He had a long face, pockmarked skin stretched over jutting cheekbones. His sparse hair was black, slicked down over a shiny skull. "It is my job to review the files of terrorists brought here in the last weeks."

"I was questioned when they brought me here, sir," Malou said in her weakest voice, eyes downcast, the way the Nazis liked it.

"Yes. Rather perfunctory, I must say. Tell me, why do you think they let you off so easily?" Krantz asked.

"Easily?" Malou said, almost laughing. "I was involved in the black market, yes. Some of the people we associated with also had Resistance connections. Terrorist connections, I mean. But money was our primary focus."

Krantz went over the details of Malou's case. The One-Two-Two club where she worked. The drugs sold there. The clientele at the high-class brothel. The arrests as the Germans prepared to evacuate Paris.

Nothing about a hotel in Rotterdam. Not yet.

While Malou stood, Krantz pressed harder for names. Names of German officers who frequented the One-Two-Two.

"Appointments were made by the owners, sir. I only entertained the gentlemen in the lounge. There were so many of them. Generals, even," she said, and began to relax. This interrogation wasn't to find evidence against her. Krantz was after names of those Germans who frequented the One-Two-Two.

"You must remember something," Krantz said, tapping his pen on the table. Malou decided to take a chance.

"May I sit, sir?"

"Yes, of course," Krantz said hurriedly, gesturing to the chair next to her. "Now think. There must have been some memorable officers there. Wehrmacht officers. Luftwaffe."

Ah. Not SS then.

"I recall a General Botsch. Also, a General Hellmich, but I think he was killed in Normandy," Malou said. "And definitely a Luftwaffe general, Olbrich, I think his name was. I'm sorry, but I was not encouraged to ask too many questions, just keep them happy."

"These generals," Krantz asked, scribbling names in his notebook, "they bought and sold on the black market?"

"Sir, generals usually have other people do such things for them, in my experience," Malou said.

"Ha! You may be a criminal, but you understand how things work," Krantz said. "You should put your talents to work here." For the first time, Krantz looked at her, studying her reaction.

"For what purpose, Major?" Malou asked, playing for time. This was the exact opposite of what she'd expected. Instead of revealing Lena as an informer, she herself was being recruited.

"They have you working at Siemens," Krantz said, returning to his file. "Extra rations, but long hours. Hard work, I'd imagine. We could reach an accommodation. An easy job here in the administrative building. Special rations. All you would need to do is report on any disruptive activities within your barracks. I suspect you are not actually a terrorist yourself, just a young woman caught up with an unsavory gang. Help us root out the troublemakers here. It will help everyone—your fellow prisoners and yourself."

"I am fairly new here, sir," Malou said, her voice hesitant as she thought through what to say. "I don't know many people here, not well enough for them to confide in me. I wouldn't want to disappoint you."

"I can be lenient," Krantz said. "Or I can be harsh. You have much to lose, as I am sure you are aware."

"I don't mean to say I refuse, Major, not at all. But I might not have any information immediately," Malou said. The last thing she needed was to lose her position at the factory because Krantz had become angry with her.

"Very well," he said. "I will have you returned to your work. But I want you to come back tomorrow and give me one piece of intelligence. There will be a reward for you. Dismissed."

"I will do my best, sir," Malou said as she stood. "May I ask a question?"

"Make it brief."

"How did you come to bring me here today? Out of all the others?"

"An intelligent question," Krantz said, leaning back in his chair and nodding his approval. "It is my job, of course. Spotting talent.

The SS is investigating corruption within the Wehrmacht and Luftwaffe, and your club in Paris came up within that context. And as you yourself said, your role was more criminal than political. I find that criminals will often act in their own self-interest. You are also a pretty young woman. The camp has not ruined your looks. Not yet. Now you may go."

Malou suppressed a shudder as she made for the door. As she reached for the handle, the door flung open and Morgen stepped into the room, blocking her exit. She stood aside, uncertain what to do.

"Judge Morgen, how can I help you today?" Krantz said, his voice oily with displeasure.

"Excuse me," Morgen said. Malou was so confused by Krantz calling him judge that she couldn't tell who Morgen was talking to. SS officers did not excuse themselves to prisoners, but Morgen was looking at her as he held the door open.

"Guards!" Krantz shouted. "Escort this prisoner to Herr Barth at the Siemens factory. And shut the door behind you."

The two guards who had brought Malou to Krantz escorted her outside. As they approached a waiting vehicle, one of them shoved her to the ground. They kicked at her and slammed their rifle butts into her ribs.

It was over as quickly as it started. It was mechanical. Controlled. Violent enough for other prisoners to notice, harsh enough to leave marks and aches, but nothing that wouldn't easily heal. Malou groaned as she pulled herself onto the truck bed where other women waited for transport to their work detail at the factory. They made room so she could lie down.

Being an informer looked to be a lot harder than she imagined.

Judge. What kind of judge did the SS employ? And what was he doing in a concentration camp?

"WHAT HAPPENED TO you?" Lena asked hours later as they carried their soup to the rough wood-plank tables in the mess hall.

"Krantz," Malou answered.

"What did Major Krantz want?" Lena said, tipping her wooden bowl to drink down the soup before it cooled.

"For me to inform," she said.

"He had you beaten for your own good," Lena said.

"Yes, although I didn't agree. As a matter of fact, I was suspicious of you. That's why I told you that story about Rotterdam," Malou said, gulping her soup. "I made it up."

"You realize they would have tortured you if I'd told them about that," Lena said.

"I wanted to know if I could trust you. Besides, I would have spun them a fairy tale," Malou said, working her bread through the remains of the soup. "It was preferable to doing nothing."

Lena looked to her friends, seated on either side of her. She smiled. "Malou, I think we're going to get along just fine."

"Good," Malou said. "You can help me figure out what to do. Krantz wants me to report on someone by tomorrow. Or else. Oh, and did you know Major Morgen is some sort of judge?"

"We know exactly what kind of judge he is," Lena said. "How did you hear that?"

"Krantz called him Judge Morgen," she said. "In a very sarcastic tone."

"What did Krantz question you about?" Lena asked.

"I worked at the One-Two-Two club in Paris," Malou said. "He had questions about army generals and the black market."

"The Mury girls working in administration have heard about an investigation the SS is running. They're questioning anyone with criminal contacts in France about corruption. Not SS corruption, of course," Lena said.

"Krantz made that obvious. But what does that have to do with Morgen?" Malou asked.

"Konrad Morgen is part of the SS Judiciary Office," Lena said. "He is charged with investigating corruption in all camps run by the SS."

Malou laughed, almost losing the last swallow of precious soup.

"This is all corrupt," Malou said. "Slave labor, murder, torture. Why would they investigate themselves?"

"Morgen's job is to root out those who steal the property of the Nazi state," Lena said. "There are plenty of high-ranking SS who have their hand in the till. Stealing valuables that are stolen from us. It's all supposed to go to the Third Reich, but a lot ends up in their pockets."

"Finish eating, Lena, you talk too much," said her friend Rachel, sitting next to her. "We know Morgen's been effective. He brought charges against the Gestapo chief at Auschwitz, Maximilian Grabner. Morgen arrested him for theft and corruption."

"How can you know this?" Malou said. It sounded unbelievable.

"I was transferred here from Auschwitz," Rachel said, rolling up her sleeve and showing Diana her tattooed number. "The Germans are nervous about the Russians getting close. They're beginning to send people west. While murdering as many as they can."

"Rachel is with the United Partisan Organization," Lena whispered, draining the last of her soup. "A combat group of Polish Jews."

"Interesting, but what does this all mean?" Malou asked, shoving down the last crust of bread.

"It means we can get our revenge on Barth," Lena said, glancing at the guards about to roust them from their seats. "It means justice, even in a place such as this."

Justice in Ravensbrück? Could it be possible?

That notion gave Malou something to think about as she worked, mechanically going through the motions of assembling machine parts, snipping individual strands of wire on each piece, hoping it made a difference.

She was not helpless. She was striking back. The taste of success with her plan to uncover Lena's true affiliations left her hopeful. These thoughts did not drive away the hunger and pain, but they did help her understand how to survive this place. She could not let

Ravensbrück rule her. She had to carve out a place in her heart for resistance, and nurture it. Otherwise, her spirit would die. Then her body. She might get her revenge against Barth now, or later. But it would happen.

THAT NIGHT, AFTER the evening meal, Lena and three of her friends, including Rachel, gathered at Malou's bunk.

"How much do you know about what Morgen did at Auschwitz?" Malou began. As much as she wanted to know about settling a score with Barth, her training demanded she know everything about Lena. It seemed terribly convenient that she knew so much about the judge, and she wondered how much a prisoner like Rachel could learn about what high-ranking Nazis were up to.

"We have a dossier on him," Lena said, "in addition to Rachel's information, which corroborated what we have."

"We?" Malou said. "Who is that?"

"The Polish Home Army," Lena said, nodding in the direction of the other girls. "We are part of Home Army Intelligence. We've been picked up in sweeps for various reasons. Mainly to work at Siemens. Small hands, you know."

"The Germans have no idea about our groups," Rachel said. "Lena and I were both snatched from the street, our papers hardly inspected. We've had Morgen's movements in Poland watched. As far as we can determine, he began investigating corruption as part of his duties. At some point he witnessed a gassing at Auschwitz."

"He became more zealous in his investigations. We think it is his way of doing what little he can," Lena said. "He's arrested SS men for unauthorized killings in some camps, unbelievable as that is."

"The Germans like their rules," Rachel said. "Morgen has found a way to exploit that. Killing prisoners who witnessed the theft of supplies is evidently against regulations."

"So Morgen is investigating Ravensbrück?" Malou said, trying to take in this strange turn of events.

"We've put out word to the Mury girls to find out what they can," Rachel said. "So far, nothing."

"This is where Józefa comes in," Lena said, resting her hand on the shoulder of a thin brown-haired girl in a relatively clean striped uniform. "She's a group leader with Mury."

"Józefa Nowak," she said, extending her hand to Malou. "We have girls in the administrative offices. We'll find out why he's here, have no worry. Did Krantz say anything about him to you this morning?"

"No, he just wanted information on army officers who were involved with the black market in Paris," Malou said. "Morgen came into the room and things were quite frosty between them. I couldn't pick up anything else, but Krantz was not happy."

"That's one way to counter Morgen's allegations against the SS," Lena said. "Come up with your own report on corrupt army generals. A distraction."

"Makes sense," Malou said. "But where does this leave us with Barth?"

"Some of the charges Morgen brought against SS officers at Auschwitz and other camps were for selling supplies on the black market," Rachel explained. "Mainly rations that were still being drawn for prisoners who had been killed. They sell the excess and pocket the proceeds."

"Barth is doing the same?" Malou said.

"Yes. We've noticed the midday meal at the factory getting worse and worse. Barth must be getting greedy, selling even more than the dead girls' rations," Lena said.

"How can you prove this?" Malou asked.

"We have a list," Lena said. "A list of over two hundred women who worked at Siemens. Two hundred dead women who are still drawing daily rations at the factory, compiled by Józefa and the Mury girls. All we have to do is get the names to Morgen."

Before Malou could reply, a young girl ran to them and whispered to Józefa, then darted out.

"It has to be tomorrow," Józefa said. "Morgen is leaving tomorrow night."

"Wait, what has to be tomorrow?" Malou said, even as she began to understand.

"You have to get the list to Morgen. Tell him to check the names against the mess hall rations at Siemens. He'll know what to do."

"How?" Malou said. "I can't just walk in there."

"Yes, you can," Lena said. "Krantz wanted you to inform on someone. We have a name for you. She's an informer, and she's been known to represent herself as a member of the Resistance in hopes of getting others to do the same. Tell them she paid you a visit tonight. You can make it work."

"But what if Krantz checks with her? He must know the name," Malou asked.

"She will meet with an accident during the night," Rachel said. "You don't need to worry about her. Just find a way to get to Morgen."

"Are you certain Morgen will act on information given to him by a prisoner?" Malou asked. She was willing to take a chance, perhaps a deadly chance, but she had to know it was worthwhile.

"The law is important to him," Lena said. "Whatever law is left in Germany. He will take the list."

"And he's a blood judge," Rachel said.

"He's authorized to issue the death penalty," Lena explained. "Remember that. He can send Barth to the executioner."

The group dispersed. Malou noted that they'd posted lookouts around the barracks, girls who melted away as Lena and the others departed. She'd had no idea the various groups were so well organized within the camp. Well disciplined.

And ruthless, of course. This was a struggle that demanded it.

As darkness settled in and the last murmurs of conversation began to fade, Lena returned, kneeling at Malou's bunk. She pressed a piece of folded, worn paper into her hand.

"Hide this," Lena said. "The name you give Krantz is Tilde Authier, a Frenchwoman like you."

"I am not a Frenchwoman," Malou whispered.

"English? I knew it," Lena said, smiling. "But don't tell me anything else. Too much information is dangerous."

"I want to say my name, in case anything goes wrong tomorrow," Malou told her, her voice even lower than a whisper, more like a prayer. "I am Diana Seaton."

"You are a strong woman, Diana," Lena said. "I can tell you my name since the Germans have killed all of my family in Poland. There is no revenge they can take on me. I am Angelika Kazimierz."

"What?" Malou said, her voice rising. "I know a Kazimierz. In England."

"Piotr?" Lena asked, the word coming out as a gasp.

"Oh my God, yes!" Malou said. "You're Angelika, of course. Piotr only learned recently that you were alive."

"He is well? Safe?"

"You wouldn't believe what he's been up to," Malou told her.

The two of them spent the next hour whispering, telling stories, exchanging confidences, and hardly believing that they'd been brought together in such a bizarre fashion. Lena shared what she knew about what they were working on in the Siemens factory. An advanced German rocket guided by an advanced gyroscopic system. Much more deadly than the V1.

They finally gave in to exhaustion, whispering each other's true name as a goodbye, with no guarantee either of them would live to hear it again.

THE MORNING PRISONER count was held in the rain, a light mist that soaked through threadbare layers and left the weakest among them shivering. Major Krantz watched the proceedings, his collar turned up as water dripped from his peaked cap. As soon as the prisoners were dismissed, Malou walked toward him instead of to the trucks. She stood until he noticed her, then gave him a discreet nod. Moments later two guards grabbed her and brought her into the building. There was less rough stuff this time, probably because the Germans didn't want to stand out in the rain. A small bit of luck that Malou hoped would stay with her.

She was ushered into Krantz's office in the Political Department. Not the interrogation room, but a proper office. The guards stood outside, with the door left open. Krantz's raincoat hung from a hook, water puddling beneath it.

"You have something for me?" Krantz said, leaning back in his chair.

"Yes, sir," Malou said. "A name. Tilde Authier. She's French. She approached me last night and said she was part of a resistance group with other Frenchwomen. She invited me to join."

"What did you say?" Krantz asked.

"I told her I was scared, but that I would think about it. I didn't know if you'd want me to join or not."

"Very smart of you," Krantz said, nodding his approval. "But you will decline. We are already watching her and her group. Let us wait until you discover something new. But well done."

"Yes, sir," Malou said, standing still, unsure what to say next. She should want something. Informers would be greedy. "Did you mention a reward?"

"I did. You don't deserve much for such a useless piece of information, but to show you I can be generous, we will find something for you. Another piece of clothing, perhaps. The days are getting colder." Krantz called for a guard and instructed him to take Malou to the storeroom and let her select one item.

Malou thanked him, bowing her head to demonstrate her abject obedience.

She followed the guard down a hallway, glancing into each office that they passed. She saw officers, clerks, and even some of the young girls who were lucky enough to get office jobs. Their attire was clean, the striped prisoner uniform worn over dresses that appeared spotless. Mury Girl Scouts, perhaps.

She hardly merited a second look. Informers must have been escorted to the storeroom before.

Malou almost stopped short. On her right, through an open door, she spotted Morgen. Seated at a desk, he was closing a file and placing it on a stack of others. His eyes met Malou's, and she thought she saw a raised eyebrow of recognition.

Then she was past the room, hurrying to catch up with the guard before he noticed she'd lagged. Two doors down, at the end of the corridor, they came to the storeroom. Malou was told to pick one item and be quick about it.

Shelves held stacks of folded clothing. Malou was stunned by the choices available while at the same time her mind was racing at how to get close enough to Morgen to pass the information. She took a sweater, too large for her, but it was perfect.

She clutched it to her chest, then worked one hand inside her clothing, pulling out the folded paper. She clenched it in her fist, hidden between the folds of the sweater. Morgen's office was coming up. Just a few more steps.

Morgen stood in the doorway, putting on his raincoat. The guard halted, Malou skidding to a stop. Morgen had one arm in a sleeve and the other pulling up the coat. He gestured with his head for the guard to proceed.

The guard walked on. Morgen shrugged himself into his coat. Malou looked him straight in the eye and received a quizzical look in return.

She gave out a small cry, fell to one knee, then collapsed.

The guard tried to lift her, but she went limp, moaning and gasping. Normally, a sick prisoner would be left where they fell, or dragged outside and dumped in the mud. But Krantz's informers apparently rated better treatment. Cursing, the guard hurried down the corridor, calling for help.

Morgen knelt. He put a hand on Malou's shoulder.

"Here," she whispered, thrusting the paper into Morgen's hand. "A list of prisoners. All dead, some killed by Barth. He's still drawing their rations and selling them." Morgen stared at the paper in his hand for several long seconds. Then he stuffed it in his pocket and stood.

"Feeling better, are we?" he said in a loud voice. "Good. You wouldn't want to be sent to the hospital. Best return to work if you know what's good for you." He stepped back, as if not wanting to get too close to this dirty prisoner. Malou was thankful for the warning. If she played sick any longer, she may well have ended up in the inmate's infirmary, a death sentence.

"Yes, sir," she said, standing as the guard returned with another soldier and Krantz close behind. "I'm sorry, I was dizzy and then found myself on the floor. I'm fine now, I can work, please."

"Get her to the factory," Krantz growled, angry over the incident, or perhaps at the sight of Morgen. "Taking your leave of us, Judge Morgen?"

"I was," Morgen said. "But perhaps I will stay a few days longer. You don't mind?"

There was nothing Krantz could say to that, and there were no sweeter words Malou could have heard as the guards hustled her out of the building.

THE NEXT MORNING Malou and the others climbed aboard the trucks outside their barracks. Dr. Herta Oberheuser stood nearby, tapping her pen against a notebook. Malou had the uneasy feeling she was observing the calf muscles of the girls as they pulled themselves onto the truck bed. But Oberheuser turned away, her pouted lips thankfully silent.

An hour after arriving at Siemens, Malou heard the screeching of tires and the slamming of car doors. Major Morgen walked through the workshop, followed by four soldiers. He did not look at the women. He didn't have to.

Within minutes, he came back through with Barth squirming and yelling, firmly gripped by two soldiers. The guards in the room looked panicked, uncertain what to do. But the authority of an SS major was not to be questioned, especially one escorted by soldiers with submachine guns.

Malou, Rachel, and Lena dared not look at each other, afraid of smiles that would bring a beating. They worked diligently, eyes glued to the components in front of them.

Revenge had come to Ravensbrück.

Later, as they walked to the mess hall, Rachel dared to point up. The blue sky was thick with white contrails, American bombers on their way to Berlin, perhaps.

"Soon," Malou whispered, hoping they could hold on. "Please."

Author's Note

THE MAIN CHARACTERS in this short story, Malou and Lena (Diana and Angelika), will be familiar to readers of the Billy Boyle mystery series. Judge Konrad Morgen and Dr. Herta Oberheuser are real historical characters. Mury was a real clandestine Girl Scout group at Ravensbrück. The Ukrainian Insurgent Army and the Jewish United Partisan Organization were real units as well.

IRISH TOMMY

...

"Aw, Jesus, Andino. How'd you end up here, lad?" Andino Maffini didn't answer. It would have been a miracle if he had, what with a bullet hole in his left temple and another one on his left side. A shot to the heart as well as the brain. Someone wanted to be sure it was lights out for Andino.

"You know this mug, Lieutenant?" Sergeant Brennan said, opening the driver's side door of the Chevrolet sedan. Maffini was on the passenger's side, his head tilted against the window.

"If you wanted to place a bet in the North End, you knew Andino Maffini," Lieutenant Daniel Boyle said, standing on the sidewalk and scanning the street. A park stood on one side, empty except for a dusting of snow on this cold November morning. On the other side sat a row of low apartment houses. Some of the windows sported Blue Star Service Banners, declaring that a family member was in active military service. A few showed a Gold Star, meaning a loved one was never coming home.

Daniel Boyle shook off the thought and watched as Brennan searched the car, grunting as he knelt to check under the seats. Daniel pulled his fedora down tight and turned up the collar of his trench coat, wondering why a small-time hood like Andino had ended up here in Mattapan, a good ten miles from his usual stomping grounds.

"Look at this, Lieutenant," Brennan said. He held a .38 revolver by the barrel, using two fingers of his gloved hand. "Shoved under the driver's seat."

"This was no simple beef," Daniel said as Brennan bagged the pistol. "Someone drove Andino down here just to kill him. Left the murder weapon behind, which means there'll be no prints."

"A professional job," Brennan said. "It was cold enough last night to wear gloves. Maffini wouldn't have been suspicious of that."

"But why here?"

"Quiet street, with the park on one side," Brennan said. "The trolley's a short walk away, so the shooter had an easy getaway."

"Or someone picked him up," Daniel said, although the fewer witnesses the better. If it had been him, he'd have taken the trolley. Scarf around the neck, collar turned up, cap pulled down over the eyes. The killer would be unrecognizable. "Who spotted the body?"

"Guy walking his dog," Brennan said. "Called it in around six-thirty."

"The policeman's friend," Daniel said. "Rigor?"

"The body's stiff, but in this cold weather it doesn't tell us much. Shot around midnight is as good a guess as any," Brennan said.

"You stay here and wait for the meat wagon," Daniel said. "Make sure the fingerprint boys go over this vehicle as soon as it gets into the garage. Understand?"

"I know the routine, Lieutenant," Brennan said. "You figure we got a gang war brewing?"

"Naw. Andino was too small-time to be the first casualty in a turf war. But he could've gotten in over his head. Maybe he's a loose end that needed cleaning up," Daniel said, tapping his finger against his jaw as he worked the notion.

"You mean the bank truck robbery?" Brennan said, his voice nearly a whisper although no one was around. It had been big news all week, even pushing the war news off the front pages. Today the coverage had faded, with the German retreat from Greece along with the RAF sinking of the battleship Tirpitz reclaiming space above the fold.

"I don't mean anything, except I got a bad feeling about this," Daniel said.

"Hey, it's a lead, isn't it? If it's connected," Brennan said. "Could be a break, me boy."

"It could be good news for us, if it is connected," Daniel said. "If so, we'll be finding more bodies real soon."

"Here comes the medical examiner," Brennan said, nodding in the direction of a van with Boston Police Department markings. "You want to talk with him?"

"No. I'm late for breakfast with the FBI," Daniel said.

"Hell, I'd rather stand out here in the cold," Brennan said. "What do those bastards want?"

"It's Sullivan," Daniel said. "No idea what he's after."

"Well, that's the best of a bad bunch, but still, watch yourself," Brennan said as the van pulled up. "All take and no give, that's their motto."

DANIEL DROVE HIS black-and-white Ford through the morning traffic, pulling up to the South End Diner ten minutes late. Getting out, he looked up Atlantic Avenue to the trolley stop at South Station. Did the killer take that route? Chinatown was a short walk away. South Boston was a little farther, but it would provide any number of places for an Irishman to lay low. North Boston was close too, just a brisk walk downtown to neighborhoods thick with Sicilians.

"Son of a bitch," Daniel muttered, opening the diner door. The warm smell of cigarette smoke, coffee, and bacon hit him with a welcoming hug.

"Lieutenant Boyle," a voice called to him through the customers' chatter. It came from the last booth, where a buttoned-up FBI agent sat with a cup of coffee centered perfectly between his hands. He wore a blue suit with a crisp white shirt and a neatly knotted tie. His hair was close-cropped on the sides and slicked back on top, like a crew cut with ambitions.

"Special Agent Sullivan," Daniel said, sliding into the booth and shrugging off his coat. His shirt was wrinkled, and he hadn't had time to shave this morning. "Sorry to keep the FBI waiting."

"Hell, Danny, you look like you've been up all night," Sullivan said with a grin.

"Hey, Johnny, you look like you've been up all night ironing that shirt," Daniel said, smiling at the waitress as she set a cup of black coffee in front of him.

John Sullivan and Daniel Boyle were friends from way back. The FBI field office in Boston and the Boston PD didn't always see eye to eye, but it was useful to keep the lines of communication open. The two agencies weren't exactly enemies, but each was distrustful of the other and jealous of its own prerogatives. So when information needed to be shared with a minimum of bureaucracy, the South End Diner was the place to do it.

"How's the bank truck job going?" Johnny asked, sipping his coffee. "Just curious. There's been no sign of state lines being crossed, and the bank wasn't part of the Federal Reserve, so it's all yours."

"That's Terry's department. He's got the robbery unit." Detective Lieutenant Terrance Boyle was Daniel's brother.

"That's right. How's Terry's boy? Hear from him lately?"

"Billy? Sure, his mother just got a postcard from some fancy hotel in the south of France. The boy knows how to fight a war, I'll say that for him." Daniel knew there was more to it, but he liked keeping it bright and easy. Somehow it helped keep up his spirits.

"You don't have much to say about the heist," Johnny said. "I thought it would be a hot topic among you flatfoots."

"Yeah, it is," Daniel said. The waitress returned, topped off their coffees, and took their orders. "And I have a suspicion it just widened into my bailiwick."

"Homicide?"

"Yeah. It's why I was late. A low-level hood name of Andino Maffini took one to the temple and one to the heart and was left in a car down in Mattapan. Revolver under the seat."

"Sounds like a contract job," Johnny said. "That why I saw you eyeing the trolley?"

"It's how I'd make my getaway. Nice and simple, no one else involved. But that's only a guess. What worries me is why Andino warranted so much attention. He was a bookie, basically harmless."

"You knew him?"

"I placed a few bets with him. Figured it would help if I ever needed information," Daniel said, seeing no need to mention how much he'd won. "Now, why are we really here?"

"We're searching for two men," Johnny said, watching the other customers as he lowered his voice. "German agents. They were landed off the coast of Maine, way up north. Both were sighted walking near the beach, dressed for the city and carrying suitcases. No hats in the middle of a snowstorm. Up in Maine, that's suspicious behavior. A couple of people called the sheriff, but he was away on a hunting trip. By the time he got back, it was too late."

"You think they're headed for Boston?"

"Could be. We had some luck and found a taxicab driver who was headed to Bangor. They flagged him down on Route One and he took them there," Johnny said. "Their story was that their friend's car had died, and they had to get to Bangor to catch the morning train. They asked to be taken to a good hotel near the railroad station and tipped the guy way too much. That made the cabbie suspicious, but he didn't say anything until we started questioning bus drivers, truckers, and cab companies."

"Too late to find them at the hotel, I'd say."

"Right," Johnny said. "But we canvassed the route between the hotel and the station. One place stood out, a radio repair shop. Turns out one of them bought a milliamp meter, a multimeter, tools, and a roll of copper wire."

"I don't know what those meter things are, but I assume it's all kit to build a radio," Daniel said. The waitress brought their plates, loaded with eggs and bacon. Daniel dug in, glancing at Johnny for his answer.

"Exactly. When they get to wherever they're going, they can buy a regular radio and adapt it to transmit. So our experts tell me," he said.

"These two speak good English?" Daniel asked.

"One does, according to the cabbie and the shop owner. Perfect American English. The other fellow kept it zipped. Probably speaks with an accent," Johnny said.

"You think they're in Boston now?"

"They bought one-way tickets here from Bangor. But that doesn't mean they stayed in town. They could've taken another train or stolen a car. But with all the military targets here, Boston could be their base."

"Yeah. And the Boston Naval Yard is full of destroyers being built and other ships under repair," Daniel said. "It's right across the Charles River."

"Now you know what we're after," Johnny said. "But we don't want to spook them. There could be Germans or Italians helping them. We need to keep this quiet, or else word is bound to leak out."

"Italy's on our side now, Johnny. Try to keep up."

"If they planted any spies here before the war, their loyalties might still be with Mussolini. And there's plenty of Germans everywhere," Johnny said.

"Well, at least we're all loyal Americans here, Johnny Sullivan," Daniel said, raising his cup.

"And good Irishmen as well."

"I HEAR YOU broke bread with the FBI," Terrance Boyle said as Daniel entered his office at police headquarters.

"Your informants are everywhere, Terry," Daniel said, taking a seat opposite his younger brother. "Have they told you about the Nazi spies in our midst?"

"Sweet Jesus and sour Joseph, that's all we need," Terrance said. "Was Sullivan sure?"

Daniel filled him in and handed over a written description the FBI agent had given him. Two men with slight builds and dark hair. One in his midtwenties, the other midthirties. The younger man spoke perfect English.

"Oh, grand, that should keep the pool of suspects down to a hundred thousand or so," Terrance said. "Hell, they could be anywhere. That train ticket doesn't mean Boston was their final stop."

"No, but we should put the word out," Daniel said. "Shops that sell or repair radios would be a good start."

"That's sensible enough," Terrance agreed. "Now, what did Andino do to deserve such special attention?"

"You have any leads on the bank truck heist?" Daniel said, leaning back in his chair and arching an eyebrow.

"Andino Maffini? You think he was involved? He was a bookmaker, ran some numbers, that sort of thing. This was a well-planned operation, not some liquor store robbery."

It had *been perfectly planned*, Daniel thought. A delivery of cash and coin was brought twice a week to the Durham Trust Company by a private trucking firm. Totaling about seventy thousand dollars, the pickup was made at the New Haven Railroad Back Bay Station. The driver then drove the bags of money to the bank, which was less than three blocks away. A week ago, he didn't make it. He was found tied, blindfolded, and gagged in the back seat of a Plymouth sedan. His truck was found a block away, abandoned and empty. He couldn't provide a description, since the assailants wore knit caps pulled down low and scarves over their mouths, and had him bound in seconds.

"I think this job had to be scouted out, well-timed. Somebody local had to be involved to watch that truck, probably for weeks, to make sure of the route and timing," Daniel said. "Andino would have been perfect for that. Then he was nothing but a loose end. I wouldn't be surprised if we see more bodies."

"An out-of-town crew getting rid of the locals, that does make sense," Terrance said. "And it was a professional bunch. The bills were all sequential, and not a single one has surfaced. These boys know how to avoid temptation."

"Who do you like for it?"

"We've been watching Mike Sweeney and the Gustin Gang," Terrance said. "But I don't think they'd make a big move like this, not without asking permission."

"Aye, it's a sad state of affairs when Irishmen have to ask Italians for permission to knock off a bank," Daniel said. "And ever since Charlie Solomon got bumped off, the Jewish boys have laid low."

"Right. That leaves Nick Bruccola. Far as I know, the Sicilian mob is dominant these days, so Fat Nick is my guess. But we can't shake anyone loose. No one knows nothin', and they'll keep on knowing it if they want to live," Terrance said.

"Well, I'll let you know if we get any leads on Andino's killer," Daniel said, rising from his seat. "I'll tell my boys about the Krauts soon as we put our heads together."

"Lieutenant Boyle?" Sergeant Brennan said, knocking on the open door.

"Aye?" said both men.

"We got another stiff, Danny. Auto accident on Boylston Street," Brennan said.

"Jesus, Brennan, tell the Traffic Division, why don't ya?" Daniel said.

"It was just a fender bender," the sergeant said. "But it popped the trunk."

"Don't tell me," Daniel said, rubbing his eyes.

"About him bein' shot in the head and the heart? All right, I won't," Sergeant Brennan said. "We have to hurry. It's creatin' holy hell with the traffic."

Brennan hit the lights and siren as soon as they left headquarters. It wasn't far down Boylston before they saw the jam. Two black-and-whites bracketed the cars involved in the accident, and patrolmen directed traffic around them. A bluecoat approached as soon as they stopped.

"Whaddya got?" Daniel said, jumping out of the patrol car.

"One shook-up lady driver and one corpse. She rear-ended that Chrysler," the cop said. "Hit it hard enough for the trunk to open."

"That'd do the trick," Brennan said, nodding in the direction of the woman's red Chevy coupe. "The front end's a battering ram."

"The other driver?" Daniel asked, knowing the answer.

"Took off on foot," the cop said. "Couple of witnesses saw him hoof it in the direction of Copley Square, but they were pretty distracted by the lady's screams. A tall man wearing a hat is about all we got."

"Let's take a look at what all the fuss was about," Daniel said, shaking his head at the inability of witnesses to actually witness anything.

"Well, well, the bastard never looked so good to me," Brennan said as they gathered around the open trunk.

"Jimmy Walsh himself," Daniel said. "Gentleman Jimmy, he liked to be called."

Gentleman Jimmy Walsh was trussed up and laid out on a stained tarpaulin, hands bound behind his back and tied to his ankles. His left temple had a blackened hole caked with blood. A matching wound was to the side of his shirt pocket. The car had been headed out of town, probably to bury the body. Andino was small potatoes, nobody needed to hide his corpse. But Gentleman Jimmy was another story. He needed to be buried deep.

"Probably what they used to carry him," Daniel said, using a pen to lift the tarp at the edges. "Find a gun?"

"Under the driver's seat," the cop said. "Snub-nose .38. So who was this guy?"

"Once upon a time, he was a famous bootlegger, one of the biggest of the Irish operators," Daniel said. "Made his mark during Prohibition and then made friends with the upcoming Italian mob. He knew the old days of the Irish gangs were passing, so he spread his money around."

"He had the ear of Fat Nick Bruccola, didn't he?" Brennan said.

"That he did. And look where it got him. This could be a break for our side, Sergeant," Daniel said. "You stay here, right?"

"Yeah. Wait for the meat wagon, get the car dusted for prints, and I hope you had a fillin' breakfast 'cause I've had none. Be careful, Danny, don't go talk to Fat Nick, not by yourself, you don't."

"No, not him, not yet. I'm taking the car, Sergeant."

"Of course you are, Lieutenant. I'll ride with the tow truck, don't you worry. But tell me where you're going in case you never come back, willya?"

"I'm going to find Joey Fisher, if he's still alive," Daniel said, heading back to the patrol car. Between the siren and the cops directing traffic, he cleared the jam in minutes. Joey Fisher was another bookie. He and Andino knew each other. Joey worked out of Southie, so they weren't competitors. For guys like them, their neighborhoods were safe territory, as long as they kept kicking a cut up to the big boys and didn't start to put on airs. But Daniel knew those two were dumb enough to think they were smart enough to pull a fast one.

Joey also did a few odd jobs for Gentleman Jimmy, or so the rumors said. Lightweight stuff, nothing too physical. But for a cut of seventy large, Joey was ambitious enough to go along. Unfortunately for Joey, ambition in the criminal world often went hand in hand with stupidity.

Last Daniel knew, Joey worked out of a luncheonette on West Fourth Street in South Boston. He had a room upstairs and took bets and ran numbers out of a booth in the back. Jimmy Walsh owned the place. It would have been natural for Jimmy to bring in Joey to scout out the truck's route and establish the driver's pattern. A job like that took a lot of time standing around on cold pavement, which wasn't Jimmy's style.

Walsh was—had been—a smart guy. He'd navigated the changing tides and stayed afloat as Prohibition ended and the Sicilians became the top dogs in the crime world. He had the brains to work this heist, but not to get out of the way when Fat Nick rolled up guys he didn't want to split the loot with. Anyone who wasn't part of the mafia could expect a shortened life span.

Daniel parked the black-and-white a few blocks away, watching for anyone staking out the area as he walked to Sonny's Luncheon-ette. The joint was on the corner, with wide windows on either side of the entrance. Not wanting to alert Joey and have to chase the kid, Daniel walked around the back of the three-story brick building, keeping away from the windows. He eased open the back door and stepped into the kitchen. A cook in a stained white apron looked up from his griddle and quickly looked away. When you worked for Jimmy Walsh, you got used to men in fedoras using the back entrance.

Four strides and he was through the swinging doors and into the luncheonette. Joey's booth was empty.

"Where's Joey?" Daniel asked the counterman. Two guys looked up from their hash and quickly averted their eyes, which seemed to be the signature move around here. "He owes me."

"Don't know," the counterman said. "Wait if you want. Can I get you something?"

"Yeah, I'll have a cup of coffee," Daniel said. "But first I gotta hit the head. Back that way?"

"Yeah, on the right," the counterman said, crooking his thumb in the general direction of the kitchen.

Daniel went back through the swinging door but hooked left, taking steps that led to a landing crammed with cleaning supplies. The stairway led to the top floor where Joey hung his hat, if it didn't already have a hole in it.

Taking the steps two at a time, and after stopping to catch his breath on the second-floor landing, Daniel came to a door at the top. He paused, listening for sounds inside, or footsteps following him from behind. All was quiet except for the beating of his heart. Being a cop for twenty-plus years meant a lot of stairs taken at the double-quick, but it also meant he wasn't a kid anymore.

He placed his hand on the doorknob and turned it. Locked. Odds were it was a decent lock, given the chance that Joey stowed stolen goods on occasion. He braced himself to take a run at the door, even though the small landing didn't provide much room for a running start.

Then he heard it. Footsteps from inside, coming closer.

The door opened.

Daniel burst through, shoving Joey Fisher back into the apartment, catching him by surprise. Joey stumbled, thrown off-balance by the suitcase he held in one hand.

"Glad to see you're still alive, lad," Daniel said. "Drop the luggage and let's have a talk."

"Geez, Lieutenant, I'm late," Joey said, screwing up his face as if he was about to cry. "Can't this wait?"

"Drop it, then turn around," Daniel said. Joey complied. "You wouldn't have a heater in your pocket, eh?"

"Hey, you know me. I don't go in for that stuff," Joey said. "No percentage in it."

"Unbutton your coat," Daniel said, patting down Joey through the layers of clothing. He pulled the coat down, pinning Joey's arms, and checked his suitcoat pockets. "Nice switchblade. There's a percentage in a sharp blade, I always say."

"What do you want, Lieutenant? I ain't done nothing wrong."

"I want you to sit down," Daniel said, plucking Joey's hat from his head and pulling a woolen scarf roughly from around his neck. "Take that coat off, and I'll tell you how I'm going to save your life."

Joey sat down, throwing his coat onto the couch.

Daniel stood, wrapping the scarf around his face like a mask. "On a cold day, it's as good as a bandanna or a stocking mask. Plus, you blend right in with all the other people trying to get from one place to another without getting frostbite. It was damn cold last week, wasn't it?"

"I guess. It's cold today," Joey said, looking lost.

"Oh, Gentleman Jimmy isn't feeling the cold, is he?" Daniel said, taking off the scarf and throwing it at Joey. "Or perhaps he is. The cold of the grave. What did he do, Joey, to get Fat Nick so mad?"

"What? What happened? Jimmy was here just this morning," Joey said.

"Oh, a lot since then," Daniel said, taking a seat on the couch and staring into Joey's frightened face. "A bullet to the brain and another to the heart. Just like poor Andino."

"Oh no, not Dino. Oh my god, what's going on?"

"They were professionals, right? Made men from out of town is the way I figure it," Daniel said. "You and Andino were brought in by Jimmy. You did all the hard work, scouting out the driver, his route, the frequency of pickups. You laid it all out for them. Stole an automobile, maybe, for the getaway."

"I never stole no car, Lieutenant."

"Settle down, lad, I'm just spinning a tale here, so you'll better understand your situation. Everything goes off like clockwork. Nicely done with the driver, by the way. He wasn't hurt and didn't see a thing. You got that done lickety-split. The loot is driven away and delivered to Fat Nick. The heavy hitters from New York or wherever they came from go home. You all sit tight. Smart, that."

"Andino? Really?"

"Sad to say, Joey, but yes. He wasn't a bad sort, was he? A good friend to you, I'm sure."

"We were pals," Joey said, head in his hands. "I can't believe this. Andino and Jimmy?"

"Listen, Joey, and listen hard. I'm not going to repeat me self. They're both dead, and you're next. But you already know that much, or why the sudden desire for travel?"

"Jimmy told me to make myself scarce," Joey said. "He came by this morning. Said they was gunning for him and maybe me too."

"He say anything about Andino?"

"No, just that he was leaving town himself," Joey said. "What are you going to do with me?"

"You're coming with me, lad," Daniel said. "You can leave the suitcase. The city will provide everything you need. We'll go to headquarters and have a talk. The more you tell me, the easier it'll go on you."

"You don't have anything on me; you can't arrest me," Joey said, trying to sound tough.

"I can bring you in for questioning, sure enough. Which will cause you to miss your train. By the time that happens, Fat Nick will have heard you've been talking to us. Then what will your chances be?"

"I'm not admitting anything," Joey said with a sigh, which meant he knew he would be but couldn't quite deal with the reality.

"We'll just have a chat. Now put your coat on and we'll go," Daniel said. Joey shrugged on his overcoat, and they moved toward the door. "Easy now, don't do anything stupid."

"I think I already did," Joey said, spitting out a bitter laugh. Daniel followed, putting a hand on Joey's shoulder as they started down the stairs.

"We'll work things out, don't you worry. If you're lucky, we won't have anyone else in custody yet. Your chance to tell the truth and work a deal," Daniel said. "Where were you headed, anyway?"

"Warwick. I got a cousin there," Joey said.

"You said you were going to miss your train," Daniel said as they reached the second-floor landing. "How were you getting to the station?"

"Called for a taxi," Joey said. "Actually, Louie called for me, I don't have a telephone."

"Louie? That the counterman?"

"Yeah. He runs the place for Jimmy."

They were downstairs and through the kitchen when things started falling into place. Jimmy had been here early this morning. Then he showed up in the trunk of a car. Who had fingered him? Not Joey.

"Hold on, Joey," Daniel said, gripping him by the arm as he opened the rear door. "The cab supposed to be around back?"

"Yeah. Louie said it would be safer in case somebody was watching the place." Safer for Louie's plate glass windows, most likely.

"Come on," Daniel said, dragging Joey behind him as he drew his pistol. He darted right, heading for an alleyway that ran behind the buildings instead of going for the street. Which is where they'd be waiting.

"Where you takin' me?" Joey whined, pulling his arm from Daniel's grasp. He looked frightened, his eyes widening as he seemed to see Daniel's revolver for the first time. "No!"

Joey bolted for the street, driven by fear, misunderstanding, and a primal desire to flee.

"Jesus, Joey, get back here!" Daniel yelled, running after him. But Joey had a good ten paces on him and was twenty years younger.

A black automobile drove up the street, brakes screeching as it halted in front of Joey, who barely stopped before slamming right into it. He waved his arms, trying to keep his balance as he slid to that sudden stop.

Three shots from the rear window settled the matter of his balance.

"No!" Daniel shouted, rage and frustration propelling him forward, pistol aimed at the car as it sped away. He got off one shot before it barreled through the intersection, narrowly avoiding a collision.

"Joey," Daniel murmured as he knelt next to the twisted body. Turning him over, Daniel saw where the slugs had hit, clustered around Joey's heart.

"I'm calling the cops," Louie said, standing in the doorway, cleaning his hands with a grimy towel.

"You do that, ya bastard," Daniel muttered, forcing himself to holster his pistol.

Ten minutes later, flashing lights and whining sirens flooded the street. Cops piled out of patrol cars, guns drawn, and circled around Daniel, who shook his head sadly.

"Put 'em away, boys, before someone gets hurt. It's all over here," Daniel said, standing next to Joey's lifeless body.

"I knew I shoulda come with you," Sergeant Brennan said, ordering three men to go inside Sonny's and take statements. "You all right, Danny?"

"I'm fine, just a bit slow on the uptake," Daniel replied. "I think Louie in there might be on Fat Nick's payroll." He gave Brennan a quick rundown of what Joey had told him.

"Ah, we'll never pin a thing on him," Brennan said. "No law against making phone calls. Want me to bring him in anyways?"

"Yeah. Can't hurt to sweat him. And have the health inspector go through this place. Be nice to shut him down for a while," Daniel said.

"Sure, but what good will that do?"

"No idea," Daniel said, rubbing his jaw as he worked the problem. "But I do wonder why Louie is doing Fat Nick's bidding. Maybe Jimmy was forced out of the bookmaking and luncheonette business. Think I'll have the property records checked. You never know."

"All this in hopes of bein' a mild irritant to Fat Nick? He'll flick you away like a flea, Lieutenant."

"Maybe so. We should get Joey's apartment dusted for prints and see who visited him recently. Let's meet up back at headquarters at four o'clock," Daniel said, checking his watch. "Meanwhile—"

"Yeah, yeah, I'll wait for the meat wagon. I've got it down to a science, laddie."

THE BOYLE BROTHERS briefed robbery and homicide detectives on the latest developments. Terrance passed out descriptions of the two Nazi spies and instructed everyone to keep their eyes peeled and their mouths shut, not wanting word of the search to spread and spook the pair into going on the lam.

Sergeant Brennan came in late, a wide grin on his face. "We found something," he said.

"Spit it out, man," Terrance said.

"Four hundred dollars in bills with sequential serial numbers," Brennan said. "Serial numbers matching the cash that was taken in the bank truck heist. Sewn into the lining of Joey Fisher's coat."

"Good work," Daniel said. "Now we know Joey was involved. I'd bet Gentleman Jimmy gave him the dough to get out of town."

"Foolish of Jimmy," Terrance said. "I wonder if that's why Fat Nick had him whacked."

"But do we have anything to directly link Fat Nick with these killings?" asked one of the detectives. "It could be a beef between some lowlifes over their cut. Maybe it was Jimmy who organized it."

"If it were brass knuckles and a couple of broken jaws, I'd think so myself," Daniel said. A clerk popped his head into the room, waving a sheet of paper. Daniel took it, read, and then let loose with a grin. "Sonny's Luncheonette, or rather the building which houses it, was transferred to the ownership of Capizzi Imports five days ago."

"That's Fat Nick Bruccola's front," Terrance said.

"And the purchase price was five times what it was worth," Daniel added, scanning the document.

"I'll bet dollars to doughnuts the agreement was to spread payments out over months, maybe years," Brennan said. "Fat Nick has Jimmy Walsh drilled and gets his property for peanuts. Plus, he eliminates a possible stool pigeon."

"This makes sense. More sense than thinking Walsh pulled off this job using his own brainpower. He wasn't stupid, but he wasn't that smart," Terrance said, catching Daniel's eye. "If Gentleman Jimmy has any heirs, they'd be smart enough not to stake their claims."

"Aye. Let's pay Fat Nick a visit. Tomorrow," Daniel said. "This day's been long enough and he ain't going anywhere, not sitting on seventy large."

DANIEL AND TERRANCE slid into their usual booth at Kirby's Tavern in Southie, and within minutes, two glasses of Guinness were set down in front of them.

"Here's to you, brother of mine," Terrance said, raising his glass. "Glad you're in one piece."

"Aye, and here's to Joey, poor lad," Daniel said, their glasses touching. "He deserved something, but not that."

"A bad end, aye. And unfortunate that we didn't have a chance to get him to talk. Sounds like you had him primed and ready," Terrance said.

"Yeah, he knew there was no alternative," Daniel said. "He hadn't admitted to anything, not out loud anyway, but he would have spilled, I'm sure."

"More's the pity," Terrance said, taking a healthy swig. Daniel raised his glass to his lips, then set it down.

"Wait a minute," he said. "That's damned odd now that I think of it."

"What?" Terrance asked.

"Joey didn't admit to a thing, which is par for the course. But he did deny one thing."

"Also par for the course," Terrance said. "What are you getting at?"

"He kept mum on everything to do with the robbery," Daniel said, rapping a finger on the wooden table. "But he denied stealing the car that was used. And he was quick off the mark with it. No hesitation."

"So, he was telling the truth?"

"I'd say so. Why else put that much energy into denying one small part, and just that one thing?" Daniel said.

"Da always said you were the smart one, Daniel. Sounds like we need to have a chat with Irish Tommy."

"Right after we visit Fat Nick," Daniel said. "It'll make for an interesting morning."

Irish Tommy was a criminal, no doubt about it. But he didn't get involved in heists, at least not directly. And he was known for staying away from murder, at least killings that were planned in advance.

"He still the only show in town?" Daniel asked.

"That he is. After Polish Tommy had his heart attack, no one stepped up to take his place." There had been two guys providing the same service, both named Tommy, so they were nicknamed by the old country each had come from. That's how every cop and criminal knew them. Polish Tommy and Irish Tommy, purveyors of automobiles, hideouts, whatever was needed for a job. Outfitters.

But not guns. There were plenty of guns around. The Tommies kept away from firearms to protect themselves from a possible date with the death penalty.

Everything else was available, for a fee. Phony identification, cars registered to nonexistent people, house or apartment rentals fully stocked with food and drink, police uniforms, witnesses who would swear to laying eyeballs on so-and-so at a restaurant or the ballpark at a designated time. Irish Tommy was good at distractions too. Calling in a fire, robbery in progress, auto accident, bomb threats, and more. No cop had ever been able to lay a finger on him. By the time the crime was committed, Irish Tommy was somewhere else.

That was a problem, but it was tomorrow morning's problem. Terrance finished his Guinness and went home for dinner. Daniel stayed, had another, and thought things through.

THE NEXT MORNING, the Boyles were driven by Sergeant Brennan and another uniformed officer to Fat Nick Bruccola's place out in Orient Heights. They were in a patrol car, accompanied by two motorcycle cops who revved their engines as they turned down Bennington Street, about as far east as you could go and still be in Boston. A nice neighborhood with churches and stores where Italian was spoken without a second thought.

Fat Nick had his import business in North Boston, but Daniel had decided to make a house call. A very visible and loud house call.

"What the hell is this?" Fat Nick demanded, standing on the wide porch of his Victorian house and staring down at the cops. Sergeant Brennan leaned against the patrol car and stared back as Terrance and Daniel walked up the short sidewalk. The two motorcycle cops sat on their machines, engines rumbling. Neighbors were already peeking out their windows, taking in the scene. "You bums know where I work."

"We're not here to talk about imported olive oil, Mr. Bruccola," Terrance said, halting right before the steps and looking up at Fat Nick. The gangster frowned, his meaty jowls weighing down his lower lip, leaving his mouth hanging open like a fish gasping for air. He wore a finely tailored blue-striped three-piece suit that failed to disguise the rolls of flesh that cascaded down the length of his six-foot body.

"Then what?" Fat Nick asked, his eyes flickering between the cops in the street and his curious neighbors.

"Can we come inside for a chat?" Daniel asked, rubbing his hands together. "It's a bit nippy out here."

"Come up on the porch," Fat Nick said. "And tell your boys to cut the racket, or I'll call the cops." He chuckled at his own joke and took a few thick-thighed steps to a wicker chair that creaked under his heft. He gestured vaguely toward two other chairs.

"You hear about Jimmy Walsh?" Daniel said as he took a seat.

"Word gets around," Fat Nick said. "That why you're here?"

"You don't seem too distraught," Terrance said. "Wasn't he a friend of yours?"

"We had some business dealings," Fat Nick said. Then, as an afterthought, "He'll be missed."

"We know all about your business," Daniel said, leaning forward in his chair. "We know about the bank truck job, and how Andino Maffini got paid off."

"Joey Fisher, too, the poor bastard," Terrance said. "He almost made it out."

"I don't know what you two are blathering on about, and I don't care," Fat Nick said. "Unless you got something important to say, how 'bout gettin' the hell off my porch?"

"I got something important to tell you, then we'll go," Daniel said as he stood. "B00230911D. I wrote it down in case you don't remember."

Daniel gave Fat Nick a notecard with the serial number sequence taken from one of the bills from Joey's wallet. Terrance held up the hundred-dollar bill with the matching serial number for Fat Nick to see. Of course, they'd know the serial numbers from the bank records. But to have evidence that a person linked to Fat Nick in any way had been in possession of some of that cash meant big trouble headed the fat man's way.

"We'll be back," Terrance said.

"Bring a warrant next time," Fat Nick said, puffing out his cheeks.

"You shoulda seen the look he gave you two," Brennan said as they drove off. "Daggers, it was. You struck home, lads."

"It'll worry him," Daniel said. "It would me. But when we don't come back with a warrant, he'll know we were bluffing."

"Even the friendliest judge, half-drunk, wouldn't give us a warrant based on guesswork," Terrance said. "But all we need is an hour or two of Fat Nick getting all worked up."

"Aw hell, it's a half-hour drive to Roxbury," Brennan said. "By the time we get there, Irish Tommy'll be quaking in his boots."

"As long as we're right about Irish Tommy," Daniel said.

"No, as long as *you're* right about Irish Tommy," Terrance said, elbowing Daniel as if they were teenagers. "We should know right away. If he's calm and collected, we'll have wasted our time."

Irish Tommy worked his outfitter racket from a used furniture store called Gallagher's. No one remembered who Gallagher was, but it was a useful front for when safe houses needed to be furnished or people moved around in unmarked trucks.

"You sure you can pressure him to rat out Fat Nick?" Brennan asked as their patrol car crossed the Longfellow Bridge.

"There's three dead men who will be a big help," Daniel said. "And we can promise not to prosecute. The DA will go along with that in a heartbeat if it helps to bring down Fat Nick."

"It'll be the end of Irish Tommy's outfitting racket," Terrance said. "We just have to make him believe it's all over anyway."

"Showtime," Brennan said as they parked in front of Gallagher's, right behind one of the unmarked black trucks. The storefront boasted two plate glass windows flanking the entrance. Couches, chairs, and tables were on display, just like in a regular furniture store. Roxbury was a good location for both ends of the business. The neighborhood was home to German and Jewish immigrants along with Negroes who'd come north to work in the war industries. They didn't always get along, but this wasn't anyone's turf. Irish Tommy could ply his trade to the criminal class without being in anyone's backyard.

"Take a look around back," Terrance told Sergeant Brennan. The driver stayed with the car while Brennan did his snooping, and the two men went inside. Threading their way through new and used furnishings, they spotted Irish Tommy at a desk behind a wide counter. He was on the telephone, and he didn't look happy.

"Look, he's still alive," Daniel said in a booming voice. "I told you they wouldn't get him."

"Not yet," Terrance said, giving Irish Tommy a cheery wave as he slammed down the receiver.

"If it ain't the Boyle brothers!" Irish Tommy said. "A pleasure to see you both." He was smiling, but the sheen of perspiration on his forehead hinted at what was going on in his scheming brain.

"We need to talk, Tommy," Daniel said, resting his elbows on the counter.

"I got nothing to say."

"About what?" Terrance asked.

"Anything."

"How about the Red Sox's chances next year?" Terrance asked.

"How about your chances, Tommy boy?" Daniel said. "Fat Nick is cleaning house. Any local muscle that was involved with the bank truck job is ending up six feet under."

"I heard about that," Tommy said, rising from his desk. He was tall, with thick shoulders and dark hair slicked back. Pushing forty or so, but in good shape, probably from moving tables and chairs all over the city. "But what's that got to do with me?"

"You know, Tommy," Terrance said. "We've just come from a chat with Fat Nick. We have cash that was in Joey Fisher's possession when he took those slugs to the chest. A messy end, as me brother can attest."

"He was just a touch slow off the mark," Daniel said. "He could've made it out of town, but where could he go? His plan was to hide out with his cousin in Warwick. Hell, Fat Nick's men would've found that hidey-hole in half a day. Where you going, Tommy?"

"Why would I go anywhere? Like I said, I heard about all this, but I'm not involved," Irish Tommy said, his voice betraying the slightest quiver. "Why are you here?"

"To give you a chance," Terrance said. "This started out as grand theft, but now we've got three deaths. Homicide. That means the chair, Tommy, even for an accessory."

"Fat Nick knows we're here," Daniel said. "He can't afford to let you sing."

"Why would I sing?" Irish Tommy asked. "I mean, if I knew the song."

"Listen, we should continue this downtown," Terrance said. "A regular interrogation is in order, don't you think, Lieutenant Boyle?"

"Yes, I do, Lieutenant Boyle," Daniel said. "We'll give Tommy a chance to come clean. Name names. Sign a confession. The district attorney will decline to press charges in the face of such cooperation, of course."

"Of course," Terrance said, watching as Irish Tommy's eyes widened, following where this was leading. "But if he should decline to help, what do we do then?"

"That's easy," Daniel said. "We thank him for his help. Very publicly. Then we give him a ride back here. Simple."

"Right. Then we bring in Fat Nick for questioning. I'm sure he and his men won't draw any conclusions," Terrance said.

"You can't set me up," Irish Tommy said. "I'm an honest businessman—I don't know about any heist or murders."

"Now here's the funny thing about that," Sergeant Brennan said, coming through the rear of the store. "You won't believe what I found lying on the ground out back next to the garbage cans."

"Hey, you got a warrant?" Irish Tommy demanded.

"I don't need a warrant to pick up litter," Brennan said, seeing no need to mention he'd knocked over the trash cans to see what spilled out. "As a matter of fact, you're probably in violation of some ordinance the way you got junk piled up in back. Look at this, boys."

Daniel took the crumpled paper from him and read down the list. It was three addresses, each with a single name. It was dated two days after the heist and headed with the notation *pick up furniture.*

"Now what are the chances?" Daniel said, smoothing the paper out on the counter and tapping his finger against it. "If I were a betting man, and if either Andino Maffini or Joey Fisher were alive to take the bet, I'd give odds that these were the safe houses you arranged for Fat Nick's heist. And the phony names they were rented under. Am I right, Tommy?"

Irish Tommy didn't answer. His face had gone white, which was answer enough.

"And you saw no reason for good furniture to be left behind," Terrance said. "So you sent your men to pick it up. Which means two things. One, they were too stupid to rip this into a thousand pieces when they were done."

"What's the other thing?" Irish Tommy managed to mutter.

"Oh, that's the beautiful one, me boy," Daniel said. "It means that somewhere in this store there's furniture with the fingerprints of the out-of-town talent. Because I don't think you bothered to wipe it down, did you?"

Irish Tommy collapsed into his chair. Answer enough.

"I want guarantees," Irish Tommy said. "In writing."

AS SOON AS they sat down in the interrogation room, Irish Tommy put on his best face. He knew he had something the cops wanted, and he was determined to work it to his best advantage.

"You'll have it all, Tommy," Terrance said. "You know us. We keep our word."

"It ain't you two I'm worried about. I ain't spilling to you until the DA agrees I got immunity from prosecution," Tommy said, leaning back and folding his arms across his chest.

"Here's how it works," Daniel said. "We need to know what you have immunity from. We need you to confirm your role in the bank truck job. What you did for Fat Nick. What contact you had with him. Then we get your immunity. Which will extend to the three murders as well. You don't want to get caught up in those charges, believe me."

"No recordings, no signed statements. I tell you what I know, then you get the DA to write up the immunity," Irish Tommy said. "If you're satisfied with it. Deal?"

The Boyle brothers whispered to each other. It sounded like he had solid information.

"Deal," Daniel said. "Anything else?"

"Yeah. I want to be relocated. A new identity. Cash to start over," Irish Tommy said.

"Hold on," Terrance said. "Only the feds can do that, and it's damned rare. We can't deliver on that."

"You better find a way. Ask the district attorney," Irish Tommy said.

"We will, I promise. But let's get moving on this. Tell us your story, and if it sounds good to us, we'll make the call," Terrance said.

Irish Tommy agreed and gave them the lowdown. He had worked with Fat Nick directly, been given a list of requirements including the safe houses and several stolen cars. Everything was to have good paperwork. The cars had been registered and the houses rented under false names. Fat Nick hadn't said what the job was, but Irish Tommy had delivered food and booze to all the houses himself. He'd heard the goons talking and knew they were planning on intercepting a bank truck.

He'd heard a rumor that Jimmy Walsh had skimmed some of the loot and that Fat Nick was on the warpath, but he thought that was just a beef between two guys, not an excuse to whack all the local witnesses.

"That enough?" Irish Tommy asked. It was. "Then get the DA down here. I want signed papers, and I want to talk about relocation."

It was a few hours before District Attorney Lewis Bailey made his appearance. Arresting Fat Nick Bruccola was worth making a deal with Irish Tommy, especially since Tommy's crimes were not violent or directly part of the robbery. According to Bailey, a good lawyer could even argue that Tommy had no knowledge of the actual plan, and the charges they could bring against him would be very minor.

"I have no problem granting immunity from prosecution based on your written statement, if it matches what you've told these detectives," Bailey said to Tommy as he opened his briefcase. "I have the paperwork ready to sign. But I can't do anything about relocating you. That would have to be a federal matter, and this isn't a federal case."

"I heard it's been done," Tommy said, returning to the arms-folded-across-his-chest position.

"It has," Bailey said, settling into a professorial tone. "The FBI has on occasion created new identity documents to protect witnesses. The legal basis for this comes under the Ku Klux Klan Act of 1871, which was passed by Congress to protect witnesses who testified against Klan members."

"Fat Nick is as bad as the Klan," Daniel said. "Can't we use that law?"

"No, we can't," Bailey said. "But the federal government could. The FBI could."

"Then bring in the FBI," Irish Tommy said. "I'll sign my statement, and we'll all be on our way."

"There's nothing for them here, Tommy," Terrance said. "Sorry to say, but it's the hard truth."

"You know what it's like, Tommy. Give and take," Daniel said.

"What if I had something else? Something the feds would definitely be interested in?"

"Definitely?" Bailey said. "I'd like to hear what that is."

"Wait, wait," Terrance said. "Before we get ahead of ourselves, why don't we get our own paperwork signed? I've had Tommy's statement typed up. We're ready to go."

"FBI," Tommy said. "Then we sign."

Sergeant Brennan brought in sandwiches and coffee while they waited on Special Agent John Sullivan to get there. Irish Tommy kept telling them they'd all be glad to hear what he had to say.

By the time Sullivan got there, the room smelled of stale cigarette smoke, bitter coffee, and corned beef.

"I hope this is good," Sullivan said, sitting across from Irish Tommy. "I'm not in the market for used furniture."

"Tommy assures us it's gold," Daniel said. "He's got the goods on Fat Nick but wants to be relocated on top of all the nice things we're doing for him. That's your territory."

"All right, spill it," Terrance said.

"First, I want you to know that it was only today I heard about those two Nazi spies you guys are looking for," Irish Tommy said. Special Agent Sullivan sat up a little straighter in his chair. "I keep my ear to the ground, ya know? So I got the description."

"Okay, Tommy, that's good," Daniel said. "What is it you know?"

"I think I know where they are," Irish Tommy said. "I can lead you right to their door."

"You think you know?" Sullivan asked.

"I know the place they rented," Irish Tommy said. "They moved in two days ago."

"I'm authorized to offer what you're after, providing the information is correct," Sullivan said. "If it's deliberately false, I'll be arresting you on charges of aiding and abetting the enemy. Think about it very carefully."

"I don't have to, my information is solid," Tommy said. "A guy came to me a few days ago and said these two guys were looking for a place in New York City. That much I tell you for free. The rest, after everything's signed."

Another two hours passed as a federal attorney from the US District Court in Boston was brought in. Sullivan used the telephone at Daniel's desk to make a call. He nodded, smiled, and hung up.

"It's a deal," he said. "Let's get back in there."

The federal attorney produced a document detailing the protection and relocation package, which Irish Tommy approved. Then he signed the witness statement and received his get-out-of-jail-free card from DA Bailey.

"They're at Thirty-Nine Beekman Place on the east side of Manhattan," Irish Tommy said. "I got a brother in the same business as me, down in New York. So when this guy says these two fellows from out of town want to find a place in New York City and keep it on the QT, I call my brother. I give him the requirements, and he comes up with exactly what they want."

"What were the requirements?" Sullivan asked.

"It had to be a building in Manhattan with no steel-frame construction. No steel beams, ya know?"

"You didn't think that odd?" Sullivan asked.

"In my business—my old business—you don't ask questions. You don't ask why," Irish Tommy said. "Like I said, I had no idea who these guys were. I just made the contact, got them on the train, and turned 'em over to my brother in Manhattan. He knows even less than I do about them; he just took them to the apartment and gave them the keys."

"Describe them," Sullivan asked.

"One guy was real quiet. The other spoke perfect English. Nothing fancy, but like he was from around here. Said his pal was Polish. Thin, dark-haired, just like in your description."

"What's the significance of the steel beams?" Bailey asked.

"Steel can inhibit radio transmission," Sullivan said. "They're obviously planning on building a radio and sending messages to Germany. Or other agents in the States."

"Hey, we good here?" Irish Tommy asked.

"Good enough. You'll be in protective custody until we verify all this," Sullivan said. "Then we'll set up your new identity."

IT HAD BEEN a long night. Armed with a search warrant, Daniel and Terrance had pounded on Fat Nick's front door at half past midnight as spotlights mounted on police cars illuminated the windows and lit the scene. They waited ten seconds, to be polite, and then let the boys with the battering ram have at it.

They found Fat Nick stumbling around in silk pajamas. That was the easy part. Getting cuffs on his fleshy wrists was harder. They'd brought the largest pair in the station but gave up trying to force Fat Nick's arms behind his back. Deciding he wasn't about to break into a run, they cuffed his hands in front.

Daniel told Nick he was under arrest and explained that they'd start tearing up the floorboards on the top floor and work their way downstairs. If they didn't find the loot, the walls were next.

"I know you and your wife have been married a long time,"

Terrance said. "Why leave her with a busted-up house? We'll not leave a stick of wood standing until we find it."

Fat Nick cursed for a moment, then caught sight of his dear wife in her nightclothes, crying at the head of the stairs.

"Guest bedroom, upstairs," he said. "Move the bed and pry up the floorboards."

Ten minutes later, Sergeant Brennan was leading a line of cops carrying bags of money out the front door, leaving Mrs. Bruccola with an intact house and no husband underfoot. A few hours of paperwork back at the station, and by dawn, Daniel was on a southbound train with Special Agent Sullivan, snoring to the rhythmic sound of steel wheels on the tracks.

"You owe me for this," Sullivan said as he and Daniel got off the train and walked through Grand Central Terminal into the bright sunlight. "Remember, you're here as a courtesy. An observer. Behave yourself."

"Oh, Johnny, don't forget who served this up on a silver platter to you federal boys. You had no idea where they were, remember?"

"Not a goddamn clue, but you never heard that from me, Danny," Sullivan said with a grin. They were met by two FBI agents, younger guys, who looked like twin Boy Scouts in their Sunday-best suits. It was a short ride to Beekman Place, where other agents armed with shotguns stood ready at the corner, shielded from view by a utility truck.

Sullivan, Daniel, and their two escorts were assigned the rear of the building. The rest of the men were going in the front door. New York City cops were assigned to block both ends of the short street.

It was over in minutes.

By the time Sullivan led the way up the back stairs, the other agents were handcuffing the two men and bundling them out the front door. Dark-haired and thin, just like the description.

"Look here," Daniel said, nodding to a table as he holstered his revolver. Coils of copper wire sat on top of an amateur radio handbook. Radio parts were spread out over the table. A large, obviously secondhand radio lay on the floor, the rear panel already removed.

"Well, thank you, Irish Tommy," Sullivan said, surveying the equipment.

"Who says the Irish are neutral in this war?" Daniel said. "Two Nazi spies captured, not to mention a crime boss brought down, and three murders solved. We need to raise a glass to old Tommy, or whatever his name will be."

"Several glasses, Danny. The FBI's paying. We've just made J. Edgar Hoover look good. For twenty-four hours, I can do no wrong," Sullivan said, his voice hushed as he mentioned the director's name.

"Oh, they have Guinness in New York City, eh?" Daniel said. "Do tell."

BILLY BOYLE: THE LOST PROLOGUE

■ ■ ■

—

BILLY BOYLE, THE first title in the eponymous series of historical crime fiction , was released in 2006. When I submitted the original manuscript to my editor (Soho Press co-founder Laura Hruska), she wisely pointed out that my long prologue, which contained no mention of Billy Boyle, would be an impediment to readers. As with all things editorial, Laura was right. So out it went. I thought I had not retained it in any form, but I recently found a copy and decided it might be of interest to fans of the series. And who knows, reading this might lead a new reader directly into the rest of the book.

"DAMNED WIND! I should be sitting in a Berlin café right now, not tramping across this wretched airfield on a fool's errand!"

Captain Johann Bischoff held his greatcoat collar up with one gloved hand and trudged, head down, holding his service cap in place with the other. Three Junkers Ju 52 tri-motor transport aircraft sat on the tarmac. In the twilight dawn, groups of men huddled next to each plane were highlighted by the faint light from within each plane as the rear doors opened to welcome them.

At precisely the same moment, nine engines roared to life, their combined prop wash adding blasts of cold air to the already frigid Arctic winds sweeping down from the surrounding mountains. Bischoff grimaced as he turned to the man at his side, shooting him a murderous look that would have been accompanied by a string of curses if he could have been heard over the crescendo of natural and man-made noises assaulting them. He leaned into the wind and staggered to the open rear door of the nearest plane as his service cap flew off and danced down the runway, touching ground several times before lifting itself on a gust and disappearing into the low cloud cover. He swore a bitter epithet.

Bischoff grabbed the ladder by the rear cargo door and hauled himself inside. His booted toe caught on the last step, and he tumbled into the aircraft, trying to maintain his dignity—such as it was—by staying up on one knee. He caught sight of twelve seated paratroopers trying to contain their laughter at the sight of a superior officer hatless, windblown, and obviously quite out of place. The trooper closest to him quickly regained his composure as he stood, delivering a stern glance to the others, quieting them quickly.

"Lieutenant Hauser, sir. I was told to expect someone from the Abwehr," the paratrooper said.

"Then you were told too much, Lieutenant." As Bischoff spoke, a figure entered the transport and stood to the rear of the compartment. All eyes turned to him. He was wearing the green-hued overcoat and gear of a Norwegian soldier. He carried a Krag-Jørgensen 6.5mm rifle but wore a Luftwaffe-issue parachute.

Hauser cast a questioning gaze to Bischoff and rested his hand on the handle of his holstered pistol. Bischoff held up his hand, gesturing that there was no need for alarm.

"As you all know," Bischoff said calmly, "your parachute company is being dropped south of Trondheim to cut off the Norwegians before they can link up with British forces landing on the west coast. Our ski troops are advancing through the mountains and should link up with you soon. This aircraft will take a different route than the others, to deliver this man to a secret drop zone before proceeding to yours. You will not talk to him or refer to his presence, ever."

"Understood, sir," said Hauser.

"Good. The pilot will signal when he reaches the first drop zone. After that, forget this ever happened, and for God's sake say nothing of the Abwehr." The Abwehr—Germany's secret service—was involved in military espionage all over the world. Hauser nodded and returned to his seat as the paratroopers returned to their quiet murmurs and waiting.

Bischoff approached the silent man and stood close, putting his arm around his shoulder.

"Well, Karl, your moment has arrived. I hope all goes well, for your sake and your father's."

"Johann," the other man said, smiling gently. "You've tried to talk me out of this every day since Canaris approved the plan. I'm glad that today you didn't; I might have agreed with you." Admiral

Wilhelm Canaris was the head of the Abwehr and had personally approved the operation Karl had proposed.

"Don't worry, old friend," Karl continued as he looked deep into Bischoff's eyes. "Everything will work out as planned."

"I'll stand for drinks at the Adlon Hotel back in Berlin in a few weeks if this crazy plan of yours doesn't work. If it does—"

"If it does," Karl said, "I'll be doing my drinking in England."

Bischoff smiled and shook his friend's hand. "I will wait for your signal that all is well. *Prodigal Son*. And I will get your father out of Dachau." He stepped back and saluted, not the stiff-armed Nazi salute, but the regular military version. Bischoff went to the door without a further word to Karl, glancing back only to give Hauser and his men a final warning. "You have your orders. Remember them." With that, he vanished into the howling winds.

The Junkers Ju 52 lumbered down the runway and lifted off slowly and laboriously, fighting the wind as well as the weight of men and equipment. Within minutes the plane rose above the churning clouds as the sun began to rise over the distant horizon. Karl ignored the others as he stared at the windblown landscape visible through breaks in the clouds. It was a stern and unforgiving land, but one he knew well. He had grown up there.

Captain Karl Frederiksen was born in Germany but had his share of Norwegian blood on both sides of his family. His father was a German citizen whose own grandparents had immigrated from Norway. His father owned a small shipping line that ran from Hamburg in northern Germany to Oslo, Bergen, and other Norwegian ports. The elder Frederiksen married a Norwegian bride and moved the family to Oslo after the First World War, escaping the destructive political battles and economic paralysis following the German defeat. Karl spent ten years in Norway, speaking the language, skiing, and living the healthy outdoor life of a normal Norwegian boy. When he was twelve, the family moved back to Germany. Karl continued his education, glad to become acquainted with the country of his birth and caught up in youthful adulation of Adolf Hitler and the rise of the Nazi Party. His father disapproved, and they argued constantly over politics, the only issue that divided them. His father told him of his experiences in the Great War, and how important it was for Karl's generation not to go through another such deadly conflict. But Karl was too young to understand, too certain in his own enthusiasm to comprehend why his father didn't think Adolf Hitler was the greatest man in the world.

When Karl turned sixteen, his father sent him to work on the Hamburg docks, to learn the shipping business from the ground up. It was hard work, and the rough dockworkers showed little mercy to the young son of a wealthy shipowner. But Karl loved the outdoor work, growing stronger as he took on every tough job he could volunteer for. He learned how to stand his ground when challenged by the older men and when to let them have their fun. And when to throw their fun back at them. He was a shrewd judge of character, and before long the Hamburg dockhands took him in as one of their own.

After a year on the docks, his father arranged to have him signed on as an apprentice seaman on one of his freighters that made the regular Hamburg-Oslo run. The night before he was to ship out, his worker friends took him out for a celebration at a tavern down by the dockyard. It was a known gathering place for Communists and other labor leaders; the men who worked the docks were mostly leftists, some of whom had participated in the 1918 naval mutinies that had helped to end the last war.

Well into the evening, a band of Nazi Brownshirts raided the tavern, pouring in with clubs and fists, outnumbering the dockworkers heavily. Fighting spilled out into the street and the police stood by, watching, as long as the Nazis had the upper hand. As more workers poured in from side streets, the scales began to tip against the Brownshirt thugs. Finally, the police joined in, but only to allow the Nazis to beat a hasty retreat. One of Karl's friends was killed, and there were many broken bones and arrests. Karl escaped with a black eye and a bruised jaw.

The next day, as his ship left the harbor, he gazed out at the receding shore. It was the first time he'd thought about the ugliness behind the Nazi marches, slogans, and promises. He thought long and hard, until his fatherland disappeared beyond the horizon.

After his sea tour, Karl returned home and promptly joined the army, telling his disappointed father he wanted a place where he could serve his country and steer clear of politics. His experience in Hamburg had disgusted and disillusioned him, but he still wanted to be part of Germany, away from the street fighting and the nighttime marches and rallies. He admitted his father had been right all along, but now the army might be the safest place for an honest man in troubled times.

Remembering that naïve comment, Captain Karl Frederiksen, now a four-year veteran of the Abwehr, smiled and let a small, bitter laugh escape his lips. It had not worked out the way he'd planned. Today he was a closely watched man, his father in the first year of a five-year sentence in the well-known Dachau concentration camp for statements made against the Nazi Party. He wasn't likely to survive the sentence. The elder Frederiksen had not had the sense to remain quiet as the Nazi storm swept over his nation. He told anyone who would listen about the lies behind the slogans and parades. He was not a particularly important or influential man, but one day they came for him anyway. The Gestapo interviewed Karl and hinted they would be keeping a close eye on him for any sign of similar sentiments.

Lieutenant Hauser had been watching Frederiksen. "Do you find all of this amusing?" Hauser asked, gesturing with his hands, taking in the men, the Junkers, perhaps even the war beyond.

"I thought you weren't supposed to speak to me." Frederiksen's voice was neutral, but the slight grin still playing at the corner of his mouth showed he didn't take the injunction seriously.

"That hatless staff officer should have come along to enforce his order. Is he the one who dressed you up in that Norwegian getup?"

"No, this mission was my own idea. Don't ask me anything else."

The plan itself was daring, but without a predictable outcome. Dressed in his Norwegian uniform, Karl was to mingle with escaping Norwegian troops and join up with the British, hoping to be evacuated to England when Norway fell. There, he was to use his false identity and language skills—he spoke excellent English—to secure an assignment that would bring him in close to the Allies' war plans. If successful, he was to contact a German agent in England and radio back the signal *Prodigal Son*. That would initiate a chain of events ending with his return to Germany via U-boat and his father's release from Dachau. Canaris had secured an agreement with the Gestapo for the release of Karl's father if Karl was successful in infiltrating the Allied High Command. An incentive that cost the Gestapo nothing and promised some share of the glory if the mission succeeded. If not, Karl's father's end would follow quickly.

What an insane plan, Karl thought to himself. *And I have no one to blame but myself. I could end up training raw recruits in Canada for all I know, and Father will die in Dachau. Perhaps Johann was right, and the mission was a fool's errand.*

The cockpit door opened and the copilot called out to Karl, thankfully interrupting his morose thoughts.

"Drop zone coming up! We will circle the clearing and then head back to our original bearing. Good luck!"

"Allow me," Hauser said as he opened the fuselage door. Karl stepped up to the edge as the Ju 52 banked slightly, offering a clear view of the flat plateau, which rose up from the mountainous terrain below. One of Hauser's men brought up the equipment canister that held skis, backpacks, and other Norwegian army supplies. Hauser clapped Karl on the shoulder. "Good luck, my silent friend. I hope our paths do not cross down there."

Karl nodded his understanding but said nothing, knowing what would be required of him if that should occur. He stood in the doorway for a moment, the wind and cold ripping into his body. Everything slowed, and he could make out every detail of the ridges and valleys he'd have to cross on his journey. Even in the freezing cold, he began to sweat. He had to stop thinking and jump.

He pushed away and vanished into the cold morning air. The canister followed him down as the Junkers completed its turn, flying away and out of sight before Karl landed in the ice and blowing snow.

Alone.

"LOOK, ROLF!" JENS Iversen grabbed his large companion by the shoulder, pointing up the mountain trail they had just descended. The morning sun crested over the high ridge behind them and glinted harshly off the crystal-white snow. The two men shielded their eyes and craned their necks, releasing fountains of frosted breath as their lungs gasped against the thin mountain air.

"Germans?" Rolf Kayser whispered, still scanning the ridgeline.

"No, a Norwegian, I think," Jens said. "On skis, perhaps following our tracks."

"Then I hope he knows the way to the coast better than we do," Rolf said with a bitter laugh. He halted as he caught sight of the skier, head down, poles tucked under his arms, taking a fast turn as the trail spilled out into open ground. "Why is he coming down so fast?"

The question was answered by a snowy blur in the distance; German mountain troops in white camouflage smocks, obtaining speed as they gained on the Norwegian. As Jens and Rolf gazed spellbound at the racing skiers, gunfire erupted from the ridge. More Germans, and they had Rolf and Jens in their sights. Snow exploded in bursts as they pivoted on their skis and pushed off, bullets plowing through snowdrifts and ricocheting off boulders.

Jens swerved off the trail, kicking off his skis as he dove for cover.

Rolf slowed, watching Jens unsling his rifle and cast a nervous glance at the ongoing Germans.

"Rolf! Get down and give him covering fire!" Jens yelled, making room behind a pile of snow-covered rocks. Rolf shook his head and removed his skis, even as Jens fired his first round, to no visible effect.

"We don't even know this fellow," Rolf grumbled, "and now you're going to get us killed over him." He sighed as he wrapped the sling around his forearm to steady his aim, then braced his elbow on the cold, hard rock. He took a deep breath and filled his sights with the lead German skier. He was only yards behind the Norwegian, who filled up most of the front sight. Rolf's eyes flickered along the trail, and then back to the sights. He waited until the Norwegian leaned into a curve, a split second ahead of the German, who was then revealed as a white form square in Rolf's sights. He gently pulled on the trigger and the German went limp, his momentum carrying him forward until he tumbled off his skis and rolled, dead limbs flopping in the frigid air.

As Rolf knew they must, the two skiers behind the dead man split apart to avoid the body. He worked the bolt, driving it forward in a single fluid motion, resighting and leading the skier who had gone to the right, away from the cover of the Norwegian ahead. That had been the German's mistake, and he took a 6.5mm bullet in the chest for it.

The Norwegian skier looked back at the fallen Germans as the last shot echoed off the mountain walls. Jens leaped up and waved him on, ducking quickly as bullets whizzed by his head. The skier sprayed snow as he executed a sharp turn, taking refuge with Rolf behind the jumble of rocks. He collapsed in the snow, working to catch his breath and unsling his rifle at the same time.

"Captain Anders Arnesen," he gasped. "Glad to meet you, gentlemen."

Jens and Rolf looked at each other in astonishment at the formality of the introduction in such circumstances. The man now calling himself Arnesen stole a quick glance at the advancing Germans, now well spread out. "We've got to get to the tree line and cover, fast. Get your skis on, now!"

"Yes, sir," both men said in unison, glad to have met up with an officer who knew what he was doing. They clamped on their skis and watched as Arnesen fixed his eye to the telescopic sight on his Krag-Jørgensen rifle. He spoke without moving as rifle fire came from the Germans, ricocheting off stone inches from his face.

"When I fire, go," Arnesen said calmly. "I'll take out two and the rest will dive for cover. It will give us a few seconds, but only that. Understand?"

"We do," Jens said. Rolf nodded, and they watched as Captain Arnesen tracked his target. Bullets whined over their heads, and Rolf tightened his neck muscles, as if a bullet might bounce off his taut skin. The firing grew more intense and accurate. It seemed like an eternity waiting for the captain to shoot. Finally, Arnesen's first shot rang out. Jens and Rolf pushed off on their skis as the second shot followed. The German fire lessened, men diving for cover as two of their own fell dead.

Within seconds Arnesen was behind Jens and Rolf, following them into the tree line where they vanished into the welcoming cloak of green firs. They skied on until they were certain they hadn't been followed, finally resting on the southern slope of a hill leading into a narrow valley, the thin rays of the sun providing the slightest warmth.

"Cigarette?" Arnesen grinned as he shook a few loose from a crumpled pack of Tiedemanns. "Don't worry, we've put enough distance behind us, and the wind is in our favor. Tell me, where are you two headed?"

"We decided to try for Molde on the coast," Jens said, accepting a light. "Rolf says he heard the British are landing there."

"Did you now?" Arnesen said, studying the two men. Jens was the younger of the two, small and wiry, talkative, and full of nervous energy. Rolf was quiet and calmer in comparison, and larger by half than his companion. "So, Rolf, what do you plan to do with the British?"

"Fight. Fight the Germans."

"Good," Arnesen said, apparently satisfied with the answer. "What is your unit? Where have you fought before today?" This time, Jens was not so quick with his answer. He looked to Rolf, who studied his cigarette and then stared at the ground. "Well?"

"We haven't exactly fought anyone before today," Jens said. "We were both called up with the 5th Division, but it never got properly organized. I sat around Namsos for days waiting for orders. Then the Germans poured through our lines, and I took off south. Most of the others surrendered."

"We met up on the trail yesterday," Rolf added. "I was with the 5th as well, in another battalion outside of Namsos. It was the same thing: no food, no orders, damn few officers. We were supposed to link up with British marines in Trondheim, but they pulled out before we got there, and the Germans moved in. Today is the first time we actually fired on the enemy."

"Well, you've got an officer now," Arnesen said, his gaze steady on the two men, leaving no doubt that he was in charge. "I wish I had food to share, but I haven't eaten since yesterday. I was with the 2nd Dragoons at Lillehammer. The Germans hit us hard and kept pushing back. We were told to surrender. However, never having done so before, I did not wish to acquire the habit."

"How did you end up here?" Rolf asked. Arnesen remained silent, staring at Rolf, who finally added, "Sir."

"I hopped a freight train to Trondheim. The Germans bombed the track near Dombås, so I took off cross-country. Lucky they did, otherwise I would have gone straight into German hands. Lucky I ran into you boys as well. You saved me."

"Well," Jens said, uncomfortable with the praise, "shouldn't we get going? There are only a few hours of daylight left."

"Yes," Arnesen replied. "Let's see if we can find shelter in the valley below. By the way, nice shooting back there. I swear I heard that first bullet go right by my ear."

"Thank you, sir," Rolf said, his chest swelling with pride. "I was the champion shot in my rifle club the last four years. How did you do with your shots?"

"It looked like I got the first one in the leg. I didn't wait to see about the other fellow," Arnesen said. "Now let's go."

THE THREE NORWEGIANS moved cross-country for three days, taking shelter in isolated villages at night, skiing over the packed snow of the Romsdal mountain range during the day. At each village, they heard the same rumors of powerful British forces landing at Molde. It sounded as if the fortunes of war had shifted, and the defeat of the mighty German army was still possible.

Early on the third day, the men descended the foothills of the Romsdal range, expecting to see the distant ocean as they topped ridge after ridge. At midday they saw hundreds of aircraft in formation, high in the clear blue sky, too far to make out if they were German or British. Several hours later, they knew with a sickening certainty. On the crest of the final ridge, they saw Molde in the distance. The city was burning. Smoke filled the sky and obscured the harbor. They exchanged worried glances, silent in the face of the terrible carnage, unwilling to believe the vision of defeat. Arnesen finally moved off on his skis, heading downhill more out of habit and resignation than anything else. His companions followed, the three tiny specks on the white landscape heading for a roiling cloud of smoke that threatened to swallow them up.

With skis on their shoulders, the trio walked through the streets against the tide of civilians pouring out of the city, carrying their hastily packed belongings and hoping to get out before the next raid. As darkness descended the smoldering fires cast a reddish hue against the walls and buildings still standing.

"Where are the British?" Each man asked the same questions as they made their way to the waterfront. "Have they landed?" No one had seen any troops, and only a few small ships were reported to be in the harbor. Some cursed the English for not coming; others cursed them for sending ships and drawing attention to their city. Most did not speak, wrapped up in their own personal world of shock and horror. The flow of civilians eased as the trio drew closer to the docks, aware they were the only uniformed men in sight.

"What are we looking for?" Jens asked, his voice trembling. "What's the use of going on?"

"Pull yourself together, man," Rolf said roughly. Arnesen ignored them as he pressed on to the sea, as if everything might be answered there.

They followed a narrow street that opened up to the expanse of the docks along the waterfront. Fires still raged, flame licking out from the wooden buildings toward the piers on their right. Not a ship was to be seen. They halted, silent at the end of their failed journey.

"Look!" Rolf pointed to the furthermost dock. Reflected by the light of the burning buildings, a warship was silently gliding into the harbor.

"What is it?" asked Jens, backing up involuntarily at the sight of a massive gray form moving closer to them.

"A British cruiser, I think," said Captain Arnesen. "Too large for a destroyer and smaller than a battleship. But that is a British ensign they're flying." He led them to the end of the dock as the cruiser steered for it. A wooden building behind them collapsed from the fire, sending swirls of sparks and thick smoke spiraling into the night air. As the cruiser neared the burning dock, sailors manned fire hoses and sprayed the pier, dousing flames and generating plumes of steam as the water hit red-hot embers.

"I guess we're the welcoming committee," Jens said as they watched sailors descend the gangplank even as firehoses still played over the dock. A party of Royal Marines, rifles at the ready, fanned out around the pier and took up defensive positions. A lieutenant approached Captain Arnesen and offered a salute.

"Is the king nearby, sir?"

"What?" Arnesen said.

"Do you speak English, sir? We are looking for King Haakon and his party." The marine officer spoke slowly, confused by the answer, even though it was delivered in English.

"Yes, I speak English," Arnesen answered. Most Norwegians learned German or English in school, a necessary task in a small nation with ties to both countries. "How would I know where the king is now? The last I heard he was in Lillehammer with the government, but that's been taken."

"I should explain, Captain. His Majesty's ship *Glasgow* is here to pick up King Haakon and his government. To take them to England."

Jens and Rolf, understanding the exchange, looked at each other in shock.

"Is the war lost?" Rolf spoke hesitantly, due to his lack of practice in speaking English as well as his reluctance to ask the question.

"It has been determined that neither the Norwegian nor the British Armed Forces can guarantee the king's safety if he stays in Norway. For him to evade capture, he must leave with us. Tonight," the lieutenant said. Seeing the anguish on the men's faces, he continued in a softer tone. "The king must leave Norway, but only to continue the war from England. He is not surrendering. And we will never surrender. Come with us to fight another day."

"Lieutenant, we have come a very long way to meet our British allies here. If we must leave Norway to continue the fight, then so be it," Arnesen said, turning to his companions. "Men?"

"I go where the king goes," Rolf proclaimed, coming to attention as he mentioned their monarch.

"Yes, I'll go," Jens said in a quiet voice.

"Vehicles approaching!" shouted a marine from his post. He pointed in the direction of the main road that led from the city center.

Three large sedans emerged from the roadway and were immediately surrounded. The lieutenant strode to the middle car, from which emerged a tall, stately figure, known to all Norwegians and now to much of the world.

"The king," Rolf said in a hushed tone.

"It *is* him," Jens said excitedly, his depression gone in a flash. "I've seen him many times in Oslo, on his morning ride." King Haakon was in the habit of riding alone in the city park, part of his unpretentious manner, and one of the things that endeared him to his people. The other was his unswerving policy of resistance to the German invasion. Jens and Rolf trailed Captain Arnesen as he joined the party and came to attention.

"We must wait for the trucks bringing the wounded from the base at Ålesund," King Haakon said. "They had to drive slowly because of the condition of the men. We cannot leave them behind."

"Yes, sir," the lieutenant said, noticing the king's eyes moving to the three Norwegian soldiers standing behind him, ramrod straight in their worn and dirty uniforms. He stood aside.

"Gentlemen," the king said softly, "where is the rest of your unit? What are your orders?"

"Captain Anders Arnesen, Your Highness, of the 2nd Dragoons. This is Rolf Kayser and Jens Iversen of the 5th Division. Our units have surrendered. We have not. We wish to go to England with you."

The king's eyes moistened as he took a deep breath and looked at the burning pier. "Destruction everywhere. It looks like the end of the world. Thank you for being here. It reminds me that Norway cannot be defeated with men like you willing to carry on. But I regret fleeing our country like this."

"Sir, you must leave," Jens said. "The people would not wish you to be captured. While you are free, you are a symbol of hope. Of freedom. You cannot serve us if you fall into the hands of the enemy." Embarrassed by his sudden outburst, Jens muttered his apology. "I'm sorry, sir."

"No, do not apologize, young man. It is good to hear you say that. I am so afraid of the Norwegian people's judgment. Your words are a comfort."

The diplomats and officials from the cars gathered close to the king. One man, dressed in an elegant long overcoat with a fur-trimmed collar, elbowed his way forward. He wore a Vandyke beard and monocle, and clutched a briefcase close to his chest. He looked ready for a day at the office in Oslo, not a night voyage on a warship.

"Who are these men, Your Majesty?" he demanded.

"My new bodyguard, Vidar. Captain Arnesen and Privates Iversen and Kayser are joining us. Since we have no other troops save the wounded, they will serve me. Captain, this is Vidar Skak, deputy interior minister." Arnesen saluted. Skak nodded quickly, then ignored him.

"Your Majesty, there is no sign of Birkeland. I warned against trusting him with such a vital assignment."

"Lieutenant," King Haakon called out to the marine officer. "Has anyone else been in contact with you?"

"No, sir. The pier was deserted except for these three men."

"We must find Knut Birkeland and the gold," King Haakon said. "That is more important than our own safety."

"Gold?" Arnesen asked. He was still reeling from the notion of being appointed the king's bodyguard, and his mind struggled to take in what he had heard.

"When the Germans took Oslo," the king said, "our entire gold reserve was taken out of the central bank hours before they arrived. It has been carried by truck and train to the coast. We must get it out of the country."

"With the gold, we can afford to continue the war and rebuild Norway when it is over," Skak said. "If the Germans get it, it will be gone forever. Which is why we must find Knut Birkeland."

"He will find us, I am sure," the king said firmly. "Now, let us board and await him."

An hour later, after constant aspersions on the dependability of Knut Birkeland by Vidar Skak, and ominous muttering by the captain of the *Glasgow* about the need to depart before the Germans showed themselves, a visibly exhausted Knut Birkeland was shown to the bridge.

Birkeland was a square-shouldered man with a full mustache and a day's growth of thick beard. His three-piece tweed suit and heavy coat were smudged with soot, and his rough hands hinted at his beginnings as a fisherman in the northern province of Nordland. Now a successful businessman who owned a fair-sized fishing fleet, he was both a friend and unofficial advisor to King Haakon, a position that earned him the jealous mistrust of Vidar Skak. Skak's responsibility in the government included the fishing industry, and the king often took his friend's common-sense advice over Skak's carefully worded memorandum.

Vidar Skak was a very proper man, a city man. As a deputy minister, he often dealt with the king on important matters. But just as Skak's influence grew, Knut Birkeland gained the king's favor. This provincial fisherman became an irritant as King Haakon more and more often called on him for advice. Birkeland was even given the vital job of moving the national gold reserve up into the northern coast because of contacts among the fishing fleets. Skak hated the idea of this important work in the hands of common fishermen.

"We couldn't get the trucks through the streets with all the bomb damage and fires," Birkeland said. "But I found an undamaged dock on the other side of the inlet. We're loading the gold on small boats right now, and they'll ferry the cargo here to the cruiser."

"Well done," said King Haakon as he shook Birkeland's hand. "I am so glad you are safe as well."

"But is the gold?" Skak said. "What happens if one of those boats capsizes? What of the gold then?"

"You!" Birkeland snarled as he turned to Skak and reached out to steady himself. He found the edge of the chart table with his hand, the whites of his knuckles showing as he tightened his grip. "You have done nothing at all! No real work to get your fancy clothes dirty, and you dare to question me, you sniveling bureaucrat!" Birkeland let go of the table and advanced upon Skak, who backed himself up against the bulkhead.

"Stop!" King Haakon's voice was enough to halt Birkeland. Skak regained his composure and stepped forward. He sniffed and looked away from Birkeland as if he were beneath consideration. Birkeland reddened with embarrassment.

"My apologies, Your Highness," Birkeland said, bowing his head. "I haven't slept much in the past three days. Skak, I am sorry for my outburst. Now, I must attend to the loading."

"Captain Arnesen, please accompany Mr. Birkeland and provide what assistance you and your men can," King Haakon said. "Mr. Skak, please refrain from unhelpful comments in the future."

Skak murmured a response and turned away to look out at the deck of the cruiser, angry at his humiliation. He watched Birkeland move across to where a small boat was tied up next to the *Glasgow*, feeling nothing but bitterness for the man.

Skak watched Birkeland as he spoke to Captain Arnesen on the pier. Bodyguard indeed! What did the king need with a bodyguard on a British ship, and with Vidar Skak at his side? Foolishness, although Skak was too savvy a politician to ever call the king foolish. Out loud.

Arnesen sent for Jens and Rolf and soon they were all working with Birkeland, the local fishermen, and some British soldiers. They crossed and recrossed the inlet in fishing boats, loading boxes of gold bars and coins from the trucks, and hoisting them with cargo nets onto the deck of the *Glasgow*. It was slow, hard work.

It was after midnight when the bombers came. Arnesen and Jens were working the hoists and Rolf was on the fishing boat below. Birkeland was on the deck watching them when he picked up the noise of approaching engines and sounded the warning. Although it was a dark, moonless night, the smoldering fires in the city cast an eerie bright glow over the harbor. They could hear the planes circling, searching for their quarry.

They were spotted.

Three Heinkel bombers swooped low over the harbor, making for the hulking form of the cruiser. Anti-aircraft guns opened up in a blaze of tracer fire as the aircraft drew closer, releasing their bombs. Arnesen could see each bomb clearly as they tumbled downward. All of them missed, but two hit the water close to the fishing boats, sending up great geysers of water and soaking the men at the hoist.

Arnesen and Jens were knocked over by the force of the water hitting them. The rope slid from their wet hands, and the cargo netting, straining against the load of several crates of gold, fell twenty feet to the deck of the fishing boat.

"Look out!" Jens screamed when Arnesen tried to grab the rope as it spun down through the pulley. Crates smashed onto the deck and wood splintered as the weight of the gold ripped boxes apart. Gold bars spilled out of one of the boxes, but most stayed tangled in the netting. The other boxes, which held Hungarian gold pieces, shattered on impact and showered the deck with brightly bouncing coins.

The bombers flew off into the night and within seconds everything was quiet. Jens looked down into the fishing boat and began to laugh. Rolf and two fishermen were on their backs, having been thrown against the bulkhead by the watery explosion.

They were covered in gold, the tips of Rolf's boots sticking out of a gleaming pile of coins that had cascaded from the broken boxes and engulfed them. Arnesen burst out laughing as did Knut Birkeland as soon as he joined them. Rolf sat smiling and unhurt as he ran his hands through the coins and sifted them between his fingers.

"I've never seen such a sight," Birkeland said, brushing a tear from his eye as he worked to regain control. An agitated Vidar Skak broke the levity of the moment as he nearly tumbled down the ladder from the bridge.

"Why are you laughing? We were almost killed!" Skak yelled.

"Well, we weren't," Birkeland said, still chuckling to himself. "But those boys were almost drowned in gold."

"There is nothing funny about this, Birkeland. The captain says the ship must depart immediately. There may be more bombers now that they've spotted us."

"You're right, Skak. Nothing funny about that. Tell King Haakon I'll return to the convoy and meet you up the coast. Namsos, in two days. All right?"

"Yes, yes, but you must deliver an accounting of the gold in your possession. We will count what has been loaded and compare that with what you deliver. We must be sure nothing has been lost," Skak said.

"I will account for every ounce, don't worry," Birkeland said. "You just be sure to stay alive to meet me in Namsos. Between German bombers and submarines, you'll be in dangerous waters for the next two days."

Birkeland was rewarded by a quick glimmer of fear from Skak as his eyes widened at the mention of further dangers. Skak turned away and snapped, "Namsos then, in two days."

Birkeland watched him clamber back up the ladder. "I don't know anything about submarines in these waters, I just said it to upset Vidar. He's not very comfortable outside Oslo, so it's easy to wind him up," he said to Arnesen. "Watch out for him. He's jealous of his position with the king. If he thinks you're in his way, he can make things hard for you."

"Mr. Birkeland," Arnesen began.

"Call me Knut, boy."

"All right, Knut. I don't plan on getting in anyone's way. I just want to fight the Germans. We came here to find the British, and we never expected to stumble upon the king's party."

"Well, you have, and King Haakon took a liking to you. Now you've got to watch out for your Norwegian enemies as well as the

Germans. Farewell, Anders. I hope to see you in two days to load more gold."

Arnesen wished him luck, and Birkeland descended to the boat where fishermen were picking up spilled coins and gold bars. Rolf joined Arnesen and Jens to watch the craft move off, its foamy wake receding into the night. Soon the *Glasgow* slowly backed away from the dock, anti-aircraft crews scanning the dark sky for the sight or sound of another air attack.

"Hard to believe we're leaving Norway and really going to England," Jens said. "My parents don't even know if I'm dead or alive."

They stood together quietly, watching the glowing remains of Molde recede in the distance. Arnesen shook out cigarettes from his crumpled package and handed them around. Rolf struck a match and they all leaned in to light up.

"Put out that bleedin' match, soldier boys! Want to get us all killed?" The shout came from a gun mount above them and was followed by laughter as they all blew out the match and looked sheepishly at each other.

"I'd say we have a lot to learn, fellows," Arnesen said. "Let's get below and try to stay out of trouble."

They got lost once as Rolf took a wrong turn, but finally found their quarters. As an officer, Captain Arnesen was given a small cabin of his own. Rolf and Jens were bunked with the junior ensigns. They were given fresh clothing, and both began to change out of their soiled and worn uniforms. Jens headed for the washroom as Rolf pulled off his tunic. He tossed his clothes down and heard a dull clink. Curious, he picked up the tunic. One gold coin dropped from the folds and rolled across the metal deck. He grabbed it and looked around. No one had seen. It was one of the Hungarian gold coins that had fallen all over him. It must have been caught up in the folds of his tunic, unnoticed.

Rolf held the coin in his hand and smiled. It felt heavy, warm, and somehow reassuring. It was only one coin; they certainly wouldn't miss it. He flipped it in the air and caught it. Yes, a good-luck piece. He'd keep it.

For luck.

Author's Note

THE STORY OF Norwegian gold, Captain Arnesen, Rolf, and Jens is continued in the first novel of the Billy Boyle series, *Billy Boyle*. In Great Britain, Lieutenant Boyle takes on his first case, which involves the Norwegian government-in-exile, a suspected German spy, and murder.

THE SECRET OF HEMLOCK HILL

■ ■ ■

"I DIDN'T EVEN know she was still alive," Deborah said, carrying another cardboard box of moldy magazines outside. "Until she died, I mean. Last time I saw Aunt Clara must've been ten years ago, and she was ancient then. Just like her house."

"What are you going to do with it?" Megan asked, tossing a garbage bag into the dumpster.

"Clean it out and sell it, I guess," Deborah said. "I sure can't live in this place; it's falling apart."

"The whole thing is strange. I mean, she died over a year ago," Megan said. "Why wait until you were twenty-one for the house to go to you?"

"No idea. Hey, thanks again for helping, and for bringing Peter and Josh along," Deborah said, brushing her long hair back from her face.

"The promise of free beer goes a long way with those two," Megan said with a grin. Peter was Megan's boyfriend, and Josh his best friend. They'd readily agreed to help clean out the old house, which had surprised Deborah. She didn't much like Megan's new boyfriend but had kept her opinion to herself. He seemed self-centered, but maybe she'd been wrong about him.

Josh came out the front door, dragging two bags of moth-eaten clothing. He threw them in the dumpster and wiped the sweat from his face with his T-shirt. "Damn, this place needs a coat of paint," he said, looking up at the two-story wooden house. The white paint was flaking.

"It needs a lot more than that," Deborah said, pointing to the sagging roof. "It looks like it's ready to cave in. What was Aunt Clara thinking, saddling me with this place? And letting it rot until my birthday?"

"Hey, everyone, look at this," Peter shouted from an upstairs window.

"What's he up to?" Megan asked.

"He found some old papers," Josh said with a shrug. "Got all excited about them, something about the Civil War."

Megan looked at Deborah and rolled her eyes. "Sorry, Deborah, but we did get a few hours of work out of him," she said.

Peter was a graduate student in American history. They all were enrolled in a nearby university, and Peter was easily distracted by anything in his area of study. Deborah had noticed the old photograph on the mantel, covered in dust. It showed a Union officer in full uniform, his hand resting on a tasseled sword. She'd planned to take that with her and clean it. Maybe it was a relative, although she didn't remember Aunt Clara ever mentioning anything about Major George Smith, the name written in faded ink on the back. It had simply been part of the furnishings, one item in an old lady's collection of dusty keepsakes.

"Peter, where are you?" Megan hollered once they went inside.

"Up here," Peter said. They found him in a guest bedroom, the very one Deborah had stayed in as a child when she'd visited. "Look at all this stuff. Letters from the Civil War. Documents from the army and old newspaper clippings. It's incredible primary source material."

Peter's face glowed with excitement. For a budding historian, this was a treasure trove. Deborah could understand a little about what Megan saw in him. He was good-looking, with long, dark curly hair that framed his face. Smart, but in her opinion, Deborah was sure Peter would take advantage of Megan. How, she didn't know. She just knew he would.

"Letters from whom?" Deborah asked, her interest piqued enough to put off work for a bit.

"Major George Smith," Peter said. "I haven't had a chance to look at everything, but one letter says he was wounded in the Battle of Antietam and sent home to recover."

"Here?" Josh asked. Maryland was home to a few major battlefields, including Antietam. If the letters were in this house, it stood to reason this is where George Smith came to rest and heal. They were less than an hour from Antietam. By car, of course.

"Was this place ever called Hemlock Hill?" Peter asked, holding up an envelope. "That's where the letters were sent."

"Yes," Deborah said, rubbing her temple as she conjured up the memory. "I remember Aunt Clara saying that was the name of the hill behind the house. There's an old cemetery up there. I guess it could have been a house name way back when."

"Well, it looks like that's where old George ended up," Peter said, pulling out another piece of paper from a box at his feet. "Here's his death certificate. Succumbed to his wounds, December 12, 1862. And an article from the local newspaper. It's nearly falling apart, but I can make out a few lines about the funeral. It says he was buried with his medals and his sword."

"Poor George," Megan said, squinting to read one of the yellowing articles.

"Where'd you find all this stuff?" Deborah asked. "I didn't see it when I went through this room."

"Under the bed," Peter said, hoisting a rectangular wooden box, about two feet wide by one foot deep, onto the table. It was thin wood, with notched pieces holding it together, not a nail in sight. He kicked the lid back under the bed with his foot. "Check it out."

"Wait a minute," Deborah said, her natural suspicion of Peter heightened by his quick footwork. He was hiding something. She reached for the lid and turned it over.

Her name was on it. Ink on wood, written in a smooth, steady hand. Not recently, but years ago by the look of it.

Deborah Collins.

"This was for me, Peter," Deborah said. "You had no right to open it, much less paw through it."

"I wasn't pawing, Deborah," he said, taking a step back and holding up his hands. "I wouldn't do that to materials like these. I'm sorry I opened it, I just wanted to see what was inside. In case it was valuable."

"Aunt Clara left it for me," she said. "So, it *is* valuable. To *me*."

"Well, I'm glad I found it, then," Peter said, taking the lid from her and putting it on the box. He made it sound like he'd magnanimously done Deborah a great favor.

"I'm going to put this in the car," Deborah said. "Then let's check out the cellar. There's still some room in the dumpster."

"Okay," Peter said, rubbing his hands together as if eager for more work. "And maybe when we're done, you'll let me look through that stuff? Maybe I could borrow it for a while. I could write a major paper with those letters."

"We'll see," Deborah said. "But first, the basement."

It was a dirt floor cellar—the earth packed hard beneath their feet. Thick timbers served to support the rafters, and they had to stoop under the low ceiling to make their way around. There was an ancient furnace, a tool bench, and pile of wooden furniture, thick with cobwebs.

"Look at these tools," Josh said. "They've got to be a hundred years old. Maybe more."

"Civil War–era, at least," Peter said, hefting a hammer. The shaft was smooth wood, well used and well cared for. "How old is this house, anyway?"

"I don't really know," Deborah said. "I think I remember Aunt Clara saying it was almost as old as the country."

"Early 1800s, I'd guess," Josh said. "I don't remember much from my history of architecture class, but that seems right. You can tell the place is old by these support beams. Basically, they used trees. You can see where they cut the branches off."

"Has it been in your family all that time?" Megan asked.

"I don't really know," Deborah said. "After my mother died, my father never wanted to visit here anymore. Clara was her sister, after all, so I always thought that was the reason."

"Clara obviously never forgot about you," Josh said. "She left you everything."

"Such as it is," Deborah said. For the first time, she felt uneasy in the house. Until this moment, it had been an oddity, a childhood memory, nothing but a distant connection. But now it was something else.

But what, exactly?

After they filled the dumpster, cold beers were pulled from the cooler and the four of them leaned against Josh's truck, staring at the house.

"You're going to need another dumpster," Megan said. "There's still a lot of junk."

"They're going to empty this one tomorrow at noon," Deborah said. "I can manage the rest; we got all of the heavy stuff today. Thanks for your help, guys."

"No problem," Peter said. "We can help tomorrow. Right, Josh?"

"Sure," Josh said with a notable lack of enthusiasm, as he drained his beer.

"Hey, let's check out that graveyard you mentioned," Peter said. "Remember where it is?"

"Yeah, I can find it," Deborah said, setting her bottle down on Josh's tailgate. "Come on." She led them around to the back of the property in the direction of a shed that looked in better shape than the house.

"Hey, more vintage tools," Josh said, opening the shed door. "Deborah, there are collectors who will pay good cash for this stuff. Don't chuck it."

"Okay, Josh, thanks," she said, circling around the shed and taking a narrow, curving path around the hillside, which brought them to a clearing at the crest.

"It's beautiful," Megan said. The graveyard overlooked rolling Maryland hills to the west. A low stone wall encompassed the burial ground, which was dotted by a dozen markers. The largest was in the center.

MAJOR GEORGE SMITH

BORN APRIL 20, 1831

DIED DECEMBER 12, 1862

"Look at this one," Josh said, standing in front of a small marker next to George's.

IN LOVING MEMORY

LUCINDA MORROW

BORN DECEMBER 11, 1841

DIED DECEMBER 11, 1862

"It's a remembrance stone," Peter said. "Not a gravestone. You can tell by the size and placement. It must have been someone close to him, maybe even his fiancée."

"Deborah," Megan said, grabbing her sleeve. "Look at this!"

"What?" Deborah said. "Oh my god!"

"She died on her twenty-first birthday," Megan said. "One day before George."

"That has to be a coincidence," Deborah said, her hand pressed flat against her mouth. "Doesn't it?"

"What do you mean?" Peter asked.

"She told you, remember?" Megan said, slapping Peter on the arm. "Aunt Clara's lawyer contacted Deborah about inheriting this property on her twenty-first birthday."

"Right, right," Peter said. "Yeah, what else could it be?"

"This is downright spooky," Deborah said, rubbing her arms as if chilled. Was there a connection between her and this long-dead woman? Why had Aunt Clara specified the age of twenty-one for her inheritance? Deborah couldn't take her eyes away from the familiar date.

"There's something else about this place," Josh said, stepping between the gravestones. "It's very well kept. You'd think an old family burying ground would be overgrown. But somebody's tended to it. Who?"

"Maybe Clara made arrangements," Megan said. "Was there anything in her will about it, Deborah?"

"I didn't really read it through," she said, standing next to her aunt's stone. "I was so astonished at getting the house that I couldn't focus on the legal details. Aunt Clara, what have you gotten me into?"

The stone was silent, revealing nothing but the fact that Clara Harland had lived eighty-one years, thirty more than her husband, Edwin.

Deborah left the small cemetery and walked down the path, trying to make sense of what she'd seen. Who was Lucinda, and was it a coincidence that she died at the same age Deborah had inherited the house? She could hear the others talking as they went to their vehicles. But her mind was clouded by questions, and she barely paid any attention. The eleventh of December haunted her thoughts.

"See you tomorrow afternoon," Megan said, as Deborah climbed into her car. "You okay?"

"Yeah. It's been a long day. Thanks, Megan," Deborah said. All she wanted was to get away and read through the legal papers, then sift through the letters and documents for any clues as to who Lucinda was.

BACK IN HER apartment, after a quick shower to wash off the grit and dust of decades, Deborah sat at her kitchen table. In front of her was the wooden box from the house. Next to that was the photograph of George from the mantel and a thick file folder from the lawyer.

The last will and testament of Clara Harland. That was where she'd start.

It all seemed like the usual legal mumbo jumbo. Pages of it. Then one phrase jumped out at her.

As Deborah Lillian Collins is the only female descendent of her line, Clara Harland hereby bequeaths all her property, the land and house commonly known as Hemlock Hill, to her on the occasion of her twenty-first birthday.

The only *female* descendent?

What about the male descendants? Deborah didn't know of any male relations, but surely there had to be someone. Why did Clara even bother to specify a woman?

There was one even stranger provision.

Deborah was prohibited from selling or transferring the property. Except to a female relative. She leafed through the document, looking for some way out of it. Then she examined the rest of the papers in the folder.

Attached to the deed was a contract with a local landscaping firm to care for the family cemetery, paid out of her estate. Not the lawn around the house, just the burial ground. She was required to maintain the plot as Clara had done.

All she found, in addition to the deed, were two previous wills.

One was that of Margaret Hauser, listing her niece, Clara McKenzie, as the recipient of the property, on the occasion of her twenty-first birthday. By the date, that was before Clara married Edwin Harland.

Strange. A tradition of handing down the property when a girl turned twenty-one? Why?

Another will, this one brittle and written in ink, showed that Margaret had inherited Hemlock Hill in 1886. On her twenty-first birthday, of course, from one Lillian Morrow Comstock.

Lillian Morrow Comstock?

Lillian was Deborah's middle name. And Lucinda Morrow had a

memorial stone next to George Smith. Comstock was obviously a married name, but not much more than an afterthought in this maternal lineage.

What was going on here? If this was the home of George Smith, how did it come into the possession of Lillian Morrow? Was she the sister of Lucinda? Deborah dove into the letters and papers, searching for an explanation. The first thing she saw was the newspaper article about the funeral. A hundred or more people had attended, a sizable crowd in a small town. According to the correspondent, George was well liked and respected, and the community was saddened not only by his death, but by the sudden death of his beloved fiancée, Lucinda Morrow, the day before he died of his wounds.

Scanning the article, written in the formal and florid manner of the times, she came to Lillian. The older sister of Lucinda, who, it was said, bore the tragedy with great dignity and strength.

There were other clippings, detailing the progress of the war and local deaths, from privates to colonels. Then, after the war, in 1868, a brief notice appeared concerning the sale of Hemlock Hill. George's mother—his father being already deceased—had sold the house to the Morrow family, stating that she would trust them to keep up the cemetery. It made no mention of where she went or why.

Or why Deborah now owned the house and land.

She moved on to the letters.

Lucinda had written to George weekly, her delicate handwriting charting out her hopes and plans for a life together after the war. She kept him informed of news from home, reporting on her visits to his parents, often in the company of Lillian. The letters were light and cheery—what a young lady might think would boost the spirits of her beloved.

There was one letter from Lillian, who apologized to George for Lucinda. She hadn't been feeling well but hoped soon to have enough strength to write. Two letters from George, written to his parents, begged for news of Lucinda. The last was postmarked two months before the battle of Antietam. It was followed by one brief note from Lucinda. Her handwriting was shaky, and the words held none of her previous joy. She ended by saying she hoped they would soon have all the time in the world together.

It was obvious Lucinda was seriously ill.

A letter from George's superior officer notified his parents of his wounding. *None too grievous, I pray*, was how the man put it. Within a month, George Smith came home. Within two months, he was dead.

As was Lucinda.

There was nothing else that could shed light on the story of George, Lucinda, and Hemlock Hill.

Deborah was exhausted. Nothing made sense. Or did it? The Morrow family obviously wanted the grave of George Smith looked after, but why give that responsibility only to the female descendants?

Was she a descendant of Lucinda? At first Deborah had wondered if she was related to George. A great-great-uncle or something? But, no, it was more likely that she'd inherited her middle name from the female side of the family. Her mother had died when she was only fifteen. Perhaps she'd planned to tell her the story but passed away before she could. Or before Deborah was old enough to understand. Her father had died a year ago, so Deborah couldn't ask him either.

She went to bed, her mind swirling with images, questions, and strangely enough, a sense of peace. A connection with the past now linked to her present. A chain of events linking the past with today and today with tomorrow.

She dreamed.

In her dreams, a soldier in a dark blue uniform stood next to a woman in a white dress. It was George, looking just as he did in the photograph. It was a wedding, a happy affair with music. Deborah waited for the bride to turn and face her as the couple walked down the aisle.

It had to be Lucinda. She smiled at Deborah, then raised her arms.

Blood dripped from her wrists.

Deborah awoke, gasping, looking around her bedroom as if she might find the rest of the wedding party.

She was alone. Alone with the certain knowledge that Lucinda had killed herself, stricken with the grief of her beloved's suffering and her own pain. Knowing George was about to draw his last breath, Lucinda had made sure she would be on the other side to greet him. To have all the time in the world together.

How could she be so certain? Because Lucinda hadn't frightened her. She showed Deborah her slit wrists to explain herself. She had graced her with a gentle smile, welcoming her into the fold. They were spiritual sisters, after all, joined together in time and place.

It was barely light, but all Deborah wanted to do was get to the cemetery. She didn't understand everything, but she did know this wasn't a haunting or anything stupid like that. It was a calling.

On the way to the house, Deborah was overcome with a sense of horror. It was as if someone had gripped her by the throat and was trying to pull her out of her own body. She barely made it to the house. She stopped the car and tried to steady her breathing. This wasn't anything like what she'd felt in the dream. This was fear and anger coursing through her body.

It was only then that she saw Josh's truck backed up beside the house.

What the hell was he doing here?

Deborah looked inside the truck. Nothing. Then she heard the noises. Grunts and curses. An argument coming down the path. Peter and Josh emerged from the woods, lugging a large canvas duffle.

"Oh no," Josh said as he spotted Deborah.

"What have you done?" Deborah said, clutching her throat.

"An archaeological dig, that's all," Peter said. "Nothing to worry about."

"You dug up George's grave," Deborah said. "That's sick. And illegal."

"We're sorry, Deborah," Josh said. "Are you okay? You don't look right."

"Never mind me. You have to put whatever you took out of that grave back," Deborah said.

"Listen, I can get a lot for this stuff," Peter said. "The sword, the brass buttons. You won't believe how well preserved everything is. We can split it."

"And you won't believe what else we found," Josh said.

Deborah felt the ground tilt around her. The horror of what these two ghouls were saying struck her like a fist, and she fell to the ground.

"Deborah, wake up," she heard Josh say. He sounded very far away. "Wake up!"

She found herself in a chair in the living room. There was plenty of room on the bare wood floor for the large two-handled canvas duffle. Peter stood over it like a victorious hunter.

"This haul is amazing," Peter said. "Wait until you see."

"*This* haul?" Deborah asked. "Have there been others?"

"Never mind," Peter said. "Are you ready for a shock?"

"There were two bodies in the coffin," Deborah said. "George Smith and Lucinda Morrow. She was wearing a white wedding gown."

"What?" Josh said, his mouth gaping open.

"How . . . how did you know that?" Peter said, his trademark self-confidence shaken.

"Let me see," Deborah said, standing and pointing to the zipper. It was strange, but she had no fear of what she was about to witness. The terror and the anger were gone, replaced by a dead-calm sense of right. "Open it."

"If that's what you want," Peter said, opening the duffle. Inside was a jumble of cloth, metal, and bone. It must have been a good-quality coffin, well sealed against the elements. Deborah touched the white silk dress and smiled as she saw Lucinda's arm draped across George's chest. It was snug in the duffel but they fit easily. Lucinda's hair was a light brown, just as in the dream.

"We had to pull them both out, they're completely intertwined," Josh said.

"Right, otherwise we'd damage the uniform," Peter said. "It's going to take some work to get it off."

Deborah saw how their limbs were entangled, like lovers in bed. In one hand, her leathery skin stretched taut over bone, Lucinda clutched a small envelope. Deborah plucked it from her grasp and stared at Peter.

"They have to go back," Deborah said.

"No. We're too far into this, Deborah," Peter said. "You asked us to do this, remember? That's what Josh and I remember. Don't get in our way, not if you know what's good for you."

"We can make a bundle off this stuff," Josh said. "The sword, his boots, the uniform, and look, that's a pearl necklace she's wearing. A three-way split is a good deal. Think about it."

"Even one original brass button is worth a lot to a collector," Peter said, reaching into the bag and ripping a button from George's uniform. "Where do you think a lot of stuff going up for auction comes from, anyway?"

"Put it back, now," Deborah said.

"Hell no. Make me," Peter said, laughing. Then his expression changed as he dropped the button. "Ow! That's hot."

"That's impossible," Josh said, picking up the brass button. "Ouch! That's red-hot."

"What's going on?" Peter said, his eyes wide in amazement.

Heat emanated from the duffle, a red-hot glow that pushed the two boys back against the wall.

"Jesus, let's get out of here," Josh shouted, and made for the door, Peter on his heels.

Deborah felt the heat but there was no fear in her heart. She moved away as the duffle began to shimmer with a pure whiteness that spread across the floorboards and climbed the walls. She backed out of the room, unable to take her eyes off the firestorm flowing out of the bag. In the doorway, she watched as the floor collapsed, furniture and ceiling beams falling into the gaping hole.

She went out the front door, stumbling backward, as fingers of fire burst out windows, shattering glass as flames enveloped the house like a giant hand crushing a child's toy.

Deborah fell to the ground and felt the heat scorch her face. She tried to move, but her mind and body were thick with shock and confusion. She pushed herself away, her heels digging into the soil as the rush of roaring flames grew louder. She raised an arm to cover her eyes as a singeing burn crept along her skin.

Deborah felt hands lift her and carry her safely away from the flames, laying her down on the grass behind her car. White silk and blue wool brushed against her skin. As the caresses of the doomed lovers faded away, these words fell like ash around her.

Thank you, dear cousin, you have kept us safe.

IT WAS ONLY much later, in her apartment, that she took the envelope from the back pocket of her jeans.

The house had collapsed in on itself, the dry wood turning to embers in the stone cellar. These old houses had no fire stops, no fireproof doors, nothing to stop the inferno. She'd stayed all day, watching the firemen hose down the smoldering remains. She'd waited until they were gone, then trudged up the hill with a shovel to fill in the looted grave. To keep the secret of Hemlock Hill safe.

Now, she held the old, brittle paper in her hands. For a century and a half, it had been held by a dead woman, close to the heart of the man she loved. Deborah knew, with a certainty that would have frightened a lesser woman, that Lucinda had taken it to her grave so that she, Deborah, could read it on this day.

She broke the seal and carefully withdrew the letter.

If these words are ever read, you will know our secret. George and I have loved each other since I was old enough to understand what love was. A cruel fate kept us apart. Not only the war that took George away, but my father's insistence that I wait until I reached the age of majority to wed. Alas, that delay brought a bullet close to George's heart and a malady into my own. The doctor told him to expect death within days. I had not much longer left. That is when I decided to defy God and take my own life, so that George and I would cross over together. A great fear of not finding him in the hereafter overwhelmed me, and I confessed my plan to Lillian. My dear sister was the messenger between George and myself. He knew of my pains and what little life I had left to live in such a pitiable state, told her his greatest wish was that neither of us would leave the other alone. He wept daily at the pain I felt, and I admit that I did as well. I never knew dying would take so long and cut to the bone so terribly. Lillian swore an oath to help me. To help us. Lillian is betrothed to Samuel Comstock, an undertaker, and a decent man. She says he will help, and I trust she knows his heart well enough. He promises to provide a stout coffin, one that will hold us for eternity, and Lillian has vowed to tend our grave on the day of my birth for as long as she lives, since it marks the beginning of the afterlife George and I shall share.

I hear her footsteps now, and I am ready. I will dress in my gown and be done with suffering and anguish. I will cross over and wait for my beloved George. He will not be far behind.

I am joyful. Please keep our secret as a sacred trust.

So, Lucinda had committed suicide. Deborah had known from her dream, but to read the confession written in Lucinda's own hand was proof. This was real. The spirits of Lucinda and George were real. They had touched her, saved her from the fire. They'd known she fought for them.

And what a sister Lillian was, to help Lucinda as she did. For a moment, Deborah wondered how they'd gotten the body in the coffin, but obviously Sam Comstock took care of that. And as a suicide, Lucinda wouldn't have been given a sanctified church burial. A quiet family affair in unhallowed ground with a weighted casket would have sufficed.

From Lillian to Margaret to Clara to Deborah, generations of women had inherited the mission of protecting the grave of George Smith and Lucinda Morrow. Deborah knew what she had to do, but it had to wait until the morning. She was exhausted, entirely spent. As she pulled off her sooty jeans, she felt something in the front pocket.

A button.

The brass button from George's uniform.

A gift from the hereafter.

IN THE WEEKS that followed, Deborah had the foundation of the house filled in, covering the charred timbers and bits of charred bone. Sod was laid down and Deborah had two hemlock trees planted next to each other. She completed the setting with a stone bench facing the trees, two intertwined hearts carved into the backrest.

That work took what savings Deborah had from the small inheritance her father had left. It took a few more years, but she managed to create a trust for the maintenance of the land, opening it to the public for hiking. She wanted company for George and Lucinda.

MORE THAN TWO decades after the hemlock trees took root, Deborah sat on the stone bench, waiting for her daughter. It was a cool, windy day. Evergreen branches danced in the breeze, and the two trees leaned into each other and touched like two lovers dancing.

Clouds moved across the sun, creating shadows beneath the trees. Or what some would think shadows. Deborah smiled as she glimpsed, from the corner of her eye, a flash of white silk and blue wool, pearls, and brass buttons. Spirits that she'd come to know, even though their presence was always unseen, hovering at the edge of perception. But as real as the button that hung on the chain around her neck.

She spotted Lucy—short for Lucinda—walking toward her, her gait brisk and athletic. Lucy had always loved Hemlock Hill Preserve from the first day Deborah brought her here as a toddler. She knew about George Smith and accepted the story of Lucinda's memorial stone. She'd explored the graveyard and the hills and trails that comprised the property. Lucy knew the land as well as anyone. But she did not yet know its secrets.

Deborah fingered the envelope in her purse. The deed. Today was Lucinda's birthday.

Her twenty-first birthday.

Lucy embraced her mother, kissing her cheek as she sat next to her. They sat in silence, listening to the whoosh of wind between the branches. Deborah searched the play of light on the greenery, hoping Lucinda and George were watching.

The wind dropped, and a pair of cardinals flew out from the branches. Birds who mate for life.

Of course, they were there.

"I have a story to tell you," Deborah said, taking her daughter's hand in hers.

VENGEANCE WEAPON

...

ANTON SCHUSTER LET the soup run down his throat and saved the few bits of rutabaga at the bottom for last. It wasn't hot; warm was the best he could expect. He licked the bowl clean, then ran his finger around it, collecting even the tiniest morsel.

His finger was dirty. He didn't care.

"Move along, you swine! This isn't a *kaffeeklatsch*!" A guard slammed his truncheon against the table, sending empty bowls bouncing and clattering. Anton shuffled into the middle of his group as it moved to the next table. Better to keep a few bodies between his own and Scharführer Kunz.

Anton watched the cooks as they poured coffee into tin cups. It was made from acorns, but everyone called it coffee, perhaps simply to keep the memory of coffee alive. Slices of brown bread, thick with mold, were handed out by the kitchen staff, men whose bodies had not yet become skeletons. Prisoners who worked with food had a chance to live. Even a few stolen bites a day meant survival. Unless you were caught.

"Hurry up, you pile of stinking rags!" Kunz shouted. Anton held his bread over the cup while he ate, capturing falling crumbs in the lukewarm liquid. Then he gulped the brew, tapping the bottom of the cup as he held it high over his mouth. He set it down on the table and formed up in a line near the door, his wooden clogs echoing against the plank flooring.

"March!" Kunz shouted, striking a prisoner who was slow getting in line. The man gasped in pain as Kunz swung his truncheon again against the prisoner's arm, smiling as he was rewarded with the crack of bone.

The prisoner collapsed, crying as he clutched his broken arm. Kunz kicked him, hard. The man tried to protect himself, curling into a ball as he spoke in Polish, the words coming out in moans drenched with tears. Anton recognized the names of the man's wife and children, long gone up in smoke and ash.

"Now 27961 cannot work," Kunz announced to the waiting line of prisoners in their dirty, worn blue-striped uniforms. "All because he was slow. Remember this lesson."

Kunz drew his pistol, shaking his head sadly as if this were such a regrettable decision forced upon him by the weight of his responsibility. He pulled the trigger, sending a bullet into the skull of Prisoner 27961. No one flinched; no one was surprised. It was another morning at Dora.

Anton Shuster marched. He kept his head down, careful not to make eye contact with any of the guards. He focused on keeping his bare feet in his clumsy wooden clogs, knowing that if one slipped off, it would mean immediate death to retrieve it. A barefoot man in the underground tunnels wouldn't last much longer either, not with the rocky floor covered with a mix of chemicals and human waste. He marched past the crematorium, past the kennels filled with snarling dogs, and through the main gate with the sign announcing what this place was.

KZ LAGER DORA-MITTELBAU

Dora. Dora meant death. Death for the slaves who worked here, building rockets for the Nazis. Death for those in London, Paris, and wherever else the V-2 rockets targeted.

"When do you think the Allies will get here?" Jerzy asked as he walked next to Anton.

"Who knows?" Anton whispered, checking for Kunz. Talking wasn't forbidden on the kilometer walk to the tunnels, but you never knew with the SS sergeant. "They're taking their time about it. They haven't even bombed this place yet."

"Good weather for it," Jerzy said, glancing at the blue sky. "But be careful what you wish for. They'll probably bomb our barracks and never even notice the tunnels."

"I'd take my chances with an American bomb," Anton said. "Better than a German bullet." It still felt odd to Anton, talking about Germans. He was German. Born in Stuttgart, where he worked as a machinist. Until the racial laws, and then every day he became less of a German and more of a Jewish problem to be dealt with. He and his parents, along with his sister, had been arrested in a roundup. They were delivered to Buchenwald, a labor camp.

Within a week, his father was killed, hung with ten others in retaliation for an attack on a guard. Weeks later, Anton heard his mother had committed suicide after his sister had died. He had nothing left, nothing to look forward to other than a trip up the chimney of the crematorium. A bomb would be a blessing.

"What day is it?" Jerzy asked.

Anton shrugged. "What month is it?" He knew it was 1945. Early spring by the hint of warmth in the air.

"April. I think," Jerzy said, after some thought. "I don't know how much longer I can last."

Anton and Jerzy had been taken from Buchenwald to Dora six months ago. The SS wanted skilled labor to replace prisoners who had been worked to death, and their camps provided them. Jerzy was an electrician from Warsaw, while Anton had graduated technical school and worked for several years producing scientific instruments before all Jews had been dismissed from the firm.

At Dora, their skills were in demand. They were deemed specialists, which only meant their labors were slightly less backbreaking than the transport crew's. Those were the prisoners who carried aluminum tanks or other heavy parts into the tunnels. Transport workers were much more expendable, their lives worth nothing.

"This must be what the gates of hell look like," Jerzy said as the tunnel entrance loomed before them, a dark, gaping hole in the mountain. Rather, two dark holes, both with railroad tracks leading inside. Each tunnel was two thousand meters long, connected by a series of cross tunnels like rungs on a ladder. Ten meters wide and nearly as high, the tunnels were the product of industrial dynamite and slave labor, prisoners who had been worked to death to create this refuge from Allied bombers. Heavy machinery and parts went in one end. V-2 rockets came out the other.

Cranes and hoists hovered over the entrance as hundreds of men marched underneath them and into the depths. The stone walls dripped water. The glare of harsh overhead lights cast strange shadows of men and machines. The echoing noise of metal on metal shredded the senses and left prisoners numb to all but the most necessary tasks.

Work. Live.

"March left, Hall Three," Kunz shouted. Other guards joined in and moved the line of prisoners, hundreds of them, into the connecting tunnel that held offices for German civilian workers and the SS. This was the realm of scientists, engineers, draftsmen, and the high-ranking SS officers who ran the V-2 program.

It was unusual to be brought into Hall Three. Unusual was not good at Dora.

"What do they want?" Jerzy whispered once they were formed into rows facing the steel walkway that ran the length of the tunnel, two meters high. The offices had been dug deep into the rock, and civilians and the SS were strolling onto the walkway, waiting for something to happen.

"Look, that's von Braun," Jerzy said. "The dark-haired one in the double-breasted suit."

"He's the head of the V-2 program, isn't he?" Anton whispered.

"Top dog," Jerzy said. "Wernher von Braun himself. That's Arthur Rudolph next to him."

Anton knew Rudolph. He was head of the V-2 production line at Dora. If things didn't run smoothly along the line, there was hell to pay. Standing right behind Rudolph was the man the devil himself sent to collect his due.

Sturmbannführer Gerhard Richter. Richter was the worst of two worlds, a dedicated SS fanatic and an expert in rocket assembly. Unlike von Braun and Rudolph, who wore their Nazi party badges on their lapels, Richter always wore his full SS uniform with its death's-head insignia. Rudolph and von Braun were aloof, men who didn't get their hands dirty. But Richter enjoyed his work, both the scientific aspect and the application of pain and suffering.

Rudolph nodded to Richter, who stepped forward and gripped the railing, looking down at the assembled workers. Anton noticed von Braun edge away from the two men and lean against an office window, his arms crossed.

"Sabotage!" Richter snarled. "Yesterday a rocket was found with electrical circuits cut through. The prisoner who did this was discovered and put to death. That was simple. But how to prevent further acts of senseless disruption?"

Richter snapped his fingers. Guards lowered a hoist with four dangling chains. Anton had seen it used before, to hold large machine parts for inspection by the civilian engineers.

"Four of you will be hanged today," Richter said. "If there is another attempt at sabotage, it will be forty. Remember this lesson."

Two prisoners were immediately dragged to the chains, then a third. Kunz walked toward Anton, who felt sweat trickle down his back. He fought the urge to flee, waiting for Kunz to pick someone else, anyone else.

"Come, Prisoner 20745," Kunz growled. He grabbed Jerzy by the collar and pushed him toward the chains. "You are invited to a dance."

Anton waited for the screams, waited for men to beg for their lives, but they never came. The silence was even worse. Vacant eyes stared at the crowd as chains were fixed around the men's necks. Jerzy, always talkative, always hopeful, kept his eyes closed.

"Watch!" Richter shouted. "Anyone who looks away will be next!

See the price of disobedience." With a flick of his wrist, he signaled a guard to raise the chain assembly. A hydraulic whine pierced the chamber as the chains grew taut, then lifted the four condemned men off the ground.

They flailed at the air, dug their fingers at steel links biting into their necks, struck each other in a frenzied dance, legs held high as if trying to climb invisible steps leading to sanctuary.

They twitched and twisted, gagged and voided, giving up their struggles slowly, until one by one, they went limp.

"Now get to work! You've wasted too much time already!" Richter folded his arms across his chest and admired his handiwork, as did the other SS. Most of the civilians nodded their approval, but some, like von Braun, studiously avoided looking at the corpses and slipped back into their offices without comment.

Kunz and the other guards moved the columns of prisoners out of the hall. It was a confused process, as everyone skirted the area beneath the hanged men. Anton looked at Jerzy, feeling he owed him that much. But the contorted face didn't look like his friend.

Anton wondered what Jerzy had looked like before the camps. Full faced? Chubby, perhaps? And what did he look like now, wherever death had taken him? Who was really the lucky one?

As Anton marched past the walkway, he caught a glimpse of a new civilian worker. He wore a white jacket and was holding a handkerchief to his mouth. Richter was clapping him on the back and laughing, seeming to enjoy the man's discomfort.

Interesting, Anton thought as he neared his workbench. Dependability was a prisoner's friend. Some food—not much—every day. You could depend on it. Brutality and killings, sadly, were dependable too. This was all part of the dependable terror of Dora. But a new face among the bosses here, that was unusual. Most of the SS and engineers had been here since Anton arrived. He knew their moods, their routines, whom to avoid, and whom to fear. A new man changed all that.

Anton began his work. His job was to remachine parts that had not met specifications due to damage in shipping or changing work orders. It was skilled labor, and it kept him alive. He focused on his tools and the turbine pump on his workbench. He understood he was fine-tuning death, ensuring an accurate delivery of a warhead to innocent civilians. He also understood that others would take his place if he refused to work.

Work meant life.

Life meant survival.

Survival meant revenge.

The Nazis called the V-2 rocket a vengeance weapon. Retaliation for the Allied bombing of German cities. Anton crafted his survival to become a human vengeance weapon. He would live. He would find Gerhard Richter when this was over.

He would kill him. For Jerzy and all the others. For his family, murdered by other Richters in this insane world.

The thought comforted him as he adjusted the turbine components and tested the tolerances. He'd undergone his own test today, and deep in his heart, he knew his tolerance for revenge was as precise and sharp as the smooth steel edges at his fingertips.

Anton's shift was twelve hours. Tins of soup were brought around for the midday meal, and it was his only chance to get off his feet. Some days he dreamed of not getting up. Letting Kunz beat him until he grew tired of the game and killed him. There was always a way to find death at Dora.

Life was harder, but Anton forced himself to stand and get to work on two servomotors, electrical-hydraulic devices that stabilized the flight of the rocket. An easy job, but his legs throbbed with pain as he began his seventh hour standing at the workbench. He let out a sigh and let his elbows rest on the bench for a moment.

He stood straighter and worked intently as he heard voices approaching.

"This will be your section, Ehrlich," Richter said. "I want a daily report on the repair and retooling of components, do you understand?"

"Yes, understood," Ehrlich said. Anton risked a quick glance as the men drew closer. Ehrlich was the new engineer he'd seen that morning.

"These five halls are devoted to remachining, of components, mainly," Richter said. "About fifty workbenches, eh, Kunz?"

"Fifty-four, *Sturmbannführer*," Kunz said, as the three of them walked behind Anton. "Not too many problems with this lot. A bit slow at times, but we know how to motivate them."

"Where is this worker?" Ehrlich asked. Anton guessed he was looking at Jerzy's workbench.

"At the end of a chain," Kunz said, giving out a sharp, rheumy laugh.

"Requisition a new one," Richter said to Kunz. "Electrician. I want him in place in the morning. Be quick about it."

"Sir!" Kunz responded with a snap of his heels. Out of the corner of his eye, Anton saw Kunz scurry off. Another figure moved closer, but in the glare of overhead lights, Anton couldn't make out who it was.

"How are you, Ehrlich? Finding your way around the place?" It was Arthur Rudolph. Stocky and balding, he had twin tufts of hair that sprouted out from behind his ears. He sounded jovial, like a friendly boss welcoming a new employee.

"Yes, sir," Ehrlich said. "The *Sturmbannführer* was showing me my area of responsibility."

"I'm glad you're here," Rudolph said. "We've been trying to obtain your services for months now. Lucky for us the Heinkel aircraft plant decided to let you go."

"The plant was one hundred kilometers east of Berlin, sir," Ehrlich said. "You might want to thank the Russians."

"No defeatist talk is allowed here," Richter said, sharply. "Be careful with your tongue."

"Don't worry, Gerhard, our wonder weapons will turn the tide soon enough," Rudolph said. "Ehrlich will be a help. Besides being a scientist, he has developed methods to increase production through quality testing. Let him review the work here and formulate recommendations. Give him anything he needs."

"Yes, sir," Richter said.

Anton thought he could read irritation in Richter's clipped response.

"Your identity papers are in order, I trust?" Rudolph asked. "It wouldn't do for our friends in the Gestapo to question your old address. Young men your age out of uniform and far from home are being hanged as deserters. You've been given living quarters, I trust?"

"Yes, in Hochstedt," Ehrlich said. "And my papers are in order. My new address has been registered with the police."

"Good, good. And, Ehrlich, waste no time. We need to launch more V-2s. Many more." Rudolph left, leaving the two men behind.

"I don't have time to take you around to fifty-four workbenches," Richter said. "Do you wish an escort?"

"I don't think that will be necessary. From the looks of these men, they don't pose much of a threat," Ehrlich said. "What languages have we here?"

"German, French, and Polish for the most part," Richter said. "The transport workers are all Russians and Ukrainians, but you have no need to speak to them. I will leave you to it."

"You," Ehrlich said, moving next to Anton. "Do you speak German?"

"I am German, sir," Anton said, keeping his eyes on the servomotor. "If that is permitted to say."

"I only care about your work, Prisoner 39482. Tell me what kind of mechanisms they bring you." They fell into a conversation about missile components and the damage done in shipping from subcontractors across Germany. From other camps too, as far as Anton knew. Ehrlich asked a lot of questions, and Anton was able to supply most of the answers.

"You were trained as a machinist?" Ehrlich said when he'd finished writing in his notebook.

"Yes, sir," Anton said, and told him about his work. As he spoke, he realized he was looking at Ehrlich. Kunz or Richter would have beat him for daring to meet their eyes. He had to be careful with this man. He didn't know the rules. Anton turned his eyes to his tools, willing Ehrlich to understand and unwilling to say anything directly.

The two men were the same size, except for Anton's emaciated frame, of course. Perhaps the same age, although Anton knew his time in the camps must have aged him. This successful, well-fed man could be living the life stolen from Anton. Before his firm fired all its Jewish workers, he was in line for a promotion. He would have been a manager. Someone to make something of himself.

"One more thing," Ehrlich said. "Do you speak any languages? In case I need help translating."

"Only English, sir. I studied it in school."

"Well, we won't need that here, will we?" Ehrlich said, enjoying a chuckle.

Not yet, Anton thought, hoping the wish in his mind had not progressed to his face.

THE BOMBERS CAME the next morning. Air raid sirens wailed as the prisoners were being marched into the tunnels. Anton ran for the entrance, pushing and yelling as the column of marching men dissolved into a frenzied rush to gain safety within the mountain. Kunz and the other guards, desperate to be under solid rock, beat workers who were in their way. The droning of aircraft engines merged with the sound of sirens. Anton glanced upward once more before he entered the tunnel. Bombers, a stream of them clear against the bright blue sky.

Civilians, guards, and prisoners panicked, their screams echoing against the walls. As far as Anton knew, there had never been an air raid drill. No one knew what to do, except for the obvious. Go deeper underground.

Shattering explosions hurled shock waves into the tunnel, knocking men to the ground and increasing the panic. The earth shuddered with each hit, and Anton felt the fear of entombment grab at his gut. He told himself the solid rock couldn't collapse.

Could it?

He fought through the crowd to reach his workbench where at least he'd be safe from the punishing truncheons. Work. Live. Survive.

He held on to his tools as the bombing continued, the sound of explosions finally moving away.

"Get to work, you lazy swine!" Kunz bellowed, strutting along the tunnel, striking any prisoner who wasn't busy at his job. Anton's hands shook as he handled the servomotor, and he gripped the device harder to steady himself. He couldn't die now. Not from bombs, not from Kunz's savagery. He was a missile, on a course set for retribution. How, he did not know. But they hadn't killed him yet, not the Nazis, not the Allies. One day, he would be the killer.

Four hours into his shift, he heard Kunz shouting. This time the guard's anger wasn't directed at a prisoner. It was Ehrlich on the receiving end.

"Shut up about the bombing, Ehrlich!" Kunz said. "Unless you want to be hanged as a defeatist traitor."

"But what is the plan? Are we to wait for the Allies to arrive?" Ehrlich said, his voice shaky with fear. He trailed Kunz farther into the tunnel, their argument fading away.

The Allies. Would the SS let the camp be liberated? Anton doubted it. He needed a way to survive, a way to avoid evacuation. He spent the rest of his shift thinking it through, observing everything going on around him. He delivered the repaired servomotors, walking through the final assembly area where sections of the V-2 were joined together.

The next day, something was wrong. The guards were on edge. When Anton arrived at his workbench, there was only a single servomotor for him to work on. Richter stormed through the tunnel, shouting orders, Kunz in his wake. Transport workers began rolling carts filled with parts toward the entrance. Six prisoners struggled with a tail fin assembly, carrying it by hand, hectored by guards every step of the way.

Desperation was thick in the air.

Ehrlich approached Anton. The engineer's eyes were wide with fear.

"What is your name?" Ehrlich whispered.

"Prisoner 39482," Anton replied, keeping his gaze focused on his hands.

"No, your name, damn you. Tell me."

"Anton Schuster." It felt strange to say it out loud, as if it were the name of a ghost.

"Anton, you must hide. Within the hour they will evacuate the tunnels. They are taking us to another camp. Bergen-Belsen. Not a good place," Ehrlich said in a hushed tone.

"Everyone?" Anton said.

"As many prisoners as can be loaded onto boxcars, I've heard. So not all. They will leave no one living, of course."

"Why are you telling me?"

"I will hide as well. When everyone is gone, you and I will go to the Americans. They will want our services, I am sure. You understand English, you can speak for me. I never harmed anyone. You can tell them."

"This is very dangerous," Anton said. "Are you trying to trick me?"

"Believe me, Bergen-Belsen is even more dangerous. When they announce the evacuation of the tunnel, hide. When everyone is gone, we will meet back here. I'll help you get away, and you help me with the Americans, yes?"

"Are they close?" Anton asked.

"Richter said two or three days. No one really knows. Well?"

"Yes," Anton said. "I will hide. Where will you be?"

"It's best we don't discuss it," Ehrlich said. "Stay hidden at least two hours. I have a feeling Richter will have the tunnels searched. He trusts no one."

"An excellent idea," Anton said, eyeing the workers moving parts out of the tunnel. They all looked nervous.

"Here," Ehrlich said, checking to be sure no one was looking. Anton found a piece of hard cheese in his hand. "Remember, I've been good to you."

The cheese went into his mouth. No one had been that good to him in a long time. Perhaps Ehrlich could be trusted. Anton finished his work on the servomotor and carried it to the assembly area. As soon as he set it on the receiving table, the public address system blared out a message.

Attention. Attention. All prisoners report to the parade ground. All prisoners report immediately to the parade ground. All skilled workers are to bring their tools.

This was it. The evacuation, just as Ehrlich had said.

The announcement created instant confusion, and soon the guards waded in, pushing and shoving the workers toward the entrance. Anton broke out of the flow of prisoners to make his way down the connecting tunnel to his workbench.

"You! This way!" It was Richter. His pistol was drawn.

"Sir, I must get my tools as ordered." Anton looked at the ground, his hands clasped together as if beseeching Richter.

"Hurry. We're going to seal these tunnels with explosives. Get your tools on the double!"

"Yes, sir," Anton said, sounding as obedient as he could manage with his heart thumping against his chest. He stopped as soon as he turned the corner, waiting for the rush of workers to pass by the connecting tunnel. As soon as the crowd went by, he looked down the way he'd come.

From the assembly area.

He ran, hoping there was no rearguard SS patrol. A prisoner rushed out from behind a stack of wooden crates, his eyes darting about for some safe refuge. In a flash, he was gone. Anton kept moving, stopping only to snatch a coiled length of rope from a peg. Then he came to them.

Six V-2 rockets. Minus the warhead and tail fin assembly. Set upright, one next to the other, each nearly ten meters high. Ready for the final inspection before the warhead and tail fin sections were fitted on in the next chamber.

A rolling ladder stood next to the first rocket, reaching two-thirds of the way to the top. Anton maneuvered the ladder and climbed as high as he could, then grabbed for an anchor hook dangling from a winch.

He missed, then tried again. This time he caught it.

Hanging from the hook and refusing to think about how Jerzy had been hanged from one, he pushed off from the ladder. It went skittering backward, wobbled, and fell over with a clatter. He couldn't think about anyone hearing it. He had to make this work.

With what strength he had, he swung on the cable, aiming for the top of the second rocket. Once, twice, three times he failed.

On the fourth try, he managed to hook one foot over the top rim. He struggled to pull himself forward, reaching out with one hand to grasp the rim and pull himself over. His hand trembled as the steel bit into his foot. He pulled harder, willing his weakened muscles to work.

He grasped the edge, hoisted his leg over, and managed to pull his body into the small space where the missile controls and warhead would go. The joint ring around the rim gave him a small bit of cover, but who would even look up here?

He let the hook go, watching it swing back and forth until its momentum was spent. He curled his back against the steel plate, keeping as much of his body out of sight as possible. Given how thin he'd become, it wasn't difficult.

He tried to rest, but lying atop a large canister of liquid oxygen and another of alcohol was less than comforting. He listened for footsteps and was rewarded by the click of bootheels on stone within minutes.

"Come out. We know you're hiding. Come out now! The charges are set, and we will seal the tunnels in thirty minutes! Come out! Save yourselves!" He didn't recognize the voice. He didn't believe the voice either.

Two hours, Ehrlich had said. Anton tried to gauge the passage of time, but in the silence of the tunnel it was impossible. When he thought it was safe, he stood and looked in each direction. No movement, no sound.

He tied the rope to a pipe running along the ceiling above him. Then he tossed it over the side, near the wall, hopefully out of sight. He wrapped a rag around each palm and grasped the rope, letting himself slide down. One clog fell off and clattered to the ground. He retrieved it as soon as he descended, straining to listen for approaching footsteps.

Nothing.

He moved carefully through the tunnel, keeping to the shadows at the edge of the wall, hiding behind crates and abandoned equipment. Twenty yards from his workbench, he melted into the darkness behind a storage cabinet. No need to announce his presence. Ehrlich seemed aboveboard, but there was no reason to take chances. No reason to rush.

"Halt!"

It was Kunz.

"Halt, or I'll shoot, you bastard!"

Anton was in shock. Was Kunz talking to him? How could he know?

"*Scharführer*, I was returning to my office. I forgot some important papers." It was Ehrlich. He hadn't been careful enough, but he was playing the hand he was left with well.

"You haven't been seen anywhere," Kunz said. "Richter sent me to root you out. He knew you'd hide and try to escape your duty to the Reich."

"No, not at all," Ehrlich said. "I will retrieve the papers and be right back."

Anton could hear Ehrlich turn, his heels scraping against rough stone.

A shot shattered the air. Ehrlich fell forward, his head hitting the ground next to Anton's hiding place. Ehrlich's eyes were open, fixed on Anton. But he saw nothing. Kunz's bullet had taken him in the back of the head.

Anton stifled a gasp. Violent death was commonplace at Dora, but one Aryan German killing another was unexpected.

Anton was sure his breathing was loud enough to alert Kunz to his presence. He worked to stay in control and keep his breaths coming in a sure and quiet pattern. Then he heard Kunz stalk off. He waited.

He waited even longer, unwilling to make the same mistake Ehrlich had. Which gave him enough time for an idea.

When he was sure no one was around, he dragged Ehrlich's body behind the storage cabinet. He began to take the man's clothing off. It was harder than he'd imagined. But not as hard as dressing Ehrlich in his filthy prison garb.

When he was done, Prisoner 39482 was dead.

Anton opened Ehrlich's wallet. Correction, *his* wallet.

Gustav Ehrlich. A fine name. Identity card, cash, house key, everything he'd need. He cinched the belt as tight as he could. It wouldn't do for his pants to fall down if he was stopped for a Gestapo identity check.

Next stop was the infirmary. It was near the engineers' offices, a place for minor cuts and injuries to be patched up. Anyone seriously injured was simply shot, but it was efficient to take care of a cut finger. Anton found a roll of gauze and wrapped it around his lower face to disguise his emaciated features. He noticed a clean lab coat and switched it with Ehrlich's, which was decorated on the back with a spray of red and gray matter.

Anton walked out of the tunnel.

The silence was eerie. Strange. He walked toward the main gate, alone. He hadn't been alone in months, and it unnerved him. But not as much as what he found at the parade ground.

Bodies. Dozens. Hundreds. The prisoners who were left behind, mowed down by machine guns. Spent shell casings glittered in the sun, displayed in arcs marking the firing positions of the killers.

Anton looked away. He had to steel himself, to remember, but not become overwhelmed. He needed strength, the strength of spirit as well as of body. He didn't have much of either. He walked out of the gate and into the world beyond Dora.

At the main road, a sign pointed to Hochstedt. Four kilometers. He had to make it, but it felt impossible. His exhaustion was all-encompassing. Hunger haunted him, and his legs burned with every step, his feet sore in the unfamiliar shoes. An automobile sped by, nearly knocking him into a ditch by the narrow lane. A farmer with a horse-drawn cart turned onto the road from a field and offered Anton a lift.

"All gone, are they?" the farmer asked, crooking a thumb in the direction of the camp. "Good riddance, I say."

Anton didn't know if he meant the SS or the prisoners. He didn't care. He agreed with the man as he climbed into the back of the empty cart. He knew his body stank, and he didn't want to risk the farmer identifying him as an escaped prisoner, whether he was friendly or not.

"Were you injured in the bombing?" asked the farmer, giving a look over his shoulder.

"Yes. They gave me medical leave," Anton said. "That's why I didn't go with the others." The farmer nodded and gave his reins a snap.

They entered Hochstedt. It was a small village with a street of shops and two-story houses surrounded by a smattering of buildings on two cross streets. Anton told the farmer a friend was meeting him here to give him a ride home. He hoped the man didn't ask where that was, since Anton had no idea of what was close to Dora. He only wanted to disguise the fact that this was his destination.

"Have you heard anything about the Americans?" Anton asked as he stood on the pavement.

"Yes. I hear they have a lot of cigarettes and chocolate," the farmer said, his tone noncommittal. "Goodbye, friend."

Seelochweg 42 read the address on Gustav Ehrlich's identity card. There weren't that many streets in Hochstedt, and he found Seelochweg after a short walk. Number 42 was a white stucco two-story building with a central hallway and a narrow staircase leading upstairs. He found Ehrlich's name above a mailbox in the lobby. Room 201.

Before taking the stairs, Anton listened. He didn't want to run into anyone. He heard muffled noises from within the ground floor rooms, but nothing from above. With an unexpected burst of energy, he took the steps two at a time, pausing only to get his bearings at the top. Room 201 was to the right. He moved across the threadbare carpet, each footfall as quiet as he could make it.

His hand shook as he held the key. He dropped it, grabbed it, and tried again. With a sharp *clack*, the lock opened. He pushed on the latch, entered the room, closed and locked the door.

It was dizzying. An easy chair and a small couch. A radio on a wooden stand. Windows. Anton stood, swaying in his weakness, unable to move. He wept at the ordinariness of the small apartment. He went to the windows and looked outside. The street was quiet. Was everyone waiting for the Americans?

Anton made his way to the kitchen table. He sat and rested his head in his hands. He didn't know what to do first. Finally, he decided upon water. He unwound the bandage covering his face and turned on the tap in the kitchen sink. He cupped his hands.

No, they were filthy. He opened a cupboard and grasped a glass with both hands, frightened of dropping it. He filled it with cold water. He drank.

Cold, clean water. A miracle.

He looked at his hands again and knew what he had to do next.

The bathroom. He ran the water in the bathtub and stripped off Gustav's clothing. He looked at his naked body, skeletal thin and caked with filth. He was embarrassed.

When he looked in the mirror, he gasped. Who was this? A man or a wraith? His cheekbones were sharp edges, dark bags were draped under his eyes. Bruises and scabs dotted his shaven head. No, it couldn't be him. That was not Anton.

Of course not. That was Gustav, in the process of being reborn. It was much easier to think of it that way. He eased himself into the water, which was only lukewarm, but it still felt like a long-forgotten luxury. He scrubbed himself, sloughing off things he didn't care to think about. He emptied the tub and filled it again. It was cold water this time, but it didn't matter.

When he was done, he cleaned the bathtub, filled it again, and dumped in Ehrlich's clothing, hoping that would drown the lice. In the bedroom, he found pajamas and a robe.

He was clean. Or at least cleaner than he'd been since arriving at Dora. Now it was time for food. He explored the kitchen. There was bread in the breadbox. Potatoes in a drawer. Cheese, the same sort Ehrlich had given him. Was that just this morning?

Anton found a jar of plum preserves. He cut the bread and spread the sweet jam across it. He ate, each bite a delight to his starved senses. He drank water and felt his body absorb it like a plant after a drought.

The bed called to him. So did the tins of food in the cupboard, but he had no energy to open them. He stumbled to the bedroom, feeling half-drunk. The bed felt like a cloud.

When he awoke, it was light. The next morning? He heard vehicles below in the street. Looking out the window, he saw trucks filled with German troops. Which direction were they going? They were heading toward the rising sun, to the east. That was bad news. Reinforcements to hold off the American advance. He sat down on the kitchen chair and sighed. How long could he last hiding in here?

Anton drank water and watched the road. The soldiers looked downcast. Defeated. Could the Americans sweep them aside? Maybe. Then he looked at the sun. It was setting, not rising. He'd slept a full day! Which meant the Germans were pulling back, retreating! Anton wanted to shout, to dance, to celebrate the end of his war.

He did all that in his mind, standing quietly as he watched the column of beaten troops pass beneath him. Across the street, a blood-red Nazi banner hung limply from a window. All Anton needed was time.

He dressed and made coffee. It wasn't real coffee, but it was better than the brew they'd been given in Dora. It contained roasted barley, oats, chicory, and acorn meal according to the package. He ate bread and cheese, chewing slowly and letting the food settle in his shrunken stomach. He'd heard stories of prisoners stealing food and gorging themselves, only to sicken violently. He couldn't chance that. Besides, he needed to conserve what food he had. That was the gift Dora had given him. He could survive on very little.

Anton slept. He awoke hungry, aware of the unusual notion that he could eat whenever he wanted. He found a withered onion, diced two potatoes, fried them, and stood over the skillet, inhaling the fragrance of his own cooking.

He ate, then sat by the window. The military traffic had lessened, and one lone civilian pedaled by on a bicycle. It was time to make a plan. He went into the kitchen and considered his food supply. He would eat the bread and potatoes first, before they spoiled. Then the tins of soup, goulash, and peas. A week's worth of food, perhaps?

He would need more. He counted out the money in Ehrlich's wallet. Seventy marks, a tidy sum. He hunted through drawers in the kitchen until he found an envelope with ration cards. They'd allow him to buy bread, margarine, jam, potatoes, and even meat. Anton had no idea if this was a normal quantity of ration coupons. It could be the SS gave their scientists more. He'd have to be careful when he used them and not draw attention to himself.

He turned on the radio, keeping the volume low. The music was thundering Wagnerian stuff, the kind of thing the Nazis loved. He turned it off and began exploring the apartment more thoroughly. In a closet by the door, he found boxes full of books and periodicals.

Scientific periodicals as well as general interest magazines. Amateur rocketry. Statistical quality control. Advances in engineering. Astronomy. Rocket engine thrust analysis. The books looked like university textbooks, dull and heavy. But the periodicals were full of the latest advances over the last ten years.

This is how Anton would spend his time waiting for the Americans.

He piled the periodicals on the table and put the books back in the closet. As he stacked the boxes, he spotted a thick envelope on a shelf in the closet. Sitting on the couch, he went through it. Ehrlich's official transfer to Dora. Travel orders from the SS. Documentation for the local police and Gestapo. A definition of his duties and responsibilities, detailing how he was to increase efficiency in the retooling and repair of V-2 parts. There were reports and technical drawings from the Heinkel factory where Ehrlich had worked, most of them concerning improvements to the jet engine for a fighter plane.

At the bottom was an organizational chart of the Dora SS and scientists.

Wernher von Braun was at the top. Then Arthur Rudolph, with

Gerhard Richter right beneath him. Ehrlich's name was not listed, but surely, he was represented by one of the boxes designated Engineering Specialist. Slave laborers were nowhere to be seen.

One sheet of paper fell to the floor. Anton grabbed it, spotting Richter's name. It was an alphabetical list of the top scientists at Dora. With addresses and telephone numbers. It was dated three days ago and included Gustav Ehrlich, although it showed no telephone number. There was no apparatus in the apartment.

But Anton had Richter's address. He might not be there now, but after the war, he'd certainly want to go home. Anton smiled as he folded the paper and hid it away.

For the next two days, Anton slept, ate, and read. He took in the technical data like a sponge. This was the life he might have lived if not for the Nazis and their war. His family may have been gone, but he could carry on, in spite of all that was done to them.

He'd avoided looking in the mirror again. But when Anton decided it was time to go out and buy bread and a few other things, he chanced it.

The first shock was his hair. It was growing in white.

The next was his color. His cheeks were almost pink, and the bags under his eyes were less puffy. Food and rest were healing him. He found a razor, lathered his face, and gave himself a shave. His hand didn't shake, a good sign.

He wound the bandage around his head, covering his jaw. He doubted anyone had become acquainted with Ehrlich in the few days he'd been in residence, but it gave him confidence to hide his face. Luckily, it was raining, so he could turn up his collar to further the disguise. Donning a fedora, he left the apartment.

He felt oddly serene as he walked down the hallway. This was now his apartment building. He was not an interloper; he belonged here. If someone walked by him, he'd give the appropriate greeting. Just right for a shy, absentminded scientist.

Out on the street, he waited while two trucks pulling artillery pieces rumbled by. One of the soldiers waved, perhaps drawn to the bandage that marked him as war wounded, even as a civilian.

Gustav Ehrlich waved back. Anton Schuster hoped the truck would miss a turn, roll off the road, and burn.

It was only a few minutes' walk to the bakery. Anton handed over his ration coupons and asked for two loaves of black bread. There was no problem. He paid, held the door open for an elderly woman, and left.

Another truck towing heavy artillery rolled by, but Anton avoided looking at the soldiers.

At the greengrocer's, the only thing available in any quantity was potatoes. Anton filled a small sack, then looked around for jam or margarine. There was none, and the woman in front of him was buying potatoes and nothing else. Maybe it was common knowledge that nothing else was available, so he didn't risk asking.

"You're not from around here?" the man at the counter asked as he tore off the ration coupons.

"Not originally, no," Anton said. "I came here for work." He nodded in the general direction of Dora, hoping that would be enough.

"We don't get much trade from you fellows," the man said. "Wish we did. But they've pulled out, haven't they?"

"Most, yes," Anton said, clinging to his sack of potatoes. "I need a few more days' rest."

"I see," the man said, his eyebrows knotted in a way that said he didn't. At that moment, the snarling sound of fighter aircraft diving low arose from outside. Anton dashed into the street, swiveling his head to find the source. The noise increased until two dark shadows passed overhead, moving faster than he could've imagined.

Twin explosions sounded, and the fighters pulled away. Smoke blossomed from the road beyond the village.

Good, Anton thought. *Serves the bastards right.* He glanced back at the shop to see the grocer at the window. Eyeing the aircraft, or him?

Anton shook his head as if saddened by the violent incursion of the Allied planes. He walked as calmly as he could down the street, away from his apartment building, taking the long way around in case that inquisitive fellow was watching.

The next two days were calm. Artillery sounded in the distance. The Nazi banner across the street vanished. Anton ate, his hunger increasing as his system became accustomed to food. He read, absorbing information as his body absorbed steaming soup.

One evening a white sheet appeared in the window where the Nazi symbol once was so proudly displayed. Anton smiled. The new flag of Germany.

The next morning, as he was brewing his ersatz coffee just after dawn, he caught sight of four German soldiers walking down the road. One wore a bloodstained bandage wrapped around his head. They all glanced back down the road, then broke into a run. A machine gun let loose a burst, bullets zinging against the pavement.

The four soldiers dropped their weapons and held up their hands. Two jeeps came into sight, braking to a halt. Soldiers jumped out and roughly searched the Germans.

American soldiers. Liberation.

Anton collapsed into a chair. So many people had died. So many brutally worked to death. Yet he was here, watching American soldiers in the street. He should feel something. Joy, relief, anticipation.

He felt nothing. He sliced bread. He ate and drank. He read journals.

He waited.

The sight of Americans in the street became normal. People gathered to watch them, curious. A column of German prisoners was marched through the village, headed to a POW camp. Without their helmets, weapons, and gear, they looked like scarecrows, their open coats flapping in the breeze.

Something would happen, Anton was sure. What, he had no idea.

He sat in his chair, reading, like a V-2 rocket ready to launch, waiting only for the right target.

Days passed. Anton fell into a routine, a routine that transformed him into Gustav Ehrlich a little bit more each day. His skin was turning a healthy pink. There was flesh under his cheekbones. He learned something from every article he read, the world of rocketry blossoming in his mind as he turned the pages. He recognized the importance of the components he'd repaired, understood how they all worked together. He saw the machined parts as more than simply steel. They were keys to unlocking the heavens.

He got used to his pure white hair and Gustav's clothing. He and Gustav became one. A new man, born of war and murder, as thirsty for knowledge as revenge.

IT WAS A warm spring morning when the Jeeps parked under his window. Two American soldiers went around to the rear of the building. Three others stomped up the stairs, the sound of their bootheels loud and harsh. One of them pounded on the door.

"Open up!" The command was forceful, spoken in German with only a trace of an accent.

"Come in," Anton said, in precise English, as he opened the door. Two soldiers brushed past him, looking around the small apartment. "I am alone here."

"Are you Gustav Ehrlich?" asked the American. By his insignia, he looked to be an officer.

"Yes, I am Gustav Ehrlich."

They were brusque and businesslike, but not mean. They told him to pack one small bag. They let him box up his periodicals and helped carry them downstairs. Gustav asked if he was being arrested. The officer didn't say yes, but he didn't say no either.

Should Gustav be arrested for his role at Dora? he wondered as they drove away. He was only a small cog in a giant apparatus of death, and perhaps not even a very enthusiastic one at that. But he could see, from his prisoner's perspective, how guilt draped itself around anyone at Dora who was not a victim. Richter, von Braun, Rudolph, Ehrlich. What was the difference? A degree of personal brutality, but that was all.

Yes. He was Gustav Ehrlich, and he was guilty. But his crime had not yet happened.

An hour later, he was in a room sitting across from another American officer. This one was older, and perhaps of higher rank. Coffee had been brought in for the two of them. Real coffee. The officer sipped as he looked through the materials his men had taken from the apartment. Spread out in front of him were Ehrlich's orders, his travel documents, and everything from his wallet.

"You are Gustav Ehrlich, correct?"

"I am."

"My name is Major Hanson. My job is to evaluate your role in the V-2 missile program," he said, glancing at Gustav as he shuffled through the papers. He held up the identity card with Gustav's photograph. "This doesn't look much like you."

"Oh yes, the hair," Gustav said. "I was ill. Pneumonia. They said I almost died."

"When was this?" Hanson asked.

"Early April, when I was transferred to Dora-Mittelbau. I had influenza, which worsened as soon as I arrived. The working conditions in those tunnels were horrible," Gustav said, watching the major for any sign of disgust or condemnation.

"Before your transfer you worked on the Heinkel 162 jet fighter," Hanson said, without acknowledging Gustav's mention of the conditions at Dora. "Tell me about that."

Gustav described the jet engine, using details gleaned from the reports in his files. Hanson then asked about the V-2 engines, and Gustav was able to talk about the problems encountered in shipping the components to Dora and repairing them. He described statistical quality control, which was news to the major. Hanson knew a little about jet engine technology but less than nothing about rocketry. Every time Gustav mentioned the slave laborers, Hanson became irritated and moved on to other questions.

Gustav asked if he was under arrest.

No, he wasn't.

He asked if he could leave.

No, he couldn't.

He asked what they were going to do with him.

No answer provided.

They fed him and gave him a room. There were no bars on the windows, but he was on an American base and had no identity papers. Where could he go? The next morning, Hanson told him.

"You've been approved for work in the United States under the terms of Operation Paperclip," the major announced.

"What? How can you make me go to America?"

"You are currently in military custody, Mr. Ehrlich," Major Hanson said. "You could be prosecuted as a war criminal. Not a very pleasant alternative."

Gustav thought about that. He could never get to Richter if he was put on trial. And after all, both Gustav and Anton were guilty. Both worked for the Nazis and helped develop weapons. Maybe this was an opportunity. If he was offered this chance, might not Richter and the others be swept up by the Americans?

"What is Paperclip?" he asked.

"A program to gather the German scientists who worked on various advanced projects. We need them to help win the war in the Pacific. And we need to keep them out of Russian hands."

"Will I be a prisoner?" Gustav asked.

"You will be in military custody," Hanson said. "You will work as you did in Germany, in your field of expertise. You will have a chance to become an American citizen."

"There are others?"

"I am sure you will be reunited with many of your colleagues," Hanson said.

"Very well. I am pleased to go," Gustav said.

There was no mention of Nazis, slave labor, or crimes against humanity. But that did not matter to Gustav. It meant that he would be the one to bring revenge down upon Richter. All he had to do was let the Americans bring them together.

IT WAS A long road. Gustav waited for a month before being shipped out. He joined ninety-eight other technicians who signed a one-year contract with the Rocket Branch of the Research and Development Division of the US Army Ordnance Corps. He ended up at Fort Bliss, Texas, where he was put in charge of a section of thirty men, due to his proficiency with English. Their job was to sift through reams of technical documentation taken from research sites across Germany in order to select the most important documents for translation. The other technicians resented the drudgery, not to mention the relative lack of freedom and the intense Texas heat. But it was salvation for Gustav. At his fingertips were the secrets of the Third Reich's rocket program.

Gustav Ehrlich became an expert. Not a brilliant scientist, but a solid technician. He understood how to make things work.

Then came the transfer to the White Sands Proving Ground in New Mexico. Gustav was astounded to learn that the US Army had secured one hundred V-2 rockets at the end of the war and delivered them to White Sands for testing. When he saw them, he couldn't help but wonder if any of them were from the tunnels at Dora. Maybe even the one he'd hidden atop in the nose cone section.

Gustav oversaw testing and retooling parts for the V-2s. He lived and worked in air-conditioned comfort, he ate well, and had freedom of movement within the base. But there was no evading the fact that the work he did was the same as at Dora.

Gustav didn't mind as long as there was hope that his path would one day cross with Richter's.

He made friends, German and American alike. People liked Gustav and his ability to get along well with everyone. A few Americans started calling him Whitey due to his shock of white hair, but he begged off the nickname.

"Call me Gus," he would say. And Gus he became. An American name. His transformation continued.

Six months after his arrival at White Sands, Wernher von Braun and a collection of other scientists arrived to witness the launch of a V-2. Rudolph was there as well. Rudolph melted into the crowd behind von Braun, who drew all the attention with his magnetic personality and handsome features. The army brass treated von Braun like a visiting movie star, keeping him away from the common GIs and technicians. There was no sign of Richter. Gustav asked around about him, and only a few of the Germans admitted to knowing him. None of them knew where he was.

Like his fleeting visits to Dora, von Braun's visits to White Sands were occasional. Gus Ehrlich wasn't allowed to get too close. Gus was a small fry, and von Braun was a rising star, frequently interviewed by the newspapers about flights to the moon, space stations, and other fantastic ideas. He was a man of the future, while Gus dragged the past around like a rusty anchor.

Gus kept asking around about Richter. Someone said Richter had landed a job at the Jet Propulsion Laboratory. No, someone else said; it was the Ordnance Guided Missile School at the Redstone Arsenal in Alabama. Or maybe it was the Joint Long Range Proving Ground at Cape Canaveral. America was crazy for rockets, and there was no shortage of research centers. Richter had to be at one of them.

Two years passed before Gus found out.

It was Redstone. Richter was part of a team designing a new missile, the PGM-11 Redstone. Gus spotted a memo debating various ideas for the best fuel mixture for the rocket. One of the signatories was Gerhard Richter, director of rocketry research at the Redstone Arsenal.

The PGM-11 rocket wasn't going to the moon. It was a short-range ballistic missile, built to deliver nuclear warheads over a distance of two hundred miles. Once again, Gus was working on a delivery system for widespread death. It pained him, but he didn't let his emotions overwhelm him, not if his work brought him close to Richter.

He put in for a transfer. By now, he'd been granted American citizenship. He was a free man, living the American dream. Redstone jumped at the chance to employ him, and within three weeks he was being waved through the gate by security at the Redstone Arsenal.

"Good morning, Mr. Ehrlich," the receptionist greeted him. "My name is Peggy, and I'll take care of your paperwork."

"Thank you, Peggy," he said, handing over the documents he'd received and signed. "Please call me Gus, unless there's some rule against it." He smiled.

"Not at all, Gus," Peggy said, brushing back her light-brown hair. "It's only that some of the German fellows who work here like the formal approach. You know what I mean."

"I left that behind in the old country," Gus said, giving her a wink. "I'm an American citizen now. No more of that *Herr Professor Doktor* stuff."

"Don't you get yourself in trouble on your first day, Gus," Peggy said. "Now sign in here, and I'll take you for your ID photo."

"I'll behave myself," Gus said as Peggy escorted him down a long hallway. It was painted bright white. Clean, crisp colors so unlike the tunnels of Dora. "I heard Gerhard Richter works here. I knew him back in Germany. The old-fashioned type, right?"

"Professor Richter? I guess so. He works on the third floor. Heavy security up there. I only see him in the morning when he comes in. He works long hours, or at least until after I leave. Here you go, Gus. Once they're done with you, come and get me, and I'll show you to your office."

Interesting, Gus thought as his picture was taken. The university where Richter claimed to be a professor was probably bombed out and behind the Iron Curtain. Who could check? Who'd care to if Richter did his job? Professor was a fine title to hide behind.

"Nice picture," Peggy said as Gus returned to her desk. "Mine is awful. But your white hair makes you look distinguished."

"It changed overnight," Gus said, embarrassed at the attention. "At the end of the war. I was sick."

"Oh, I'm sorry," Peggy said. "I didn't mean anything by it. And we're all on the same side now, right? Follow me."

Peggy's heels clicked as they entered another hallway, this one just as white and antiseptic. Showing their ID cards to a guard, they went into a large room filled with file cabinets, drafting tables, and an oval conference table. A row of small offices ran along the wall across from them. To their left, a large plate glass window afforded a view into a single spacious office.

"You'll share this office with Victor," Peggy said, knocking on an open door. "Victor, this is Gus. Take him to meet Dr. Haber, will you? I have to get back. Good luck, Gus."

"Victor Neumann," his officemate said, standing and offering his hand. "Welcome to Alabama. I hear you come from White Sands."

"Yes. I came to escape the heat," Gus said.

"Oh, very good," Victor said. He looked about ten years older than Gus, and still spoke with a distinct German accent. "We haven't met before, have we?"

"I don't think so. Where did you work in Germany?"

"Listen, my white-haired friend. If you see an old comrade, keep it quiet, all right? No need to delve into the past. It doesn't matter where we worked. It only matters that we are working together now. To keep the Russians in their place. Understand?"

"Of course," Gus said. No one wanted to hear an uncomfortable truth. "What's the boss like?"

"Dr. Haber? He's all right. Knows what he's doing, doesn't get in our way," Victor said. "But if we're late on anything, he turns into a tyrant. Keep to the schedule and you will be fine. Come, I'll bring you to meet him."

The door to Haber's office was shut, but through the plate glass window, Gus could see Haber standing over his desk, intent on a design rolled out in front of him. A second man was seated across from Haber. Victor knocked twice and opened the door.

"The new man is here, Dr. Haber," Victor said. "Do you have a moment?"

"*Ja, ja*," Haber said, his voice distracted. "Come in. And excuse me. We must stay away from our native tongue and speak English. Some of us need practice, yes? Remind me who you are?"

"Gus Ehrlich, Dr. Haber," he said, coming to a halt as the man facing Haber turned toward him.

It was Richter.

Gus felt his breath leave him. Sweat trickled down his spine. He tried to stop staring at the man, remembering he needed to act like the new employee meeting the boss.

He wrenched his gaze away from Gerhard Richter, who looked nothing like the devil in the SS uniform who roamed the tunnels of Dora. This Richter had a paunch, bent shoulders, and a graying beard. The very picture of a kindly professor.

"Welcome to Hades, Ehrlich," Haber said, chuckling at his little joke about the Alabama heat.

"I've come from White Sands, sir. I'm used to it." Gus worked to keep his voice steady as a tumult of emotions raged through his body. Shock, rage, fear, and horror.

"Indeed, you must be. This is Professor Richter, director of research," Haber said, returning to the drawings on his desk.

"Ehrlich? Do I know you?" Richter said, offering his hand. "I don't think I'd forget that head of hair, but the name is familiar." Gus shook the hand of the man who had summoned the chains to hang Jerzy and the others. Richter's skin was clammy. Gus tamped down revulsion.

"I don't think so, Professor. I haven't had the pleasure of meeting you." True enough. Nothing about encountering Richter had been close to pleasurable.

"I'm sure it will come to me," Richter said, returning his attention to the technical drawings. "I have an excellent memory."

"Thank you," Victor said, tugging on Gus's sleeve. Their time was up. Gus shut the door behind him as he followed Victor out. Gus felt his legs weaken, but he kept walking, hardly believing he'd touched the man he came to kill.

He glanced back as they entered their office. Richter was standing at the window, watching him, stroking that neatly trimmed beard. He looked like a man trying to solve a problem. The problem of a name and face that didn't match.

In the days that followed, Gus watched for Richter. Not to avoid him, but to demonstrate he had nothing to hide. He was just another man named Ehrlich, not a common name, but not singular in any sense. Gus felt that if Richter saw him often enough, the new Ehrlich would replace any buried memory of the Ehrlich from Dora. After all, the fellow had only been there a short time, and it was more than ten years ago.

The work was demanding. At Redstone, they were developing a new missile. A bigger version of the V-2. Everyone was nervous about the Russians beating them to a nuclear weapon that could target Europe from behind the Iron Curtain, and the pressure was on to get the PGM-11 operational. Dr. Haber indeed proved to be a harsh taskmaster whenever they fell behind. Design changes were constantly demanded. Gus and Victor teamed up to improve the function of the oxygen turbopump. Days went by when Gus never even thought about Dora or Richter.

The nights were different.

Alone in his small house, visions of Jerzy in chains and Kunz brutalizing workers drifted through his dreams. He'd dream he was lost in the tunnels of Dora, descending deeper and deeper until all was darkness.

He needed a plan. Fate hadn't brought him here to do nothing.

But what, exactly? Gus liked his life. He liked being alive, and as much as he daydreamed of plunging a knife into Richter's heart, he didn't want to face the electric chair. No, not after everything he'd gone through. He wanted to make friends. Take a girl on a date. Be normal. He'd been a victim. He'd changed his identity. He was on a mission, an avenging angel of death. But he wanted something after that.

He wanted a normal life. The life that had been stolen from him.

But he couldn't allow Richter to live either. The ghosts of his parents and sister wouldn't allow it. They'd haunt him forever if he didn't bring a measure of justice to the one war criminal who was within his grasp. The Americans obviously didn't care about war crimes committed by Nazi scientists, so it was left to Gus. There was no one else.

There had to be a way.

One evening, after working late, Gus left the facility and spotted Richter ahead of him, walking to the parking lot. He watched Richter ease into his gleaming black Cadillac, as black as an SS uniform. Gus folded himself into his used Studebaker coupe and followed Richter. He had no plan but began to wonder about a car crash.

No, that wouldn't work. Richter's car was a tank compared to his. Gus hung back, keeping several car lengths behind Richter. It wasn't a problem on the crowded road, but soon Richter took a left, heading into a residential area. Gus watched him slow and take a right turn onto a street lined with shade trees, their shadows lengthening as the blazing sun dipped close to the horizon. Single-family houses sat back from a wide sidewalk, lawns green even in the summer heat. A pleasant street. Richter pulled into number 48. Gus drove by and looped around the neighborhood. A creek, mostly overgrown by brush, ran behind the houses on Richter's street. Gus followed the road on the opposite side of the stream, then doubled back, driving past Richter's house. A light was on in one room.

Did Richter live alone? Gus drove home, thinking about the layout of the houses and the creek bed. He could approach the house from the rear, hidden by the vegetation and the sloping bank. But then what? A gun? He didn't have one, and it would be too noisy anyway. A knife? There'd be blood everywhere. It would splatter on him, but maybe it would wash off in the stream? He had to think this through. It had to be just right.

The next night, Gus worked late. He waited until dusk, then left. Richter's car was still in the parking lot. Gus drove past Richter's house and found it dark. Odds were the man lived alone. Good.

He spent the rest of the evening thinking of ways to kill the man. If he knew about poisons, he could break into the house and put some in Richter's food. But he had no idea about doses. How much rat poison would it take to kill a human rat? Strangle him? Smash his skull with a baseball bat? Wearing gloves, of course.

IN THE MORNING, Gus listened to the car radio as he drove to work. The local station played country music, which wasn't his favorite, but he liked listening to the disc jockeys to pick up new American jargon. As he parked, Gus noticed Richter pulling in.

"Good morning, Professor," Gus said, a forced grin on his face. "Another hot one." That was the standard greeting he'd learned from his American colleagues.

"Unpleasant," Richter said. He already looked wilted from the heat. "I still haven't placed you, Ehrlich, but I am certain we've met." Richter kept his eyes on Gus, studying his features. Gus returned the gaze and noticed the heavy, dark bags under Richter's eyes. The man's skin was pale, probably from long hours working inside.

"I've been told it's best not to talk about where we worked in

Germany," Gus said. "But I'd be glad to compare assignments if that might help jog your memory."

"No," Richter said, one eyebrow raised. "Some things are best forgotten, yes?"

"Some things, yes," Gus replied. He slowed his gait to allow Richter to keep pace. That extra weight was not good in this heat. He watched as Richter puffed to take in air, beads of sweat breaking out across his forehead.

Gus opened the door for him, the expected courtesy to be shown to a senior man. The cool air hit them like a welcome arctic blast. Richter mopped his head with a handkerchief and motioned for Gus to sign in ahead of him.

Gus scrawled his name, said good morning to Peggy, and walked down the hall. As he checked in with the security guard, he glanced back at Richter. He was leaning against the receptionist's counter. Chatting? Or did he need to rest before walking to the third floor?

Perhaps he didn't want Gus to see him out of breath. Men like Richter were vain, especially when it came to looking weak in front of others. Did it pain Richter to exist in a world where others failed to quake at his approach? Where his bloated, sweating body rebelled at carrying him up a flight of stairs?

"Hot enough for you?" Victor said as he came in. No matter how hard Victor tried, American phrases didn't flow off his Germanic tongue. Each word was too precise, clipped, and hard.

"Hotter'n blazes," Gus replied, giving Victor a grin and a lesson in American slang. In no time they lost themselves in fuel calculations. They'd received the specifications for the W39 warhead. The damn thing weighed sixty-nine hundred pounds and had forced a rethinking of thrust and fuel requirements. The fact that the W39 was also a thermonuclear weapon hardly mattered. Unless you thought about it, which wasn't useful at all.

Just before ten o'clock the sirens sounded.

Redstone had its own military hospital, and by the time Gus

looked out his window, he saw the flashing lights of an ambulance and a military police car. He joined the others who rushed to see what was going on.

Peggy was standing at her desk, hands held over her mouth.

"What happened?" Gus asked her, spotting Dr. Haber coming down the stairs and then standing aside as medics with a stretcher ran by them.

"Poor Professor Richter," she said, her eyes wide and brimming with tears. "He had a heart attack, or something."

"The ambulance is for Richter?" Gus asked. "Is he okay?"

"Of course he's not okay," Victor said. "Not if he's had a heart attack."

"Victor!" Peggy said, admonishing him as tears seeped through her fingers.

"It's terrible," Gus said, and meant it. He didn't want Richter dead, not yet. Not without knowing it was Prisoner 39482 who was killing him.

"Dr. Haber, how is he?" Peggy said, waving a damp handkerchief in Haber's direction.

"Conscious, at least," Haber said. "He said he wasn't feeling well but thought it was the heat. The poor fellow has been working so hard lately."

"Was it a heart attack, Dr. Haber?" asked Victor.

"He clutched his left arm, which is a sign of one, I believe," Haber said. "We shall know more soon, I am sure."

The medics carried Richter down the stairs, strapped onto a stretcher. He wore an oxygen mask with a cylinder at his side. He waved a hand weakly in Haber's direction.

"That's a good sign," Peggy said, sniffling.

"A very good sign," Gus agreed. "Let's get back to work. It's what the professor would want."

Dr. Haber went off to the hospital, and everyone else returned to their offices, buoyed by Gus's optimism. *It* was *a good sign*, he told himself. Richter would endure pain, but not die. Not right now, anyway.

The next morning was blisteringly hot and humid. Walking from the parking lot, Gus fingered the damp hair on his forehead. It was getting long, too long for this heat. He didn't mind the white color, not at all. But white or brown, it felt like wearing a felt hat in the desert.

The cool air of the foyer greeted him like a welcome friend. Peggy and Dr. Haber were at the desk, and by the smile on Peggy's face, there was good news.

"Professor Richter is going to be okay," Peggy said, jumping up and down in excitement.

"With rest and a change in diet," Dr. Haber said, raising his hands as if to hold back Peggy's exuberance.

"That's great to hear," Gus said. "So it wasn't too serious?"

"Oh, it was serious," Haber said. "The doctors said it was very close. The stress of our work demanded too much of the professor's heart. Overworked it, I think they said. They gave him nitroglycerin and blood thinners and prescribed a period of rest from any physical or emotional stress."

"Professor Richter won't be returning to work then?" Gus asked.

"Not for at least a month, if he wants to live," Haber said. "If he is well enough in a week, they will discharge him. But he must stay at home. No work, only relaxation."

"It will be hard for the poor man," Peggy said. "He's used to working such long hours."

"Any undue stress could kill him, the doctor told me," Haber said. "We must work all the harder so Gerhard knows he can relax and heal, yes?"

"Yes, we will. Right, Gus?" Peggy said. "We don't want the professor to worry about a thing."

"Absolutely," Gus said. "Professor Richter deserves a good, long rest."

Richter might have gotten a good rest in the hospital, but there was none at Redstone Arsenal. A test rocket blew up on the launch pad at Cape Canaveral, and that threw everyone into a frenzy of recalculation and recrimination. By the time things calmed down, Dr. Haber reported that Richter would be released from the hospital for home rest in two days.

Gus left work as early as he could get away with. He had errands. First, he got himself a haircut. Not a trim, but a crew cut, extra short. A lot of the younger technicians had them, and they looked cool in the summer heat. Then he went shopping. He bought a pair of white cotton pajamas, a can of blue paint, brushes, sewing needles, and heavy thread.

Gus went home and worked on his project in the garage. He laid out cardboard saved from boxes and placed the pajamas on it. Using a ruler, he marked out rows across the front and back. When that was done, he started painting the stripes. Blue stripes on white. He worked carefully, slowly, keeping the lines straight and the paint light so it wouldn't get brittle. It took three nights to finish.

He cut a small rectangular piece of fabric and inked 39482 on it, then stitched it onto the pajamas, over his heart. The final touch was the Jewish star. Using fabric from one of his shirts, he cut out the star and sewed it on.

Gus, no, Anton—right now he was Anton Schuster—tried on the uniform. The paint had dried perfectly. Only a few spots were wrong, but no one would notice. Not in the dark, not in the middle of the night.

Tomorrow night, he would be Prisoner 39482 once again. After that, he would be free.

The next day passed slowly. Gus checked the weather report on the radio and watched the sky. Rain was the only thing that would stop him, and there was none in the forecast. But it was another scorching day. The temperature wasn't expected to dip below seventy-five degrees all night. Perfect.

"I think I'm finally used to that haircut," Peggy said as Gus left for the day. "It's growing back a bit."

"The barber did cut it a bit short, didn't he?" Gus said. "I'll have to talk with him next time. But I like it." He rubbed his hand over his scalp, feeling his skull as he used to back in Dora.

At home, he was too excited to eat. He could barely wait until midnight. He dressed, putting on a light jacket over the pajamas, checking to be sure his wallet was in the pocket. If he was stopped by the police for any reason, he wanted his driver's license close at hand. His story would be he couldn't sleep, and he hoped the cop wouldn't take note of the pajama bottoms.

He drove by Richter's house. It was dark, as were the rest of the houses. As he had so many other times, he counted the homes. Richter's was the ninth. He drove around the block, crossing the small bridge over the creek, and parked on a side street, in the shadows cast by an old tree. He locked the car and hid the keys underneath a bush.

Gus looked around. No one in sight. No late-night drivers. He took a deep breath and moved through the bushes, making his way to the creek. When he reached the bank, he rolled up the legs of his pajamas. The creek was knee-deep at most, and the cool water chilled him as he waded in. He kept his jacket on, figuring there was no reason to display white stripes at night.

He counted houses. Seven, eight, nine, and he was there. He scrambled up the bank and knelt on the grass. He listened. Small animal noises rustled in the undergrowth. Somewhere in the distance a dog barked, but not at him.

It was time. He removed the jacket and his sodden shoes. He put on socks to disguise his footprints. He moved to the garbage can in the backyard, the same kind he used to burn his garbage. He rubbed his hands in the soot, dabbed it on his prisoner's uniform, and then finally on his face and shaven head.

Then the gloves, and it was time.

As Gus approached the house, he could hear the whirr of fans. In this heat, you had to keep the windows open, otherwise you'd smother in your sleep. He stood and looked in the window at the back of the house. The kitchen. Around to the side, he could make out a dining room table. That was his best bet. Less furniture to bump into, and there was no reason for Richter to be in there.

Gus tested the screen window. The wood frame emitted a creak before one corner popped out. He ran his fingers along the opening at the bottom until he came to a hook. He worked it loose, and the screen hung open, giving him just enough room. He boosted himself up, stuck his head in, and lifted his body with his arms.

He kept his legs limp, willing them not to scrape against the house. He wriggled one arm in, then pushed against the sill with the other.

He heard a noise. A snort. Snoring from the next room. The living room.

Gus didn't move. His muscles ached with the effort, but he waited until the snoring became deep and regular again. Richter was sleeping in the living room. He was close.

Gus moved farther in, his center of gravity drawing his legs in after him. His two hands hit the floor, but he managed to keep one leg on the windowsill to keep the screen from slamming shut.

He was in. He latched the screen, leaving no evidence of a break-in. His stocking feet were quiet on the wood floor as he moved toward the living room. It reminded him of the shuffling gait he'd had to adopt at Dora simply to keep his clogs on his feet.

He thought of all the prisoners who had no shoes, their feet a daily bleeding reminder of what was to come. He thought about Jerzy, going silently to the chain.

Then he was over Richter, who was stretched out on the couch, a thin sheet covering him. His mouth gaped open, gasps of air escaping him in throaty snorts.

"Prisoner 39482 reporting for duty, *Sturmbannführer*," Anton Schuster said.

Richter rolled on the couch, the sheet slipping away, revealing his heavy belly sagging over stained pajama bottoms.

"Prisoner 39482 reporting for duty, *Sturmbannführer*," Anton repeated, louder, but not too loud. A prisoner would never speak to an SS officer in that tone, and Anton wanted Richter to momentarily sense he was someplace else, in the past, the man he used to be.

"What?" Richter slurred the question, his eyes barely open.

"Prisoner 39482 reporting for duty, *Sturmbannführer*, as requested."

"I didn't," Richter said, rubbing his eyes, slowly coming awake. "*Mein Gott!*"

"Yes, let us speak in our native tongue," Anton said, switching to German.

"No, no," Richter said, moving back on the couch, holding up one hand as if to ward off the nightmare he'd awakened to. "Where am I? Who are you?" He pushed himself back, nearly climbing the back of the couch.

"Prisoner 39482 reporting for duty, *Sturmbannführer!*"

"Ahhhh!" Richter moaned, then leaped from the couch, running through the house, making for the front door but falling short of it. He crawled on all fours, his hand reaching for the doorknob. Anton swatted it away and stood over him, watching the panic fester in Richter's eyes. It wasn't human, it was primeval. The great horrible fear of retribution from beyond.

"I will come every night. Prisoner 39482 will always come for you, Richter."

"Ahhhhhhh," Richter cried again. But this time it was a grimace, a shuddering moan as Richter gritted his teeth and flailed, clutching his chest. His mouth flapped open, but nothing but a gasping breath emerged.

"Remember the chains, Richter? I do," Anton said. "Remember Jerzy, Prisoner 20745? I do."

Richter blinked, as if trying to make sense of what was happening. But he couldn't. He shook his head, a final denial of what his eyes were seeing. A ghost of Dora. He blinked one last time, and then his eyes took in the last thing he ever saw.

Prisoner 39482.

Anton waited until he was sure Richter was dead.

Then he searched the house. Not for incriminating papers, he knew there would be nothing like that. But when he found the study upstairs, with the portable typewriter on a small desk, he knew exactly what to do.

He made the call from a telephone booth, well away from any witnesses. He didn't stay on the line long, just a concerned neighbor saying he heard noises. Then one more call, and he went home.

"Oh my God," Peggy said as soon as Gus arrived at work. "Did you listen to the radio this morning?"

"No, I didn't," Gus said, professing ignorance. "What's up?"

"Professor Richter, he's dead," Peggy said. "But he left a note. He confessed to some horrible things. I can't believe it."

"Did he kill himself?" Gus asked.

"No. The police said he'd written about what he did during the war, in those concentration camps. Because of his heart attack. He wanted to confess before he died. And then he did."

"Confessed?"

"And died. Can you believe it?" Peggy said.

"I'll believe it when I read it in the paper," Gus said. He watched as Dr. Haber took the stairs to the third floor. It might not make it into the newspapers. Police reports can be faked, and a local radio station news item can be written off as overenthusiastic. A story in the local newspaper can be spiked. The men of the third floor were experts at hiding the truth. But for one brief moment, in this small town, the truth had been told. Some people might remember.

Most importantly, Richter had died knowing Anton had come for justice for Jerzy. A vengeance weapon, set on a true course years ago at Dora, had found its target.

Now, all that was left for Gus was to set a new course, a trajectory that might lead to a sense of peace.

Perhaps, even joy.